Queen
of the
Reformation

About the Author

Author Charles Ludwig grew up on the mission field in Kenya. He brings to his historical novels with BHP an impressive writing experience, having more than forty books already published, several of which have been read or dramatized on worldwide radio. Ludwig also has a rich pastoral and evangelistic ministry, having preached across Europe and in many other countries. He and his wife make their home in Tucson, Arizona. Biographical novels with BHP include:

Queen of the Reformation—Katie Luther
Mother of an Army—Catherine Booth
Champion of Freedom—Harriet Beecher Stowe
Defender of the Faith—Queen Victoria

Queen of the Reformation

Charles Ludwig

BETHANY HOUSE PUBLISHERS
MINNEAPOLIS, MINNESOTA 55438
A Division of Bethany Fellowship, Inc.

Published by Bethany House Publishers
A Division of Bethany Fellowship, Inc.
6820 Auto Club Road, Minneapolis, Minnesota 55438

Printed in the United States of America

Library of Congress Cataloging-in-Publication Data

Ludwig, Charles, 1918–
   Queen of the Reformation.

    1. Luther, Katharina von Bora, 1499–1552—Fiction.
2. Luther, Martin, 1483–1546—Fiction.
3. Reformation—Germany—Fiction. I. Title.
PS3523.U434Q4   1986   813'.52   86–11754
ISBN 0–87123–652–4

For Mary,
my Katie von Bora
during the last
half century

Author Charles Ludwig grew up on the mission field in Kenya. He brings to his first historical novel with BHP an impressive writing experience, having more than forty books already published, several of which have been read or dramatized on worldwide radio. Ludwig also has a rich pastoral and evangelistic ministry, having preached across Europe and in many other countries. He and his wife make their home in Tucson, Arizona.

Contents

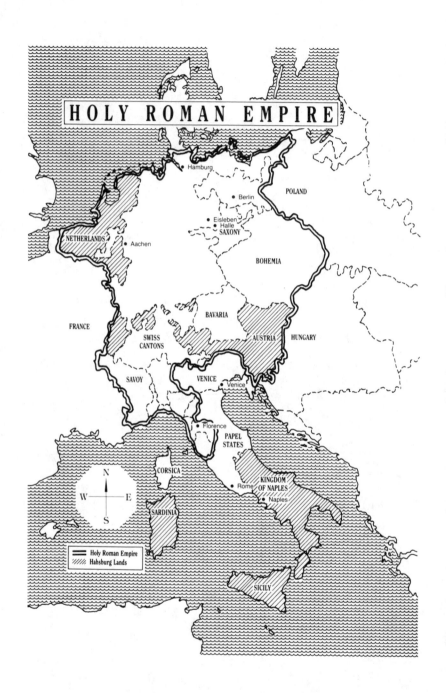

Preface

She had lost her mother when she was a child, and not being accepted by her stepmother, Katie's world was even darker than the dark world around her. Moreover, Katie viewed her world from a cell in a convent where her family had discarded her.

Unloved and alone, Katie frequently sobbed herself to sleep, curled up in her narrow cell. Deep in her heart she desired to make her life count for something; and occasionally, sometimes during mass, she felt a dim confidence that maybe it would be worthwhile. But the high walls and routines of the convent had a way of blurring that confidence. Convinced there was no way of escape, Katie smiled artificial smiles and longed for death.

Six years before Katie was born into the home of Hans von Bora and the former Katherine von Haubitz on January 29, 1499[1] the *Nuremburg Chronicles* was published in Nuremburg—one of the most progressive cities in Germany and the envy of all Europe. The authors of that book stated they were writing about "the events most worthy of notice from the beginning of the world to the *calamity* of our time." They

---

[1]This date and the name of Katie's mother are not certain.

declared the world was in its "sixth" stage, and the seventh period, which it was entering, would be finalized by the Day of Judgment. Moreover, the seventh period would be one of indescribable wickedness.

The authors had reason to be pessimistic. Europe was engulfed in ignorance and corruption. Even the church had strayed. Bribery was an accepted way of life. Bishoprics could be purchased with money, and greedy financiers were anxious to lend that money. The loans could be repaid by the sale of indulgences. Alexander VI, the current pope, had even made his son a cardinal.

Popes were supreme. They insisted that since Peter was the only apostle to walk on water, occupants of his throne had divine authority to rule the world. To them, Europe was like a chessboard and the popes had the right to shift kings and queens as they wished; consequently, ambitious rulers often found themselves in conflict with the pope. However, the rulers always lost, for the pope had access to wealth— and the wills of the people. Decrees by His Holiness, scriptural or not, were final.

Smallpox, leprosy, and the plague were epidemic, sometimes destroying entire villages. This was not surprising since medical treatment was very primitive, the normal prescription being an enema, prolonged sweating, or the letting of blood. In drastic cases all three methods were combined, but few survived.

Slowly things began to change, and a new era dawned. One of the most revolutionary changes was the invention of movable type by Johann Gutenberg, introducing the first printed Bible in 1456. Because of printing, learning spread quickly with Nuremburg leading the way. New hygienic measures were instituted. The City Council even decreed that pigs could be kept only in the backyard and had to be driven through the city to the river once a day. It also shocked owners by demands that they scoop the droppings and cast them into the river *downstream* from the city.

This was progress and it saved lives.

But not all discoveries were appreciated. To most, the voyages of Columbus to the New World were merely something to shrug about. "It's all a lie," sneered the skeptics.

Discoverers of truth feared for their lives. Stakes with humans attached were easy to light, and many a bored citizen was entertained by watching the flames snuff out the life of any victim with a new idea.

John Wycliffe escaped the stake because of the intervention of a fatal stroke in 1384. But forty-four years later his remains were unearthed, burned, and his ashes scattered in the river Swift. However, John Huss was not so fortunate. For his crimes of agreeing with Wycliffe and opposing the pope, he died in the flames of a stake in 1415. And in 1498, the year before Katie was born, Savonarola was hanged in Florence. His crime? He declared that Alexander VI was the representative of Satan. But in spite of dungeons, gallows, exile, boiling oil, and the stake, men—and women—continued to proclaim what they considered to be the truth. The outstanding thinker of this time was Doctor Martin Luther, the "wild boar" of Wittenberg.

Although outlawed and excommunicated, Luther did not know the meaning of fear. His battle cry was *the just shall live by faith!* (Rom. 1:17).

Through the providence of God, Katie made a daring escape from her convent, discarding the vows she had made earlier at sixteen, and married the man about whom more books have been written than almost anyone else who has ever lived.

This book is about that marriage.

1
Nimbschen

Although the convent bell had stopped booming, Katie had been so engrossed in Luther's tract that she had neglected to don her wimple. Now, terrified at the consequences of being late, she yanked the starched covering over her newly shaved head and descended the steps two at a time.

By the time she had squeezed onto the front bench with the other nuns, she was panting. While trying to calm herself, she forced her eyes to the front where the abbess—her dead mother's sister—always appeared. This morning her aunt was missing. "W-what happened to her?" she asked, whispering hoarsely into the ear of Ave von Schönfeld, the stiff-spined nun on her right.

But before Ave could answer, Katie remembered: *she had forgotten to hide Luther's tract!* The memory was like the sight of a striking cobra. Her heart thudded in her chest. *Could it be that the abbess had already discovered the tract on the bed in her cell?* Suddenly her body was drenched by a cold sweat. Eyes wide, she unconsciously rubbed her hands together.

As she tried to control herself, Katie remembered the warnings of a nearly toothless nun just before she took her vows. "Keep in mind, Sister," she had said, wagging her finger, "there is no escape. None! Now that I'm retiring, I must tell you about Florentina.

"Desperate to escape, that determined girl risked her life writing to Luther. Imagine, writing to Luther! Betrayed by a nun, Florentina was subjected to the furious, almost insane wrath of the abbess. In fury she sentenced Florentina to remain in an unheated cell for a month. Since it was late in the fall, she almost froze to death. We felt so sorry for her, but we were unable to help her." The aged nun shook her head sadly.

"At the end of the month, Florentina was allowed to attend the public prayer sessions. At the first one she was forced to stand and publicly confess her crime. After that, she was commanded to prostrate herself on the floor, so the other nuns had to step over her body as they marched to their choir stalls.

"This horror continued for three days. Yes, for three *long* days!

"Her vengeance knew no end. Soon that hardhearted abbess had a new idea. 'You will wear a straw hat and eat on the floor,' she ordered. At the end of this three-day ordeal, Florentina was placed under the observation of five supervisors, who guarded her in shifts." She tapped her tooth, remembering those terrible days.

"Ah, but she smuggled out another letter," she continued. "This time she was flogged, shackled—and locked in a cell. One day the jailer neglected to lock her door and she escaped.[1] Let me repeat, Sister Katie: there is *no* escape; *never* leave Nimbschen until you're dead or transferred. Never!"

Suddenly the door opened and Katie was shocked into reality. As she stared, the abbess strode onto the platform. By the light of the morning sun streaming through the tall window, Katie noticed that her aunt's normally pale cheeks had blanched until they were merely a shade darker than the wimple squeezing her thin face.

---

[1]Luther published her story in a tract, *Luther's Works*, vol. 43, pp. 85–96.

Luther's tract was in her hands, and from her front-row seat, Katie had a clear vision of its scorched edge. She could even read its title: *The Babylonian Captivity of the Church*. As she stared, her aunt's imposing figure loomed before her like a huge triangular candle.

Katie, gripped with fear, held her breath.

"I've seen many dreadful writings," stated the abbess, shaking her head, "but this is by far the worst." She slapped the tract and her face became grim. "As all of you know, our Holy Father, His Holiness, Pope Leo X, issued a bull against Luther, the criminal who wrote this tract. This morning, I shall quote a few sentences from that bull."

She twisted her face in disgust as if she were holding a filthy piece of paper and recited:

> Arise, O Lord, and judge thy cause. A wild boar has invaded thy vineyard. Arise, O Peter, and consider the case of the Holy Roman Church, the mother of churches, consecrated by thy blood. Arise, O Paul, who by thy teaching and death hast and doth illumine the Church, whose interpretation of Scripture has been assailed. We can scarcely express our grief over the ancient heresies . . . revived in Germany. We are the more downcast because [Germany] was always in the forefront of the war on heresy. . . .[2]

At this point she lifted her eyes and swiveled them across the rows of wimpled nuns. Like fresh eggs in a tray at the market, the nuns' expressionless faces stared back. Katie nervously rubbed her hands together.

Then stepping over to her niece, the abbess shook the tract under her nose. "Now listen, Sister Katherine von Bora," she hissed, "and you will learn why you should never read any of Luther's writings!" Her voice crept higher until it nearly cracked. In a half-scream, she continued:

> We can no longer suffer the serpent to creep through the field of the Lord. The books of Martin Luther . . . are to be examined and burned. . . .

[2]This bull, issued on June 15, 1520, is identified by historians as *Exsurge Domine* (Arise, O Lord)—the Latin version of the first three words.

"Did you hear that?" she demanded, her voice trembling with anger. A pale ring encircled her lips as she continued. "The Holy Father called him a serpent, S-E-R-P-E-N-T,"—she slowly spelled the word—"and ordered that all his books are to be burned. That's right: B-U-R-N-E-D! And by the burned edge on this tract, I can see that some lost heretic rescued it from the fire. Also, no one is to own, or even read, Luther's New Testament. That is the decree of Duke George! This horrible tract and all the writings of Luther are the works of Satan."

"I disagree!" interrupted Katie, leaping to her feet. "That tract tells the truth! It teaches that the Lord's cup is for everyone—"

"And that's one reason the Holy Father condemned it to be burned!" snapped the abbess. "When a priest blesses the bread and wine, it becomes the actual body and blood of our blessed Lord. The bread is for all Catholics who have been to confession. The wine is only for priests."

"Why?" Katie's voice was now loud enough for all to hear it.

"Because that's what the church says! And the church is right. Consider how terrible it would be if one drop of God's blood were spilled on the floor." The abbess shuddered, closed her eyes, and shook her head.

"That's not according to the Bible," Katie blurted out. "Jesus and Paul taught that the wine is for everyone. Everyone! If you don't believe it, read *The Babylonian Captivity*." Katie knew her danger, but she had to speak the truth no matter what the cost.

The abbess stared, incredulous, her form slowly taking on the appearance of an old Roman statue.

"Do you know what you said?" she finally demanded, fastening angry eyes on her niece.

"I do! No priest has the power to change the wine into blood or the bread into flesh. Yes, I've heard our priest say, *Hoc est corpus* [This is the body], but those words don't affect the bread and wine in any way. It's from those words the

English jugglers get their expression, hocus-pocus!"

"Be careful, Sister Katherine. Heretics are still being burned at the stake."

"Yes, I know. John Huss was burned alive because he taught the truth about the cup!"

"Silence, Sister Katherine!" screamed the abbess. "We are living in the part of Saxony ruled by Duke George. And Duke George is a very devout man. He studied for the priesthood, and he hates heresy."

"Yes, I know that too," Katie stated, disregarding the abbess's demand. "He even had a man put to death because he helped a nun escape from her convent."

"And that man deserved to die! A nun's vows—your vows—are for life. You took your vows when you were sixteen. And before you took them, I read to you the words: *Ecce Lex, sub qua militare vis; si potes servare, ingredere; Sis non potes, liber discede.* Is that correct?"

"It is, and those words mean: 'Pay heed, this is the law under which you are willing to serve; if not, you are free to leave.' But at the time I was too young to understand their full meaning." Gaining courage, she continued, "Now I have a question for you. If you were starving in a dark tunnel and you suddenly saw a dim light at one end, what would you do?"

The abbess hesitated, but Katie's eyes remained firm. Finally the older woman said, "I'd go toward the light."

"Well," Katie said adamantly, "I've seen some light. Erasmus has shown that Jerome's Vulgate is full of err—"

"It's Saint Jerome," the abbess interrupted, "and don't talk about Erasmus to me! He's contemptible, a snake in the grass," she hissed. "I heard of a priest who keeps Erasmus' picture on his desk so that he can spit at it whenever he's annoyed!"

"Nonetheless, Erasmus has shown that penance is false."

"Go to your cell!" screamed the infuriated woman, shaking her finger toward the door. "Go! Go! Go!"

At the door, Katie paused with her hand on the knob. "The

whole idea of pilgrimages, climbing steps on one's knees, and wearing hairshirts is false. Erasmus has proved by the words of Jesus that—"

"Silence!" The abbess glared, and her jaw sagged until every nun had a glimpse of the gap-teeth in the back of her mouth. "You, Katherine von Bora, are a disgrace to everyone here at Nimbschen! I'm even ashamed that I'm your aunt. It's fortunate that your mother is dead. She was an energetic person and very sensitive. If she were alive now, your actions would kill her!"

"If Mother were alive now, I wouldn't be in this horrible convent," returned Katie. "The only reason I'm here is that my stepmother didn't want anything to do with me." Overcome by emotion, she began to wipe her eyes with a handkerchief.

Mysteriously, the abbess softened. "Sister Katherine, you may go back to your bench," she said, a tone of forced kindness squeezing into her voice. "Most of you do not know how really poisonous this man Luther is. And since I am obligated to protect you from evil, I will tell you about him. A friend of mine attended school with that miserable heretic and told me his story.

"Martin was born into the home of Hans and Margaretta Luther in Eisleben on November 10, 1483. I remember that date because it was nine years before Columbus discovered the New World. Hans Luther was a prosperous miner. In time, he owned six foundries.

"The year after Martin was born, his parents moved to Mansfeld. Hans and Margaretta were devout Catholics, and they raised their children in the proper way. All of them went to mass, sang hymns, and marched in processions. In no way can Martin Luther blame his parents for what he is doing. They raised him right! Martin loved school and in each school he did well. In his youth he was undecided what he wanted to do. But his father wished him to become a lawyer, and so at the University of Erfurt Martin studied law.

"Then on a warm July day, while he was returning to the

university after visiting his parents, a stroke of lightning slapped him to the ground. Rising, he prayed, 'St. Anne, help me! I will become a monk.' St. Anne is the patron saint of miners. In those days Martin Luther was very sincere. There were twenty cloisters in Erfurt; he chose the Augustinian because of its strictness.

"As the prior stood in charge before the altar, Martin prostrated himself on the floor before him. Then the prior asked, 'What seekest thou?'

"Martin's reply was: 'God's grace and thy mercy.'

"After lifting him up, the prior asked the usual questions: 'Are you married? Do you have a secret disease? Are you a bondsman?' When Luther answered no, the prior described the difficulties of monastic life. He told him plainly that his clothes would be rough, that he would be required to spend long hours in prayer, to go on long fasts, to have poor food, to suffer the humility of begging, to work long hours, and to endure poverty the rest of his life.

"Next, he asked him, just as you were asked, 'Are you ready to assume these burdens?' Martin's firm answer was: 'Yes, with God's help and so far as human frailty allows.'

"Following this promise, Martin Luther entered a nearby room. There he exchanged his normal clothes for the habit of a novice. Upon returning, he knelt on one knee while a barber shaved all of his hair except for a slender rim, the crown of thorns, around the edge of his skull. As the barber worked, the choir sang the solemn hymn, 'Hear, O Lord, our heartfelt pleas and deign to confer thy blessings on this thy servant, whom in thy holy name we have clad in the habit of a monk. . . .'

"In the midst of this hymn, Martin Luther prostrated himself on the floor again and pushed out his arms in the form of the cross. He then stood, was kissed by each of his fellow monks, and was received into the order.

"The prior closed the ceremony by quoting those most solemn words, 'Not he that hath begun but he that endureth to the end shall be saved.' "

Head cocked to one side, the abbess asked, "Was Martin Luther forced to become a monk?"

"No," answered several.

"Is he not to be blamed for breaking his vows?"

"He is," chorused an even larger group.

The abbess then pointed to Katie. "And what do *you* think, Sister Katherine?" A sneer distorted her face.

"I . . . I don't know," replied Katie, a crimson flush spreading over her cheeks and neck.

"Well, Martin Luther has been excommunicated, and that means he will burn in hell unless he repents," concluded the abbess. "Follow me and I will show you what I think of him."

She solemnly led the nuns to the enormous fireplace in the kitchen where the meals were cooked. Here she ripped Luther's tract into pieces and burned it bit by bit in the flames. After the last shred had been reduced to ashes, she said, "A year ago one of the nuns here in this convent was wicked enough to write to Martin Luther. Fortunately her treachery was discovered, and she was punished. Now I have a warning for all of you. If anyone here ever writes to Luther or reads any of his poison, that person will be severely beaten." The woman of authority glared. Then, with arms akimbo and her eyes focused on Katherine, she snapped, "Have I been understood?"

More than half the egg-white wimples nodded, and a shrill voice shouted, "You have been understood!"

"Very well." Her lips drew together like the blade of an ax. "All of you," she said, glancing at Katie, "except Sister Katherine, are dismissed."

As the nuns pushed out of kitchen, Katie studied the enormous painting of Duke George on the wall near the chimney. The nearly bald, long-bearded, wide-moustached ruler seemed to be defying the world. His thin ears and cold eyes expressed unyielding determination.

After the nuns had disappeared, the abbess thrust her face at Katie. "As I said, I'm ashamed I'm your aunt. Our convent is one of the finest in the Holy Roman Empire. That's why only girls of noble blood are allowed to enroll here." She pursed her lips and stared.

"If I weren't your precious mother's sister, I'd give you a severe flogging! You're proud and you talk too much. You will remain in your cell for two weeks, with only bread and water for food. And while you're imprisoned, you'll write a three-page history of the Holy Roman Empire!"

Katie froze. "Where will I g-get the b-books?" she stammered.

"I'll bring them. Also, I'll supply paper and ink."

Shoulders slumped, Katie turned toward her cell.

"Before you leave, tell me about the errors Erasmus discovered in the Vulgate." The abbess's voice was eager. "I . . . I want to check . . ."

"I'm sorry. That story is too long." Katie hung her head. "Besides, it will make you angry."

With that, Katie started up the stairs.

2

Misery

Alone in her cell, Katie knelt on the bare floor by the window and gazed out at the wide meadow, green fields overflowing with crops, the sparkling springs, and the fringe of forests beyond the stone walls of the convent. As she studied these scenes, her mind returned to her childhood.

Katie's memory of the little village of Lippendorf where she was born was vivid. The handful of thatched houses was less than an hour's walk south of Leipzig. But memories of her mother were dim. Still, she remembered the way her mother had dressed for special occasions and the gentle kindness of her voice as she held Katie on her lap.

"What was Mother like?" she had inquired of her brother the week before she took her vows.

"Her eyes were deep blue just like yours, and her hair was curly and tinged with the color of the setting sun on a summer evening."

"Was she kind?"

"Oh, yes. She was very kind. Night after night she sat up late mending our clothes, and when we returned from school she was always waiting with an apple or pear or some grapes. And she always told us that we should make our lives count."

"Was she a good cook?"

"Of course! I can still see—and even smell—the table she prepared. She had an artistic way of arranging dishes in order to make us hungry. One specialty was trout served with milk and cakes loaded with honey. Mmm! That was a tasty combination." He licked his lips and sighed. "And it didn't matter what kind of fish she had; she made it fit for the best restaurant in Nuremberg.

"Once she sent me to our pool to catch trout for special company. 'Get big ones,' she said. But all I could catch were some small common fish about as long as my hand. That didn't matter. Mother cleaned them, baked them in thick batter, sprinkled them with bread crumbs, and stuffed them with figs and grapes. Even the pope would have asked for more!

"Meatless days didn't bother Mother. On holy days she baked pies filled with shredded crab and figs. Occasionally she studied Grandma's cookbook. But not often. She knew all of the recipes by heart and invented new ones. Mother could make a great meal out of nothing, and her sausages were great. I used to tell her that our pigs hated to see her come!"

As Katie daydreamed of the past, she remembered the unhappy days following her father's remarriage. Every little thing loved by her mother had to be kept out of sight. Also, her father's new wife refused to allow Katie ever to speak of her mother, and once, when she did, she was packed off to Nimbschen.

Katie's first schooling had been at the Benedictine school at Brehna where a relative was in charge. At Nimbschen she became a member of the Cistercian Order and was molded in the precepts of Bernard of Clairvaux—a mystic and hymn writer who had flourished in the twelfth century.

Her father had visited her once a year, always bringing a present. Once it was a handkerchief, another time it was a supply of fruit which she shared with other nuns, and later, in 1521, it was a devotional book published in Nuremberg.

Katie's stepmother never visited her.

After removing her wimple, Katie viewed herself in a mirror. Her head had not been shaved for a month, and now her bald skull was covered with short, reddish hair like a fertile meadow. While twisting her head at various angles, she tried to imagine what her appearance would be like if she were permitted to let her hair grow. From her childhood, she remembered that it had been slightly curly.

Katie was in the process of imagining herself dressed in fashionable clothes with her hair pinned high when the door squeaked open.

"I brought you some books for your essay," said the abbess, laying them on the narrow bed crowded into the corner formed by the reddish brick walls.

Katie frowned. "And why do you want me to write about the Holy Roman Empire?" she asked, her voice slightly sarcastic.

"Because I want you to realize the power of the church."

"Should I mention some of the wicked popes such as Alexander VI, John XXIII, and the female pope, Joan, who was put out when she had a baby?"[1]

"You may write the essay in a way that suits you. But you must draw a map indicating the whole area of the Holy Roman Empire in our time," said the abbess. Then her tone and facial expression softened. "What do you know about Erasmus?" she asked a little anxiously.

Katie studied her out of the corner of her eye. "Are you looking for another heretic to burn?"

"Of course not! Erasmus has never been excommunicated."

"All right, I'll tell you what I know. Erasmus was an illegitimate son of a man who became a priest. He was born in

---

[1] Alexander VI (1492–1503), the former Rodrigo Borgia, was one of the most corrupt popes of the Middle Ages. John XXIII (1410–1415), not to be confused with John XXIII of Vatican II fame, was deposed in 1415 and imprisoned. The story of Joan, believed in Luther's day, is now shrugged at as a legend.

Holland and became a monk. He's the most famous writer of our time. He—"

"Tell me about his finding mistakes in the Vulgate."

Katie bit her lip. "Are you scratching for heresy?"

The abbess shook her head. "No, I'm just wondering where that passage about penance is to be found."

"If I tell you, will I be punished?"

"No, you'll not be punished in any way."

"All right then. But you must keep your word. It's in the Gospel of Matthew where Jesus is talking about the kingdom of heaven being at hand.[2]

"The Vulgate, the Bible we use, translated by Jerome in 404 into common Latin, translates the original Greek into the Latin *poenitentiam agite*, which means do penance. Erasmus discovered that this is incorrect, and so he changed it to *poeniteat vos*—be penitent. There's a lot of difference between being penitent and doing penance!"

"How do you know all this?" demanded the abbess. Her face had become a question mark.

Katie dropped her head.

"Tell me!"

"Will I be punished?"

"No."

"From the writings of Doctor Martin Luther."

"Do you have more of his tracts?"

"N-not n-n-now."

"Where are they?"

"I don't know."

"Are you sure?"

"Yes, I'm sure."

"How did you get them?"

"That's a long story."

"Tell me."

---

[2]Although Stephan Langton, who was elected archbishop of Canterbury in 1207, had divided the Bible into chapters, Robert Stephanus did not section it into verses until 1551. In modern versions this passage is Matthew 4:17.

"I can't."

The abbess rubbed a dark mole on the right side of her chin. Then half to herself she muttered, "If Erasmus is right, doing penance is wrong, and I've been wearing out my knees climbing to holy shrines for nothing." Catching herself, she exclaimed, "I shouldn't have said that! Don't repeat it. It's close to heresy."

Soon after the abbess had gone, the tantalizing smell of baked herring drifted up to Katie's cell. Already hungry, Katie tried to ignore it by concentrating on her assignment. First, she decided that she would draw a map of the Holy Roman Empire. Two of the books brought by the abbess had such maps in them and all she had to do was to make a copy.

With the largest map before her, Katie began to make a freehand copy. Having to dip her quill constantly into the ink and then blot what she had done with sand consumed a lot of time. But it was interesting work. She had just drawn the dark line separating France from Germany when the supper bell began to ring. The sound of the bell increased her hunger. But knowing she had to remain in her cell, she continued with the map.

When she was nearly halfway through, Katie was interrupted by the abbess. "I brought your water and bread," she said. "I want you to know that I hate to do this. But, Sister Katherine, we do have to keep order and we must not allow heresy to creep into Nimbschen!" As she started to leave, she added, "The bread is fresh from the oven."

From the dining room Katie listened to the sounds of laughter as her sister nuns dined. By this time the smell of herring and cabbage was very strong. Choking back her anger, Katie ate the bread and drank the water; then she returned to the map. She had made a mistake on the first try by making Bohemia too large. Starting with fresh paper, she again dipped the quill into the ink.

As Katie drew and blotted, her mind somersaulted back

to St. Bernard, a founder of her beloved Cistercian Order. She and the abbot, born in 1090, had many things in common. Like her, he had been born into a noble family, and like her, he had lost his mother. His loss had been later, at the age of seventeen; nonetheless, Katie knew that he had experienced the indescribable pangs of this loss.

Sometimes Katie was teased by fellow nuns because of her love for this man who had been canonized in 1174. Once when flies swarmed over the food, a sister had said, "St. Bernard had a weak stomach. When the flies in the church at Foigny bothered him too much he *excommunicated* them and they all died! Why don't you do the same?"

Now as Katie thought about this man whose passion was simplicity, she remembered a miracle credited to him that had real meaning. A distinguished lord had approached Bernard in order to confess his sins before he died. But when he opened his mouth he was unable to utter a word. Puzzled, Bernard sang a mass; and while he sang, the lord's speech returned. Then, three days after his confession and restitutions, he died. This was Bernard's first miracle.

As Katie considered the event, she had an inspiration. *Could it be that she might be used by the Lord to lead others into the light and to show them that salvation is obtained by faith and not by penance, good works, or endless repetition?* Excited by this idea, she accidentally labeled Bohemia, on the southeastern border of Saxony, Bavaria. This ruined the map and she had to start a new one.

When St. Bernard had decided to go into a spiritual retreat, he had persuaded thirty-one of his followers to follow him. Turning this over in her mind, Katie shuffled toward the window. An inward impulse impelled her to open and then close it. *Yes, it was large enough for a slender girl to pass through! However, it was a long distance to the ground. But the woodshed almost straight beneath the window could make a jump feasible. One would merely have to jump a little to the right, and then from the roof to the ground.* Strangely inspired, she began to sing her favorite St. Bernard hymn:

> Jesus, the very thought of thee
> With sweetness fills my breast;
> But sweeter far thy face to see,
> And in thy presence rest.

Katie had just drifted into sleep when there was a tap at her door. A moment later Ave von Schönfeld tiptoed over to her bed. By the light of the candle in her hand, Katie noticed that she was carrying a flat package. Without her wimple, Ave's dark hair was like a worn brush all over her skull.

"I've brought you something," she said softly.

Catching a whiff of herring, Katie whispered, "You'd better put it under the bed. The abbess is next door. Her long nose is like that of a hound! Let's wait until she starts to snore."

"How long will that be?"

"I don't know. But she's in bed now. It won't be long. And while we wait, you can look at my map of the Holy Roman Empire."

Katie spread the map on her bed and held her candle close. "It was easy to do, for I merely had to copy another map. But in my hurry I ruined the first two."

"While you were doing that map, I did one of Saxony. And mine is the one that's really important," whispered Ave.

"What do you mean?"

"As you can see, Nimbschen is just on the edge of Albertine Saxony—that part ruled by Duke George. Duke George hates all who have new ideas. If he caught anyone helping us to escape this dreadful place, that person would be hanged!"

Katie's eyes grew large. "Escape?" she questioned.

"Look at the map," replied Ave, avoiding a direct answer. "We could go east in a wagon. By the time we got to Torgau, we'd be safe because that city is in Ernestine (Electoral) Saxony, the part ruled by Frederick the Wise. Although he's a Catholic, Frederick respects Luther and his followers."

"But what if the wagon were stopped before it got to Torgau?" Katie's throat had gone dry and she began to lick her lips.

S A X O N Y

N
W   E
S

● Wittenberg

ELECTORAL SAXONY
(Frederick The Wise)

● Torgau

ELBE RIVER

● Leipzig
● Grimma
● Nimbschen

ALBERTINE SAXONY
(Duke George)

● Dresden

"That's easy." Ave ran her little finger along the escape route she had drawn with a series of dots. "At all times we'd be near the border of Frederick's territory. If we're discovered we can turn north."

"But what if there's no road?"

"Katie, we must trust the Lord!"

Sounds of loud snoring filled the quiet air: "Ngho, ngho, nghoo, ngo. Mmm. Nghooo. Mmm . . ."

Ave began to unwrap the package.

"Not yet!" cried Katie. "She's a light sleeper. We must wait until each set of snores is followed by a whistle."

"A whistle?" Ave's face had creased into wrinkles.

"Yes, a whistle! When she's in deep sleep she'll go *ngho, nghoo, Mmm. Shruuu*. The *shruuu* will mean we're safe. In the meantime, tell me how Saxony got divided between Duke George and Frederick the Wise."

"That story's a little complicated," replied Ave, who was hoping to be a history teacher. "Briefly, this is what happened. For more than half a century the sons and grandsons of Frederick the Valiant jointly ruled all of Saxony. But in 1485—two years after Doctor Martin Luther was born—the heirs, Ernest and Albert, decided to divide Saxony so that each could be a sole ruler over his territory. Historians call this division the *Leipzig partition*. That partition created *Albertine* and *Ernestine* Saxony.

"Now since Frederick was the oldest heir, he became the elector."

"And what's that?"

"I can see you haven't started your homework on the Holy Roman Empire," said Ave. "In the Holy Roman Empire there are always seven electors, each of whom inherits his position. Thus, since Frederick the Wise is an elector, his oldest son will inherit his position. These seven electors are the ones who elect the Holy Roman Emperor. When Charles V was elected, he had to make a deal with Frederick to vote for him, and it's partially because of that deal that Frederick has to have mercy on Doctor Luther and his followers. But that's another story.

"At the time of the Leipzig partition it was decided that since the eldest son had the advantage of being the elector, he should divide Saxony and give his younger brother the right to choose which part he wanted. It was because of his father's position that Duke George is now the ruler of large sections of Albertine Saxony.

"I—" she was interrupted by the *shruuu* whistle of the abbess. "Do you think it's safe now?" she asked.

Katie listened for a long moment. Then she smiled. "Yes, she's asleep. Open the package."

After making the symbol of the cross, Katie started on the herring. She ate as if she were famished. While she was devouring the fish and bits of cabbage, Ave withdrew a letter from a concealed place at the bottom of the package. "Look at this," she whispered, holding the candle close for a better view.

Katie took a quick look and gasped. The letter began, "Dear Dr. Luther: I'm writing you from Nimbschen . . ." The shock was too much for her and at that moment she choked on a bone.

Eyes closed, Katie began to cough.

"Be quiet!" begged Ave, holding a hand over Katie's mouth. But she couldn't stop. "*Akhu! Akhu! Akhu!*" she exploded. Finally she managed to say, "H-hide the letter, and—*akhu!*—slap me on the back."

Ave slid the letter under the map of Saxony. Then she gave Katie three mighty whacks. The third whack dislodged the bone. And at that moment the snoring stopped. Frightened, both Ave and Katie stared at the door. A brief moment later it was flung open.

Candle in hand, the abbess stood before them. Seldom had she been seen without her wimple. And now, in spite of the tenseness of the situation, Katie stared at her onion-bald head covered with closely clipped gray hair. "Are you sick?" she mumbled as she held her candle high.

"Katie was choking, but I helped her," explained Ave.

The abbess studied them doubtfully while she rubbed the

mole on her chin. "The bread was fresh," she said at last. "I don't see how you could have choked on that." Then she began to sniff. "Do I smell fish?" She quickly sank to her knees and sniffed under the bed. Getting up, she held the remains of the herring in her hand.

"What's this doing here?" she demanded, shaking the tail.

"Well, well, you see it's . . . it's l-like this," stuttered Ave; "we know that you want us to be as much like Jesus as possible. And when He fed the five thousand, He supplied them with bread and f-f-fish. Right?"

"Yes, but the boy's fish which He used were small, and this is a large herring!" Her faded blue eyes drifted to the map of Saxony lying on the bed. Lifting it up, she scanned it closely. "I told you to draw a map of the Holy Roman Empire, not Saxony!" She then held her candle close to the map for a better view. "And what are these dots that lead from Nimbschen to Torgau and then to Wittenberg?" She traced them with her finger, a scowl creasing her face.

"The dots, the dots, the d-d-d-dots . . ." spluttered Ave. "The dots show how close we are to Wittenberg."

"And why would anyone want to know that?" The abbess scowled. "Wittenberg is a sewer. That's where those vile tracts are printed!" She studied the map a little more, and her face became even more sinister. Raising her voice, she demanded, "And why have you shown the location of Grimma?" She crushed the map into a ball.

"What's wrong with Grimma?" asked Ave innocently.

"Haven't you heard? The prior of the Augustinian Hermits in Grimma, together with several monks, read some of Luther's slop, were poisoned, and gave up the true faith."

When neither of the girls answered, the abbess half-shouted, "Tell me! Why did you put Grimma on that map?"

"Did I make a mistake and put it in the wrong place?" asked Ave, her voice still as smooth as honey.

"Don't avoid my question! Tell me, why did you indicate the location of those cesspools and show the way to Wittenberg with those dots?"

As Ave ransacked her mind for a suitable answer, Katie viewed the exposed letter to Dr. Luther lying face-up on the bed. It was more dangerous than a bear trap. Her heart was thumping so wildly, she was afraid her aunt would hear it. *What was she to do?*

Suddenly she had an idea. Thrusting her map of the Holy Roman Empire at the abbess, Katie angled it in such a way as to turn her eyes from the bed. "D-did I do a good job?" she managed. Then, her eyes still on those of the abbess, she motioned frantically with her left fingers for Ave to scoot the letter under the bed.

Eyes focused on the map of the Holy Roman Empire, the abbess examined it with the care of a jeweler. Finally, after thoughtfully considering it she said, "Sister Katherine, you did an excellent job. If you do as well with the history part, I'll be happy. Say your prayers. Get some rest. I'll see you in the morning."

As the abbess closed the door, the faint trace of a smile brightened her lips and a tiny glow shone in her eyes.

After her aunt had left the girls, Katie whispered into Ave's ear, "Did you see that smile?"

"I did."

"Maybe, just maybe, the abbess doesn't hate Dr. Luther as much as she pretends."

"You may be right," agreed Ave as she scratched her bald head.

Tormented by the happenings of the day, Katie was unable to sleep. As she rolled and tossed, she was haunted by one question: *Is it right for me to break my vows?*

3

Escape

As the days of her bread-and-water sentence crept by, Katie kept busy researching the history of the Holy Roman Empire. Each night a friendly nun slipped her a snack to eat.

Katie, certain that her aunt was aware of the food being smuggled into her room, was puzzled that she didn't object. During the second Monday of her "imprisonment," Ave sneaked her a plate filled with bread and sausage. While she was eating, Katie said, "Ave, I'm not certain that I want to escape."

Ave cocked her head to one side and frowned. "Why not?"

"I made my vows . . ."

"But perhaps you didn't understand them."

"True. Still I made them."

"Many nuns are escaping and a lot of monks are leaving their monasteries. Even the prior of the Augustinian Hermits left Grimma."

"I know. Nonetheless, I want to do what is right!"

Ave smoothed her wimple. Then cupping her chin with her right hand she said, "I sent the letter to Doctor Luther by the hand of Leonard Koppe of Torgau, the one who brings a wagon of supplies each week. The next time he comes I'll ask him to bring a tract of Luther's about breaking vows."

"I hope the abbess never discovers what Koppe is doing. If she does"—Katie shuddered—"if she does, Duke George will have him hanged!"

Ave laughed. "She won't. Koppe's a clever man. He's a member of the town council, and he used to collect taxes for Frederick the Wise. He's retired now. But he doesn't know the meaning of fear."

Day after day as Katie remained in her room, she made notes on the Holy Roman Empire. It was hard work, for the actual beginning had many roots. Finally, after several tries and the waste of a lot of paper, she completed her *essay* three days before the end of her two-week term of punishment.

Her story was brief and to the point:

> When the western section of the Roman Empire fell to the Vandals in 455 and then ceased to exist in 476, the church was dismayed. This was because the Prophet Daniel had prophesied that during the fourth kingdom (the Roman), God would set up "a kingdom which would never be destroyed." It then occurred to many that only the temporal kingdom had fallen and that, as St. Augustine had suggested, the spiritual kingdom would continue.
>
> With this in mind, Pope Leo III crowned Charlemagne as *Carolus Augustus, Emperor of the Romans*, on Christmas Day in the year 800. Charlemagne's coronation by the pope was merely the beginning of what would become the Holy Roman Empire. Then, nearly two centuries later, in 962, Otto I of the Saxon dynasty was crowned by Pope John XII. Otto's coronation was the foundation of the Holy Roman Empire—even though that title was not used until 1254.
>
> In our time, as my map shows, the Holy Roman Empire includes a big circle in central Europe and a large section of northern Italy.
>
> Although crowned by the pope, many of the Holy Roman Emperors have disagreed and fought against him. Still, the Holy Father has had great power over these emperors. This is because he has the power to excommunicate and proclaim an *interdict*. An interdict could prohibit its victims from saying mass, burying their dead, or even blessing the bread and wine and thus transforming it into the blood and body of Christ.

Having this power, the pope usually had his way. Because he was in trouble with Pope Gregory VII in 1075, King Henry IV of Germany called a meeting in Worms the next year and declared the pope "deposed." Gregory then excommunicated Henry and released all his subjects from their obligation to obey him. In the end, Henry was forced to kneel before Pope Gregory and ask his forgiveness. At the time, Gregory was in his castle in the Apennine mountains, and before he allowed King Henry to come inside, he forced him to stand outside in the snow for three days. The poor king had to obey!

Maximilian I, the emperor who reigned from 1493 to 1519, was the first Holy Roman Emperor who was not crowned by a pope; neither was his grandson, our present emperor, Charles V. Emperor Charles was crowned in Charlemagne's cathedral at Aachen. And since Pope Leo X didn't approve of him, he was crowned by the archbishop of Cologne on October 23, 1520.

After reading Katie's paper on the Holy Roman Empire, the abbess said, "Katie, you did a good job. I'm so pleased, I'm ending your punishment today."

Katie smiled and couldn't help saying, "It seemed to me as I looked up the material that the pope is gradually losing his power. He didn't crown either of our last two emperors. Perhaps God is leading us into some new truth." When she finished, her deep blue eyes were sparkling.

The abbess scowled. "Sister Katherine," she reprimanded angrily, "you are as stubborn as ever! You're just like your mother! I think your trouble is that you need to go outside. From now on I want you to work in the fields."

Working in the fields was exactly what Katie longed to do. To her, nothing was more pleasant than to have her hands in the soil and to watch the crops grow. But to keep her aunt from knowing that she really liked this assignment, she remained stonily silent.

Tired from her work in the fields, Katie was unable to sleep. As she rolled and tossed, she was haunted by one question: *Am I doing the right thing?* True, she was tired of the discipline, the never-ending routine of bells, masses, fasts, repetition of the same prayers, the dependence on relics—and the decrees of the popes rather than just the authority of the Bible.

Heavily burdened, she knelt by her bed and began to pray.

"Do I have a right to break my vows?" she asked. Without receiving an answer, she prayed about Luther's teaching that *the just shall live by faith*. As she prayed, she received assurance that on this subject, the leader at Wittenberg was right. Indeed, she had been convinced by her own experience. She remembered occasions when she had privately sought God's forgiveness for a shortcoming and had accepted God's promises by faith. On each occasion a sense of peace had convinced her all her sins were gone and Christ dwelled within her.

She was still considering whether it would please the Lord for her to escape when she fell into a deep sleep. The next morning she got up early and knelt by her bed to pray before she started the many weary routines of the day.

Katie had been busy cultivating cabbages when Ave showed up. "Have good news," she said.

"Yes?"

After carefully looking around to make certain there were no listeners, she said, "I received a reply from Dr. Luther."

Leaning on her hoe, Katie asked, "And what did the doctor say?"

"He said that he will make a way for all of us to escape, that we will be contacted by Leonard Koppe."

"How many do you think want to escape?"

"About a dozen."

Thoughtfully, Katie dug around a cabbage plant and pulled up two or three weeds. "As I said before, I'm not sure I want to escape. I keep thinking about those vows—"

"Don't let them bother you. Koppe gave me Doctor Luther's tract on marriage." She looked around to make certain no one was either watching or listening, and then she removed the folded tract from her bag filled with vegetables, and began to read:

> For the Word of God which created you and said, "Be fruitful and multiply," abides and rules within you. . . .
>
> Don't let yourselves be fooled on this score, even if you should make ten oaths, vows, and adamantine or ironclad pledges. For as you cannot solemnly pledge that you will not be a man or a woman (and if you should make such a promise, it would be foolishness and of no avail since you cannot make yourself something other than what you are), so you cannot promise that you will not produce seed or multiply. . . . And should you make such a promise, it too would be foolishness and of no avail, for to produce seed and to multiply is a matter of God's ordinance.[1]

"That sounds very convincing," said Katie.

"Oh, but there's more. Listen!" As Ave continued, she emphasized each word:

> No vow of any youth or maiden is valid before God, except that of a person in one of the three categories which God alone has himself excepted. Therefore, priests, monks, and nuns are duty-bound to forsake their vows whenever they find that God's ordinance to produce seed and to multiply is powerful and strong within them . . .[2]

"Now what do you think of that?" Ave waved the tract in a gesture of triumph.

"It's great. Still . . ." she frowned and dug up some more weeds. "But I'm puzzled by those exceptions. Maybe we're in one of them!"

"Oh, no. That's impossible. Here's what Doctor Luther said." She again read from the tract:

> In the third place, from this ordinance of creation God has himself exempted three categories of men, saying in Matthew 19 [v. 12], "There are eunuchs who have been so from birth, and there are eunuchs who have been made eunuchs by men, and there are eunuchs who have made themselves eunuchs for the sake of the kingdom of heaven."[3]

---

[1] *Luther's Works*, vol. 45, p. 18.
[2] Ibid., pp. 18, 19.
[3] Ibid., p. 19.

Katie laughed. "I'm sure that doesn't include any of us," she said. "But let me study the tract on my own so that I can be convinced."

"Fine. But you must keep it hidden."

"Don't worry. I've thought of a special place in my cell where no one will ever think to look."

That night as Katie waited for the abbess to begin snoring, she thought about her possible escape to Wittenberg. Each bit of the journey had its own terror. What would happen if they were caught? And what would she do if she did manage to get to Wittenberg? She had no clothes other than her convent costume, her shoes were in shreds, and she was still completely bald. Where would she stay? And what would she do? She had never worked for wages. As she considered the future, a hollow place formed in her stomach and kept expanding.

Soon the abbess began to snore and then to whistle. Encouraged, Katie spread out the tract and, holding her candle close, began to study it. As she was rereading the passage about vows, there was a sudden sound at the door. She froze and waited. It was merely a large gray mouse. The mouse looked in her direction, blinked, and scampered for a hole. Katie sighed with relief.

After a long session of prayer, Katie felt that it would please God for her to break the vows she had made in her immature youth. Completely satisfied, she hid Luther's tract behind the picture of St. Bernard, pinched out her candle, and went to sleep.

While Katie was working in the field the next day, Ave approached her. "I have the names of seven other girls who want to escape," she said. "They are my sister, Margaret, Elsa von Canitz, Ave Gross, Margaret and Katherine Zeschau, Magdalene von Staupitz, and Laneta von Goltz."

"Magdalene von Staupitz is a younger sister of John von Staupitz, and he's a special friend of Dr. Luther," said Katie.

She spoke with more enthusiasm than usual. "But I'm worried about your sister Margaret, and especially Elsa."

"Why?"

"Because they giggle all the time. It would be terrible if we were all hanged to an oak tree. Duke George—"

"Don't worry. I'll warn them."

It was now April. Lent came early in 1522. "We will be entering the forty-day period before the Resurrection during the last week of February," announced the abbess in solemn tones to the assembled nuns. "Lent is a most sacred time. These near-six weeks will help us to remember the sufferings of Jesus which ended on the cross on Good Friday. In order that we, too, might experience some suffering, we must keep our conversations to a minimum. Years ago we had to remain hungry most of the day, for, as you know, the rule is we can't dine before Vespers. But now His Holiness allows us to have Vespers early so that we can eat soon after midday. There will, of course, be no meat eaten during the forty days of Lent."

Two weeks after the beginning of Lent, Ave nodded to Katie just after Vespers, signaling for her to follow.

"Yes?" questioned Katie, standing in the shadows of a large oak.

"Three more nuns are considering escape. But two are worried about their vows. Could you get Doctor Luther's tract for me so that we can share it with them?"

"Of course. I will bring it here tomorrow, right after Vespers."

As Katie swallowed her last spoonful of the watery soup which contained nothing but a few bits of carrots and a cabbage leaf or two, she was so hungry she could have drained another five bowls. But the limit was one bowl for each nun.

Deep inside, Katie was anxious to go to her cell for rest and to make sure the tract was still in place behind the picture. But fearing that hurry would arouse suspicion, she lingered at the table with the other nuns. Finally, when she felt the time was right, she got up.

"Sister Katherine, I want to speak to you," said the abbess.

"Yes?"

"The woman who washes our dishes is not feeling well. Could you go into the kitchen and help her for an hour or two?"

Inwardly, Katie sighed. But there was no escape.

As Katie was finishing her sixth pile of bowls, the cook said, "I have a little cabbage left over. Would you like some?" Instead of answering, Katie wolfed it down as if she were famished.

After closing the door of her cell, Katie cautiously lifted St. Bernard's picture from its nail on the wall. The tract was gone! Sick at heart, she slowly sank to her bed. *What could have happened to it? Had she accidentally put it in another place?* Frantically, she searched under the bed, in the closet, in her bedding. She even looked behind the slender crucifix near the window. Slumped on the bed, she unconsciously began to wring her hands. Numb with fear, she sped down the steps three and four at a time and knocked at Ave's cell.

"I can't find the tract!" she cried. "It's . . . it's disappeared!"

Ave stared. "You can't find the tract!" she exclaimed in a hoarse whisper. "Oh, Katie, we're in trouble! Let's go to your cell and look."

After closing the door, Katie lifted the picture of St. Bernard, and Luther's tract thumped to the floor. She picked it up and stared. Then she leafed through it. "Yes, it is the same one! I . . . I . . . I can't believe it." Staring as if she had been confronted by a ghost in the graveyard, she reread the section about vows. This time her eyes all but popped, for that part had been clearly encircled by a faint line of ink!

Ave stared at the ink markings. "M-maybe the devil borrowed it . . ."

"What will we do?" wailed Katie. "Our plans have been discovered!" She rubbed her hands together and her eyes bulged in fear.

Ave shrugged. "Even if they have been, it's too late to change them now. While you were washing dishes I talked to Koppe. He's bringing his canvas-topped wagon on the Saturday before Easter. He'll be here at nine o'clock in the evening. All the sisters will have to be ready at the right time."

"But the moon will be bright! How can we keep from being seen? Duke George—"

"Koppe will keep his wagon hidden in the shadow made by the oak tree. The wagon will be full of empty herring barrels."

"Are we to get into the barrels?" Katie's eyes widened.

"I doubt if they're big enough! Still—"

This conversation was suddenly interrupted by a scratching at the door. The girls froze. Then they laughed. Going to the door, they found Methuselah, the convent cat. He slipped in and began to rub up against them. Katie picked him up and scratched him behind the ears. "You should have been here yesterday and caught the mouse that scared me."

Methuselah's only response was to increase the volume of his purring and to rub his whiskers on her wimple. "I'll miss you," said Katie, gently dropping him on the floor.

"From now on, we've got to get the girls organized," said Ave.

"And we must keep our plans secret." Katie crossed her lips with her finger. "And that frightens me. Some of the girls on the list are pretty talkative. Laneta can't seem to keep a secret for more than five minutes! What will we do?" She began to rub her hands again.

"I'll warn her that if we're caught, we may be hanged," replied Ave grimly.

As the moon began to enlarge toward the first week of April and Good Friday, Katie's heart kept speeding. Each evening she knelt by her bed and prayed for God's help. "I do want to do the right thing," she pleaded. "Make my life count. Show me, help me to obey."

Mysteriously, the entire dozen nuns who planned to escape squeezed onto the same bench during Good Friday services. This worried Katie, for they had all sat together on three recent occasions, and it had seemed to her that the abbess had studied them with a knowing look. That night Katie opened her window again and considered how she would jump to the woodshed and then to the ground. As she considered this way of escape, she wondered if the shed roof could stand the impact of her jump. She had meant to test it but had forgotten.

The moon on Saturday night was unusually plump. Its golden light pushed eerie shadows over large sections of the convent grounds. Katie studied the place where the wagon would enter the narrow gate in the wall. Then her eyes followed the path it would take to get to the splotch of shadows on the far side of the oak tree.

Since she would no longer be a nun, Katie considered leaving her wimple. Perhaps a remaining nun could use it. But no, this wouldn't do. She already had the beginnings of a cold. Also, her bald head would appear grotesque on the streets of Wittenberg if it were not covered. Moreover, a chill wind was now stirring the leaves in the oak tree.

While thoughts of Duke George and his executioners stirred in Katie's head, the abbess opened her cell door and Katie could hear the usual sounds she made as she prepared for her night's rest. She listened to the opening and closing of drawers, the pouring of water, a deep sigh, and the mumble of words as she repeated her evening prayers. Having nothing to pack, for she owned nothing, Katie was obliged to just sit and wait.

Outside, an owl hooted. Then a pair of tomcats got into a fight. Katie hoped that if Methuselah was one of them, his ears would not be chewed too severely. The dark shadows under the oak were now fluttering with the movement of the wind as if they were writing on the ground. Then she saw the silhouette of a wagon pull through the gate. *Was this Leonard Koppe?* If it was, he was early.

As Katie waited, the thumping of her heart speeded, sounding like the hoofs of a running horse. Then she noticed three shadows approaching the wagon and climbing inside. At the same time she began to hear the abbess's snores.

Watching, listening, Katie followed four more shadows mounting the wagon. As she concentrated, the snoring sounds seeping through the wall became more and more regular. The *nghos* were becoming interspersed with comfortable *mmmmms*. Excellent! But before she dared leave, there would have to be a series of whistles. While she waited, two more shadows flitted across the grounds. Still, there were no *shruuus*. Terror clutched her insides. *Would she be left behind?*

Then between the mournful hoot of an owl and the cry of a distant wolf, Katie began to hear the satisfying sleep-whistles: *shruuu, sh-s-sh-shruuuu, shruuu.* Those nasal sounds were music.

Her time had come!

Slowly, Katie lifted the window, taking care not to make the slightest noise. Encouraged by more *shruuus*, she began to ease her way out. She had just pushed her feet through the window when the door was noisily flung wide. A terrifying glance revealed the abbess. Pale as a sickly ghost, the yellow flame from her candle shimmered on her closely clipped skull.

"Come here, Sister Katherine!" she shrilled. Strangely, there was a wee note of kindness in her voice.

Dry as a baked brick, Katie's mouth sagged. She feared her heart would bump out of her chest. Feet like boulders, she was unable to move.

"Come here, Sister Katherine!" repeated the abbess.

Katie made an effort to obey. But she was paralyzed.

Her aunt then rushed to her. She threw her arms around her and between sobs murmured, "Oh, Katie, I wish I were going with you! And please forgive me for pretending I was asleep. I'm a curious old woman and it's easy to make snoring sounds! I've heard everything you and Ave have discussed from the beginning. I know all of your plans. The walls in this building are too thin." She dabbed at her eyes.

"I'm the one who borrowed the heretic's tract on marriage." And I believe there is a possibility that he may—I said may—be right." She went to the door. "Wait for me. I'll be back."

Returning from her cell, the abbess brought a shawl. It was a long, heavy one—the color of cream. "This shawl belonged to your mother. It was knitted by our grandmother. My sister wrapped you in it when you were born. The weather's cold this evening. Drape the shawl around your shoulders. When you get to Wittenberg you can wear it on your head until that beautiful red hair you have has grown out. I can still remember the pretty curls you had when you were little." She held Katie tight, kissed her soundly on both cheeks, and whispered, "*Auf Wiedersehen!*"

As she regained her balance on top of the woodshed, Katie looked upward at the window of her cell. Her eyes and those of her aunt met and lingered for a moment. Then her aunt waved, rubbed the mole on her chin and began to wipe her eyes.

4

Wittenberg

Because of her long dress, Katie had some difficulty in climbing into the wagon. By the light of the moon she could see that almost every space around the empty barrels had been taken. However, there was an empty spot toward the rear. Here she crouched in the midst of three barrels.

Nodding at each nun, Koppe counted, "*Ein, zwei, drei, vier, fünf . . .*" He concluded on an upbeat with the word, "*zwölf* [twelve]." Then, after looking fiercely around, he said, "I am doing a very dangerous thing. If I am caught in Duke George's territory, I will probably be hanged. This means that all of you must be very quiet and keep your heads down. Undoubtedly we will be challenged when we come to the border of Albertine Saxony. I know the guard at that place very well. He hates Luther and all of his followers. He told me that when Luther is burned at the stake, he wants to light the fire.

"I'm now going to cover you with a canvas. Please remember that we must all keep silent. Don't even breathe loudly!"

After these instructions, he pulled the canvas in place and flicked the horses with his whip.

In spite of the canvas, Katie was cold and was thankful for the shawl. She pulled it tightly around her shoulders and tried to relax. For a long time there was an eerie silence. Then a giggle broke the quiet. Katie shuddered. The giggle seemed to be coming from Elsa who was crouched up front. Elsa giggled at everything, and her giggles were contagious. She giggled when she spilt the milk; she giggled when a fly lit on the nose of the priest during mass; she even giggled when the abbess sentenced her to live on bread and water in her cell for a week.

Suddenly the wagon squeaked to a stop. "We must be quiet!" scolded Koppe angrily. "We're not far from the border. If I'm caught with a wagon full of nuns, I'll be executed. Remember, I have a wife! When we cross the border into Ernestine Saxony, I'll roll up the canvas and you can giggle all you like. You can even sing. But now each of you must remain as quiet as a corpse."

Gradually the wagon wheels began to turn again. Katie busied herself by praying in the depths of her mind. "Lord, guide us. Help us. Teach us. Make us useful," she pleaded. After what seemed an eternity, the wagon stopped and a sleepy male voice shouted, "Halt!" Then, after a painful moment of silence, the voice said, "Remove the canvas!"

Unconsciously, Katie began to wring her hands.

"And smell up the country?" asked Koppe. "The wagon's full of empty herring barrels. Can't you smell them?"

"Yes, I smell them, and they make me hungry. Lent has made me so hungry I could eat one all by myself—bones, tail, fins, eyes, and all."

"Friend, if I had one I'd give it to you," laughed Koppe. "But I left them all at Nimbschen. Lent is over and the nuns are famished."

"All right. All right. Keep going."

Several miles farther on the wagon eased to a stop at the foot of a small hill. Koppe rolled up the canvas. "Now you can breathe better and giggle all you like," he announced with a chuckle. His words were met with silence. Most of the former nuns were asleep.

As dawn was breaking and the dark outline of Torgau

loomed in the distance, Katie was overwhelmed. It seemed that each golden finger from the blotch of red was reaching toward her. "Wake up! Wake up!" she cried. "It's Easter morning! Jesus rose from the dead on this day, and so have we!" After all of them had stretched or yawned, she said, "Let's celebrate our freedom by singing." She led them in singing the third verse of St. Bernard's famous hymn. With enthusiasm, they sang:

> O hope of every contrite heart!
> O joy of all the meek!
> To those who fall, how kind thou art!
> How good to those who seek!

After another hour, the wagon stopped on the outskirts of Torgau. Here, three of the nuns climbed out to join their waiting parents. "*Danke! Danke!*" exclaimed one of the men after he had embraced his daughter. "You are another Moses. Wife and I can't thank you enough. *Danke! Danke!*"

A short time later, Koppe hitched his horses to a post in front of a sprawling frame house. "We'll remain here all day and leave for Wittenberg on Tuesday morning. Fill your stomachs and get some rest," he said.

Later that day, when Katie responded to the knock at her door, she found the long table was loaded. The many plates were heaped and overflowing with sausages, herring, rabbit. And there was a huge bowl of steaming vegetable soup. Katie laughed inside as she watched the man and his wife making efforts not to notice them. She knew their nine bald heads must have seemed very strange. She was finishing her last bit of sausage when a heavy-jowled man stepped through the door.

"I'm Gabriel Zwilling, a former monk and a close friend of Dr. Luther," he announced importantly, after he had removed his bright feathered beret. "It will be my pleasure to ride with you to Wittenberg. If you have questions, ask me."

"Where will we stay when we get there?" asked Katie.

"At the Black Cloister."

"And what is that?" questioned Ave von Schönfeld, speaking around a mouthful of cabbage. Her frown indicated doubt.

"Yes, the Black Cloister! It's the monastery where Doctor Martin and I and the other monks lived. It's called the Black Cloister because the monks wore black. Actually, it's made of red brick."

"But you're not dressed in black," objected Katie.

"True. When I learned that salvation is through faith alone, I removed my cowl. Carlstadt and I are radicals! Martin is more diplomatic. He still wears black."

During the day as Katie rested, her mind kept slipping back to Nimbschen. *Had she done right in breaking her vows? What would her father think?* There was no crucifix in the room where she was resting. This was most unusual. Also, neither the husband nor his wife, as generous as they were with the food, had crossed themselves before they ate. Instead, the man had closed his eyes and prayed out loud, requesting God's blessings on the food. This was strange! Deeply troubled, she prayed, "Lord, guide me . . ."

Early on Tuesday morning, after the girls had climbed into the wagon, Zwilling seated himself on a high box at the front. "You will be entering a new world," he said as they awaited Koppe. "Dr. Luther has asked me to explain things to you so that your new lives will not be a shock. As you know, he's a professor at the University of Wittenberg. He's extremely busy. Along with his writing, he preaches, settles disputes, and makes great efforts to calm the radicals." He laughed again. "Don't tell him I said so, but he desperately needs a wife. He hasn't made his bed for two years!"

The wagon was leaving Torgau when the back right wheel slipped into a sharp hole. Having no springs, the wagon leaped high and returned to the cobbled street with a spine-shaking thud.

"Hail, Mary!" exclaimed Katie.

"Oh, you mustn't say that!" scolded Zwilling. "There is no record that any of the apostles ever prayed to a saint."

"Then to whom should we pray?" asked Ave Gross.

"Jesus taught us to pray, 'Our Father who art in heaven . . .' "

After the wagon and its passengers had endured a morning of innumerable jolts, twists, and swaying caused by long ruts, the noon sun was reaching its zenith and beginning to move slowly toward the west. "We are now a little more than halfway to Wittenberg," announced Koppe, after he had stopped at an inn. "While the horses rest, we can get something to eat. Dr. Luther has kindly provided money to pay for everything. Order and eat anything you like."

This was the first time Katie had ever sat at a table in a public eating place. "And what would you like to eat?" asked the waiter.

"Soup," she managed after a long hesitation.

Winking at a man at another table, the waiter said, *Danke*," wiped his plump hands on his apron, and went to the kitchen.

Not one of the girls was wearing a wimple, and their bald heads attracted curious glances and scowls from the patrons.

The inn was just a short distance from Lippendorf, and Katie wondered if someone, perhaps a distant relative, might recognize her. Pushing this thought from her mind, she bowed in prayer, and for the first time in her memory began to eat without having crossed herself. She was half finished when an old man limped toward her on a crutch.

"Excuse me," he said. "Are you a nun?"

Glancing at his flat face and the long hairs growing out of his nose and ears, Katie had a feeling of revulsion. But forcing a smile, she said, "No. I used to be, but I've changed my faith. I'm now following the teachings of Dr. Luther."

"Luther!" the man shouted. "Luther! A fine girl like you following Luther?" He shook his head and massaged an ear. "Luther is the ambassador of Satan."

"And what are you going to do about it?" asked Zwilling.

"If we were in Duke George's territory, I'd have you and all of these apostate nuns arrested. Every one of you should be rotting in jail!"

"But we're not in Duke George's territory," replied Zwilling, pushing his face close to that of the old man and lifting his voice. "We're in the territory ruled by Frederick the Wise, who is also an elector of the Holy Roman Empire!"

"True," replied the flat-faced man, backing away, "but remember, George and Frederick are both Catholics. Also, they are first cousins! One of these days Elector Frederick will see the light, and when he does"—he gleefully rubbed his hands—"and when he does, Luther and Melanchthon, and that turncoat monk, Gabriel Zwilling, will be burned at the stake."

"And what do you have against Zwilling?" asked Zwilling.

"What do I have against him?" "Flatface" shook his head. "He's a renegade monk. Even Luther is ashamed of him."

Zwilling started to answer, but it was too late. "Flatface" had backed out the door. It was obvious he had not recognized Zwilling.

Everyone in the wagon was silent as the horses plodded along. Finally Zwilling said, "Since we'll be in Wittenberg this evening, I'll give you a short history of the town. Wittenberg is a small place. Only about 2500 people live there. But the city has a long history.

"The Elbe, as you will see, flows northward through this country and empties into the North Sea. In our part of Saxony—some call it Ernestine, others Electoral—the Elbe makes a sharp bend to the west, that is toward the Netherlands and France. In this area, there was a large hill of white sand. The Flemish immigrants from the west called this place *Witten Berg*. In Flemish that means White Mountain.

"The area began to be inhabited about 1174. However, there is a rumor that the Romans were there centuries before. When you get there, you will find that, in contrast to many German towns, the streets are straight. Indeed, they are at a right angle to the original marketplace. They are like that due to the original Wends who lived there before Albert the Bear brought in the Flemish immigrants . . ."

As Zwilling droned on, Katie wondered why he had not explained the accusations made by the old man at the inn.

Could it be that he was a wicked, immoral man? Then an even worse thought snaked into her mind. *Could it be that Koppe had deceived them and that he and Zwilling were going to sell them into slavery—or something even worse?* She closed her eyes and shuddered.

Suddenly Zwilling's "lecture" was interrupted by the clatter of the wagon's wheels on a bridge. "We're crossing the Elbe," he explained. "We'll be following it on its east side clear to Wittenberg. The Elbe is a mighty river. It's second only to the Rhine in usefulness. It starts in Bohemia, flows northward through Prague—the city where John Huss preached—and empties into the North Sea."

"Are there fish in it?" asked a girl eagerly.

"Yes, it's full of sturgeon, salmon, chad. It was the Elbe that helped make Wittenberg famous, for not only did it supply fish and water, but it was also useful for navigation. This is the reason the early inhabitants protected their city with a moat, thick walls, and fortifications."

Zwilling might have gone into more detail had it not been that the women were so tired many of them had stopped listening.

The sun was a crimson flame in the west when Koppe stopped in front of the Black Cloister. "This is where you will be staying until Dr. Luther can make better arrangements," he said. As Katie studied the massive building, a rather thin man of medium height strode up to the wagon. "I am Dr. Luther," he announced. "Welcome to Wittenberg—and to freedom."

After the girls had stepped out onto the lawn, Luther motioned to a man standing nearby. "Wolf," he said, "take their luggage to their rooms."

"Oh, but we don't have any luggage," laughed Ave Schönfeld.

"Then just show them to their rooms and get them something to eat. They've had a long journey."

5

The New Faith

When Katie opened her eyes, sunlight was streaming through the window onto the floor. She had overslept! Not wanting to miss anything, she quickly ran to the window. *What a dreary place!* she thought disappointedly. The brick buildings, tiled roofs, high chimneys, and little carts moving about seemed terribly impersonal—and unfriendly. In contrast to Nimbschen's tumbling streams, wide fields, and fertile valley patched with trees, Wittenberg was grotesque. Moreover, this morning the walled city was heavy with patches of smoke, and the smell of breweries and stale garbage bit at her nose.

Before her escape, Katie had visualized the joy she would experience when she first opened her eyes in Wittenberg. She had been mistaken. Instead of joy, she felt depressed. *Everything is so different*, she mused. Then brightening, she stated firmly, "But at least I'm free!"

Spotting the basin on the stand near her bed, Katie began pouring the water. As she scrubbed, she wondered what the day held for her. Lingering before the mirror, she twisted her head one way and then another. Yes, her hair was making progress. Indeed, the little scar which she had acquired on the peak of her skull when she was in pigtails at the age of three was almost completely covered.

At the table during the first meal of the day, Katie sat next to Ave von Schönfeld. There was plenty of food: a huge overflowing plate of scrambled eggs, a platter of sausage and crisp bacon, large pitchers of milk, fresh bread, and several dishes filled with an assortment of vegetables. There was also a tray crowded with fresh pears. But instead of heartily eating, most of the girls merely picked at their food.

"Has someone died?" asked Katie finally, hoping to dissipate the gloomy atmosphere.

No answer.

"Are all of you sick?"

No answer.

"Are you afraid of Duke George?"

No answer.

"How about you, Elsa? Can't you even giggle?"

A faint smile crossed Elsa's lips, but her eyes were glassy, expressionless.

"Well, if no one else will speak, or eat, or giggle," offered Ave, "let's persuade Katie to lead us in her favorite Saint Bernard hymn. Maybe that will cheer us up with memories of our imprisonment at Nimbschen."

Katie got to her feet and, facing her eight companions, began to sing, "Jesus, the Very Thought of Thee." But only Ave joined Katie in the hymn. Then with the suddenness of a stone crashing through a window, Martin Luther strode into the room. "I'm sorry I'm late," he apologized as he approached the table. "I had an early class."

As the doctor spoke, the nine sets of eyes watched in curious silence. He started to pull out a chair at the head of the table. Then leaving it where it was, he said, "Excuse me, I'll be right back." Katie followed him with her eyes as he moved toward the door. She noticed that his head angled slightly upward and that his back tilted backward. His posture was that of a person who has great confidence.

When Luther returned, he had a sheaf of paper in one hand and a lute in the other hand. He laid the sheaf of paper on the table, pulled out his chair, seated himself, and cradled the lute. "Now let us sing that hymn of Bernard of Clairvaux," he said. "He was one of the greatest Christians of all times. I love both his hymns and his writings." Then, as he ran his fingers across the strings, he led them in singing the well-known hymn.

Katie was impressed with Luther's deep baritone voice. It had both volume and range. She was also impressed by the way her friends responded.

At the end of three verses, Luther stood up. "I have a feeling that some of you are bewildered and a little afraid. Let me assure you that all of you are perfectly safe while you are here in Wittenberg. Frederick the Wise is a very generous and understanding man.

"Also, I know that some of you are a little embarrassed because you don't have shoes or street clothes. Don't worry. The people here are gathering clothes and shoes for you, and before long each of you will also have a home to go to. The Lord helped you escape, as He has done for others." After glancing at the clock, he continued.

"Escaping Nimbschen and coming here where we don't believe in penance is a shock—especially to a lady who has been raised in a convent." He smiled. "It's like jumping from a hot bath through a hole in the ice of a frozen river. But perhaps I can ease that shock by telling you how I escaped that false doctrine and was gently led by the Holy Spirit to agree with dear brother Paul that 'the just shall live by faith.' Learning the real meaning of those words took several years."

He paused and ran his fingers through the curly dark hair that covered his head and ears. "When I entered the Augustinian cloister at Erfurt, I was determined to be just as dedicated as Saint Bernard. As you were at Nimbschen, we were kept busy saying prayers, going to confession, celebrating the eucharist. All of us were awakened by a bell at one or two o'clock in the morning. Each of us then hurriedly made the sign of the cross and donned our white robe. At the sound of the second bell, we went to church. There, we sprinkled ourselves with holy water, knelt before the high altar, and prayed.

"Following this period of worship, we had another. Then another. And another. We worshiped seven times each day. In this fashion we crowded all of our waking period with worship and more worship."

As Luther spoke, Katie sat with her mouth slightly ajar. The doctor's words flowed like a mountain stream, and his gestures were perfect, dramatic. When he spoke about the cup, his artistic hands shaped one in such a way that Katie visualized a silver chalice filled with wine. But his eyes were the most captivating part of his personality. Brown as berries, they glowed, sparkled, commanded, radiated life.

"As you may know, my father, Hans, wanted me to become a lawyer. When I refused and decided to become a monk, he was brokenhearted—and angry. Finally, it was time for me to say my first mass. Since this would be a highlight in my life, I invited him to come. And he did. In addition, he brought a generous gift to the monastery. Finally, it was time for me to don my vestments and proceed.

"Soon, in most solemn tones, I recited the words: 'We offer unto thee, the living, the true, the eternal God.' At these words I was utterly stupefied and terror-stricken. I thought to myself, 'With what tongue shall I address such Majesty, seeing that all men ought to tremble in the presence of even an earthly prince? Who am I, that I should lift up mine eyes or raise my hands to the divine Majesty? The angels surround Him. At His nod the earth trembles. And shall I, a miserable little pigmy, say, 'I want this, I ask for that'? For I am dust and ashes and full of sin, and I am speaking to the living, eternal and the true God."

Katie had become so interested in this part of the speaker's story that she unconsciously pressed her palms together as if she were at prayers.

"That first mass," continued Luther, "inspired me to be even more dedicated. In order to please God, I went on long fasts, slept without coverings even in the coldest part of the winter, wore only enough clothes to be decent, and prayed during all the time I was awake. I was a good monk, and I kept the rule of my order so strictly that if ever a monk could get to heaven by his monkery, it was I. All my brothers who knew me will bear me out. If I had kept on any longer, I should have killed myself with vigils, prayers, reading, and other work.

"But still I was convinced that I wasn't doing enough. Dark temptations assailed me. At that time I had fasted so much my fellow monks could see my bones. What was I to do? Fast more? No, I couldn't fast more; that would have killed me.

"I followed the teachings of the church!

"According to that teaching, the saints had more merit than necessary to get to heaven, and so their surplus merits are pooled into a spiritual bank. Since this bank was available to me, I sought to avail myself of their surplus merits in order to cover my deficiencies. Alas, the bank of merit is controlled by the pope! Moreover, when he allows merit to be transferred, this is called an *indulgence*."

Luther glanced again at the clock and then, as he paced back and forth, continued:

"In 1510, due to a dispute in the Augustinian Order which only the pope could settle, another brother and I were chosen to go to Rome and represent Erfurt. That was an exciting trip! I enjoyed every mile. Some of the scenery, especially in the Alps, was magnificent. Since there were many monasteries on the way, we always had a pleasant place to stay.

"One of the reasons I longed to visit Rome was that the Eternal City has more relics than any place in the world. Viewing these relics would provide me with a vast number of merits. But the city was a disappointment. It smelled even worse than Wittenberg! Still, I determined to take advantage of my stay. With a travel book in my hand, I located and visited many famous shrines. Since I don't have much time, I'll tell you about only one—the *Scala Sancta*. This is the staircase which allegedly stood in front of Pilate's palace in Jerusalem which Jesus ascended when He faced him on Good Friday.

"I trembled in awe before those steps. The idea that I, Martin Luther, the son of a miner, would be climbing the very steps Jesus had climbed, was overwhelming. In my mind I could hear the crowd below as it shouted, 'Crucify Him! Crucify Him!' And since some pope had decreed that anyone who climbed them on his knees could select a soul to be released from purgatory, I climbed all twenty-eight steps and groaned a fervent *Pater Noster* on each one. As I prayed and moved upward, I almost wished my parents were dead so that I could release them from purgatory. But since they were both alive, I compromised. I prayed for the release of Grandpa Heine.

"However, I must confess that even at that time I was not a total believer. When I stood to leave, I muttered to myself, 'Who knows whether it is so?'

"Why was I a doubter? In Rome I had seen too much! At one place I almost disbelieved my ears when I heard an Italian priest address the sacrament, 'Bread art thou and bread thou wilt remain, and wine thou art and wine wilt thou remain.' But that wasn't all. I was horrified at the flippancy of some priests who were saying mass for the dead. Some could rattle through six or seven masses in the time I could say one. And when I was in the midst of saying a mass, they would nag me, '*Passa! Passa!* [Get a move on!]' Even today I shudder at the time I spent in Rome."

He picked up the sheaf of papers by his plate. "While I was in the Wartburg Castle hiding from the emperor, Charles V, I translated the New Testament into German. I had hoped to present each of you one of the first copies. But the book won't be off the press until September. Lucas Cranach, one of our close friends, has been making the woodcuts and I don't think he has finished all of them. Since I don't have copies, I've printed some of the key verses that led me into the truth." He handed copies out to all the girls and then continued. "Each of those verses is just as important as the compass was to Columbus. That compass enabled him to discover the New World. Study each scripture and commit them to memory. I will discuss them with you later."

He glanced at the clock and almost ran toward the door. "I have another class," he mumbled over his shoulder as he left.

After Luther had disappeared, Katie said, "I wish I had asked him about Gabriel Zwilling. That man puzzles me."

6

A New World

The following day as Katie stood looking at herself in the mirror, she wasn't altogether unhappy with what she saw. Her smile revealed two rows of even teeth. She saw a firm chin, sky-blue slightly slanted eyes, full cupid lips, reddish eyebrows and a matching brush of hair now allowed to grow, and street clothes in place of her habit.

Turning from side to side, she studied her hair and considered how she would wear it when it was sufficiently long. Her high-collared blouse was a little snug around her shoulders. Otherwise, it was perfect, as was the matching skirt that reached to her ankles. The black shoes were those of a peasant. The outfit might not be up-to-date, but it was nice— and she was free. The realization brought a surge of joy to her heart.

The atmosphere at the long table during the first meal of the day was completely different from the day before. Dressed in their new attire, the former nuns were full of chatter, feeling now that they could fit into the new society. Elsa giggled in her customary way, and all of them emptied their plates and asked for second helpings. Halfway through the meal, Martin Luther stepped in.

"I see that you are happier than you were yesterday," he

said, taking his place. "New clothes can brighten a woman's heart I'm told."

"But our hair is so short," complained Ave.

"Don't worry. Your hair will grow. Mine was shaved in the center in order that I might have a crown of thorns. Look at it now! If it weren't for my cowl, no one would know that I had been a monk." After bowing his head for silent prayer, he began eating voraciously.

Fascinated, Katie watched Luther empty his plate and heap it again. The day before, she had observed his brown eyes, encircled by a golden-like border. She also noted their piercing eagle quality.

After Luther had consumed his meal, he got up and said, "Yesterday, I presented you with some scriptures printed on sheets of paper. But I neglected to tell you that you should bring them to each meal. And now, if you don't mind, I think it would be proper for each of you to go to your cells—I mean your rooms!—and return with your copies. If you're like most of the priests and nuns I know, you've never studied the Bible. To us, the Word is far more important than tradition."

Katie rushed up the steps, picked up her sheet, and returned to the table. After all were assembled, Luther said, "Perhaps I could answer any questions you might have. I have to leave soon for a class."

Hand high, Katie said, "Please tell us about the mistake Erasmus discovered in the Vulgate."

"In [Matthew 4:17], Erasmus discovered that Jerome had translated the Greek word *metanoia* into the Latin *poenitentiam agite* which means do penance. This is incorrect. And so he changed it to *poeniteat vos*. Those Latin words mean: be penitent. There is, you can see, a vast difference between the two translations. Later, Erasmus had more light on the subject and changed *metanoia* to *resipiscite* which, as all who understand Latin know, means: change your mind.[1]

---

[1]This passage in the KJV reads: "From that time Jesus began to preach, and to say, Repent: for the kingdom of heaven is at hand."

"As you can see, there is a vast difference between changing one's mind and doing penance!

"I was teaching here at Wittenberg when Erasmus made that discovery. It opened my eyes and became more important to me than the discovery of the New World!"

"Now tell us how you learned that 'the just shall live by faith,' " said Ave.

Luther glanced at the clock. "That's a long story and time is short. But briefly, this is what happened. On Tuesday, August 16, 1513, I gave a lecture to my students on Psalm 31. As I was preparing that lecture, I was puzzled by the words *In Justitia tua libera me*—'In thy righteousness deliver me.' What did those words mean? I searched the commentaries for an answer. There was none. I reasoned, How can I, made of dust, avail myself of the righteousness of God? It seemed impossible. Then I came across the same idea in another place, Psalm 71:2. There I read, *'Deliver me in thy righteousness.'* I paced the floor seeking an answer. But I did not find one." He glanced at the clock again.

"Almost two years later in April 1515, I was reading in the Book of Romans, and I saw 'the just shall live by faith.' Since I was then lecturing on Romans, I did some searching. Soon, I was confronted with nearly the same words in Habakkuk 2:4.

"Then, as I was struggling with my digestive process, the words *righteous* and *righteousness of God* struck me like flashes of lightning. All at once, I felt as if I had been reborn. In the same moment the whole of Scripture became apparent to me. My mind ran through the scriptures as far as I could recollect them, seeking analogies to other phrases such as the 'work of God,' 'that which God works in us,' 'the wisdom of God,' 'by which he makes us wise,' 'the salvation of God,' 'the glory of God.' This passage of Paul, 'the just shall live by faith,' became to me the very gate to Paradise." He glanced at the clock again.

"I'm going to be a little late," he continued. "But I want to mention something else. During the following year I came across the discovery Erasmus had made—the one we've discussed. His book confirmed my belief that 'the just shall live by faith.' Now, since I may have bored you with all this heavy theology, I'll sing you a little song." Accompanying himself on his lute, he sang:

> He said to me: "Hold thou me,
> Thy matters I will settle;
> I gave myself all for thee,
> And I will fight the battle.
> For I am thine, and thou art mine,
> And my place also shall be thine;
> The enemy shall not part us. . . ."[2]

As Luther sang, in his beautiful baritone voice, the words brought hope and encouragement to the girls. God had helped them escape. *He would hold them. He would help them through their problems. He would fight for them.*

As Luther stepped out the door, he said, "I've arranged for Gabriel Zwilling to show you about the city—"

"May I ask a question?" interrupted Katie.

"Certainly."

Katie related what "Flatface" had said about Zwilling at the inn. Then she asked, "Are we really safe in his company?"

Luther laughed, rubbed his hands together, and laughed again. "Of course you'll be safe with Brother Zwilling! He's just a little radical. I had to straighten him out in the same way Aquila and Priscilla straightened out Apollos."

"But what did he do?" persisted a voice.

"That's a long story. You don't have the background to understand it. After I've explained how I was outlawed by Charles V, was kidnapped and went into hiding, I'll tell you what happened. But now I must leave."

Outside in her street clothes, it seemed to Katie that everyone was staring at her. Soon Zwilling appeared. He was wearing a yellow-striped coat and sporting several crimson feathers in his beret.

---

[2]*Luther's Works*, vol. 53, pp. 219–220.

As they journeyed through the city, Zwilling began to expound. "Wittenberg is an important city," he said. "But it isn't very large. Many hold it in contempt. Duke George once remarked, 'It is intolerable for a single monk living in such a hole to launch a reformation.' " Zwilling laughed. "But as you know, God's ways are not our ways. And someday, the reformation that is being born here will sweep the world." He pointed to the Elstertor gate on the far east side. "From that gate just over there to the Coswiger Tor gate on the west side is only a little more than a thousand paces. Anyone can walk across the city in ten minutes. Then from the Elbtor gate on the south side to the Franziskanerkolster gate on the north side is a mere four blocks. But first, let's talk about the Black Cloister where you've been staying."

He pointed to the many chimneys and windows. "At one time as many as forty monks lived there. You should have seen them! Dressed in black, they were a sight! Follow me." He led them to a tall pear tree. "Luther and his friends used to gather here to discuss the fine points of theology. I remember those days very well. It was under this tree that John Staupitz—he was the first dean of the Wittenberg theological faculty—persuaded Martin to prepare for his doctor of theology degree."

Zwilling nodded toward a pigsty and henhouse. "These places are filthy. Our friend, Dr. Martin, needs a wife to keep them clean. There's enough space here for a good woman to raise a large garden and supply enough bacon and eggs to make any man happy." He sighed. "But Dr. Martin is not about to get married."

"And why not?" asked Katie, raising her voice a trifle.

"He's too busy. He's always lecturing and writing books. Also, he's afraid of being burned at the stake."

"Is that really possible?" asked Ave von Schönfeld, frowning.

"Of course! Duke George would have him burned today if it weren't for his cousin, Frederick the Wise."

"Why?" asked several.

"Because Duke George hates heretics. Come, let me take you through the Elstertor gate."

This gate, which penetrated the high wall encircling the city, was less than a quarter of a block to the east of them. As they passed through the wall, Zwilling said, "Many despise our city. Consequently, across the centuries armies have attacked it. That's the reason for the wall—and the moat just beyond."

"How large is the moat?" asked someone.

"It flows around the city, and in places it's more than fifty feet deep. The walls and cannon and moat give us a lot of protection. But let's cross the bridge. I must show you something that's far more important than human fortifications."

While crossing the wooden structure, Katie kept putting a hand to her nose. "Why the smell?" she asked, unable to endure the stench any longer.

"Because this is where the Wittenbergers burn their infected clothes and slaughter their animals. Look at the bones and bits of skin. Try to put up with the smell for a bit, for this is a very dramatic place, and I want you to see it. History was made here!" Motioning with his pudgy hands for them to gather around, he asked, "How many of you have heard of the pope's bull, *Exsurge, Domine*?"

They all nodded, and Laneta von Goltz said, "The abbess at Nimbschen recited to us the part which commanded Luther's books to be burned."

"Did she read the section in which His Holiness threatened excommunication if Martin Luther didn't recant?" Zwilling tweaked his feathers as he awaited an answer.

Following a whispered consultation, Katie replied, "No, we don't remember that section."

"Well"—Zwilling threw his shoulders back as if he were about to make the world's most important announcement—"in that bull which was published on June 15, 1520, Pope Leo concluded:

> Now therefore we give Martin sixty days in which to submit, dating from the time of the publication of this bull in

his district. Anyone who presumes to infringe our excommunication and anathema will stand under the wrath of Almighty God and of the Apostles Peter and Paul.

"Those were sneaky words! How did Dr. Luther respond? At 9 a.m. on December 10, 1520—remember that date—the university students assembled here. Luther's books had been burned all over Germany. Now it was time to burn some of the pope's books! Soon a fire was going. Then various books crammed with dogma were tossed into the flames. You should have seen the way those students worked.

"Martin Luther was thoughtfully silent as the smoke curled upward. Suddenly his eyes gleamed. From within his gown he withdrew the papal bull, and as if it were a poisonous snake, threw it into the blaze. As it burned, he solemnly remarked, 'Because thou hast destroyed the truth of God, may the Lord consume thee in these flames.'

"It was a spine-tingling moment!" Zwilling's eyes widened.

"After the faculty had returned to the university, a student dressed like Leo X sauntered across the bridge. He was even crowned with the papal triple tiara. This was too much!" Zwilling clapped his hands. "The students stripped him and burned his robes."

"Very interesting," commented Katie. "But, please, Herr Zwilling, what had Dr. Luther done to cause this commotion?"

Zwilling stared. "What! Don't you know about the Ninety-five Theses?"

"Never heard of them."

"How could that be?" Zwilling shook his head.

"Convent walls are high. We were cut off from news."

"Then why did you escape?" Zwilling tweaked his feathers.

"Because we learned through Dr. Luther's tracts that salvation is attained through faith, not penance."

"Then you learned that it was Erasmus who discovered that truth?"

"We did," affirmed several.

Zwilling laughed. "Today, Erasmus and Luther have parted. Still, Dr. Luther credits Erasmus for opening the door of truth to him. The trouble is, Luther charges through a problem like a wild elephant, while Erasmus tries to walk barefoot on rotten eggs without cracking them. Strangely, the book which confirmed Luther's conclusions was dedicated to Leo X!" He smiled and clapped his hands. "The good Lord has a way of providing humor for His children." He led them back across the moat and through the gate.

"Where are you taking us now?" asked Katie.

"I'm taking you clear across the city to the Castle Church where Dr. Luther started the storm by nailing his theses on the church door." A few minutes later he stopped in front of a five-story building.

"This is the home of Philip Melanchthon, one of Luther's best friends. As you can see, he lives only a stone's throw from the Black Cloister. He's brilliant. He came to Wittenberg to teach Greek when he was only eighteen. He has a slight impediment of speech and twists his shoulder when he walks. Once I heard a student ask Luther what Paul was like, and he replied, 'I think he was a scrawny shrimp like Melanchthon!' Now please don't tell him I told you that. It would embarrass him." He laughed.

"Is he married?" asked someone.

"Oh, yes. His wife's name is Katherine."

The group had just started up the street when Melanchthon's door opened and a young man stepped out. "Well, Gabriel," he said, "I see you have a lot of girlfriends."

"They are former nuns, just escaped form Nimbschen. I'm showing them around Wittenberg," explained Zwilling. By the frown on his face it was apparent that he didn't relish being called by his first name, nor did he recall the stranger.

"My name is Jerome Baumgaertner," replied the young man as he took Zwilling's hand in a firm grip. "You ought to remember me. I was here in school from 1518 to 1521."

Zwilling peered long and hard into his dark eyes. Then

his face lighted. "Yes, of course. You're from Nuremburg and from a distinguished family. Right?"

"Correct. And now, Father Zwilling, do you mind if I tag along?"

"Suit yourself. But I'm not Father Zwilling!"

"Sorry. Just teasing."

As the young ladies followed the men along the Collegien Gasse, the German name for Street, nine sets of eyes studied Jerome. They all longed to discuss this dashing young man, but they feared being overheard. Katie was especially curious about his dark beret, so wide that it lapped over the well-groomed hair covering his ears.

At the market, halfway across the city, Zwilling stopped. "Collegien Gasse ends here," he explained. "From here to the western wall, the street's name is Schloss Gasse. Now look north," he directed, pointing with his arm fully extended. "The building you see with two spires—actually there's a third one, but we can't see it from here—is the City Church. Johannes Bugenhagen is pastor. He's a good friend of Dr. Luther—translated his New Testament into Low German—"

"And that's where Dr. Luther attends," broke in Jerome.

"Bugenhagen is a good preacher," continued Zwilling. "But he's long-winded. A while back a man returned from services and found that his dinner was only half cooked. 'What's the matter?' he complained. 'I thought Bugenhagen would preach,' answered his wife, 'and so I took my time. You must have had a guest preacher.' 'We did,' he said. 'Dr. Luther preached, and he knows when to stop!' "

"Another thing about Bugenhagen is that he was the first monk in Wittenberg to marry," added Jerome. "By doing that, he founded the Lutheran manse. Rumor is that he courted one woman and married another."

"Before we proceed," said Zwilling, a slight note of annoyance in his voice, "I want you to take a long look at those towers. There are three bells in the main towers: big, medium, and small. The large bell is rung only on very special occasions, such as the funeral of a well-known person. It is also rung when a master's degree is given. In 1519, it was rung to celebrate Luther's doctorate. The little bell in the tower you can't see is used to summon the children to their classes. But let's go on to the Castle Church."

At the west end of Schloss Gasse, the group came to the castle—a large, five-cornered stone building which formed a huge inner open space. The Castle Church with its tower was on the southwest side.

Facing the door of the church, Zwilling said, "These buildings were first erected about a century ago. Then when Elector, Frederick the Wise, came into power, he had them completely rebuilt. He spent money lavishly and we are all happy with the result. This Castle Church is used by the university for convocations, the conferring of degrees, and so on.

"Now please look at the door. This door has served as a sort of bulletin board. All kinds of notices are tacked on it." He touched one with his finger. "Here's an announcement that Melanchthon won't meet his four o'clock Greek class on Monday. Well, one day Dr. Luther was so disturbed by the way Tetzel was selling indulgences that he dashed off ninety-five theses attacking them and other problems in the church, and tacked them to this door.

"Each thesis—a proposition for argument—was written in the strong language Doctor Luther often uses. The reason he posted them was that he wanted to debate each issue with a well-informed opponent. He had no idea that this act would set the world on fire.

"Now it so happened that Doctor Luther nailed the ninety-five theses to this door at a very special time. November 1, 1517, was the Festival of All Saints. That is a very special day, especially here in Wittenberg, for on that day Frederick the Wise always displayed his huge collection of relics.

"Martin Luther had his document ready to post on October 31, which is the eve of All Saints' Day. That year Wittenberg was crowded with pilgrims who had come for miles to see the relics. Those relics, gathered by Frederick the Wise, are fascinating. For example, he has—" Suddenly he clamped his jaws shut and sealed his lips with his index finger. "Oh, I forgot," he groaned. "Dr. Luther told me to reserve that story because he wants to relate it to you himself so that you'll get it straight. Sometimes this big mouth of mine gets me into all sorts of trouble!" He glanced at the sun. "The time has really slipped by. Do you think you can get back to the Black Cloister on your own?"

"I'll go with them," offered Jerome.

7

Cornerstones

It was the first Sunday after their escape, and Katie and her friends were enjoying a dinner of roast beef and cabbage with Dr. Luther at the cloister. When they had finished their meal, Dr. Luther made an announcement. "Places are opening for some of you," he said. "And since many of you will be moving before the end of the month, I want to explain a few of the cornerstones of our faith. This is important, for you will be working with other families or raising your own children, and it is expedient for you to understand our complete trust in the Bible."

Luther then led the nine girls up to his study in the tower. The austere-looking room had a double window overlooking the Elbe. It was furnished with dark paneled walls, a five-tiered stove, and a wide table where Dr. Luther worked. The table overflowed with books.

In solemn tones, and with his fingers on his cowl, Luther said, "This room is to me what the burning bush was to Moses. It was in this room that I learned the true meaning of justification. But since I've already spoken to you about that, I want to tell you about those ninety-five theses that almost sent me to the stake—"

"Herr Zwilling mentioned your ninety-five theses," cut in Katie.

"Did he explain them?" demanded Luther, a shadow crossing his face.

"No. He started to and then he stopped. He said that you wanted to explain them yourself."

"Good for him!" From a corner, Luther picked up a tightly rolled manuscript. "This is a copy of those theses. Now follow me and I will tell you how I came to nail them to the door of the Castle Church. As we walk along I will also explain to you the history of relics and indulgences."

As the thin man clothed in the garments of a monk led the way downstairs, his gown caught on a nail. "Let me mend it for you," offered Katie and Ave von Schönfeld almost as one voice.

"Never mind," replied Luther hurriedly. "When I was a monk I learned to repair my own clothes. Besides, the rip isn't very bad." He laughed.

At the bottom of the steps, Luther pointed up the street with the roll of manuscript and said, "Come this way." While heading along the Collegien Gasse toward the Castle Church, he stopped in front of Melanchthon's house. "Gather close," he said, "while I explain something. Archbishop Albert didn't have to search long to find an energetic candidate to sell indulgences. Germany, as always, was full of energetic men who wanted to earn a little extra money."

"And who was Archbishop Albert?" asked Katie. "And what did he have to do with indulgences? I thought only the pope could issue indulgences!" She and several of her friends frowned.

"The answer to your questions," replied Luther with a note of amusement in his voice, "goes back to Rome's constant thirst for money. Pope Leo X, the pope who died last year, felt that he needed rivers and then oceans full of money. Part of the reason for this was that he was the son of Lorenzo the Magnificent, the tycoon of Florence, to whom money was like snow and had to be shoveled away in order to get rid of it. And so, first of all, we must know about him.

"Leo—his real name was Giovanni—had a very good

mind. He could read when he was only three and a half years old. The lad received his tonsure before he was eight."

"Tonsure?" enquired a voice.

"Yes, the top of his head was shaved to show that he was not a layman. When he was thirteen, Pope Julius II made him a deacon cardinal. He was the youngest person ever to receive that honor. If that's an honor!" Luther chuckled.

"Leo was more interested in art than theology. I doubt if he ever really studied the Bible. When he was elected pope in 1513 he faced a problem, for he had never been ordained. The authorities solved that difficulty by ordaining him a priest on March 15, a bishop on the 17th, and crowning him pope on the 19th.

"Hunting was a sport that Pope Leo really loved. He said he enjoyed the fresh air. Sometimes he invited a thousand or even two thousand of his friends to go with him."

"Didn't that cost a lot of money?" asked Ave.

"Of course. But, as I said, money meant nothing to him. He had a vast income, which he spent freely. Those hunts caused another problem, for when he was on one he didn't like to take off his boots, and that annoyed his master of ceremonies."

"Why would that annoy him?" asked Katie.

"The master of ceremonies—his name was Paris de Grassis—was annoyed because those boots made it impossible for anyone to kiss his master's toe!" He laughed, the girls joining him in his merriment.

After they had stopped laughing, Luther adjusted his beret and continued. "But Pope Leo's great problem was to finish St. Peter's, the massive cathedral started by Pope Julius II. At first he raised money by selling offices in the church. He ordained 31 new cardinals and made a profit of 500,000 ducats."[1]

"How could anyone pay that much?" asked Laneta von Goltz.

---

[1]Approximately sixty million 1986 U.S. dollars.

Luther shrugged. "That *is* a lot of money," he replied. "But remember, many of the cardinals have incomes of 30,000 ducats each year."

Elsa giggled. Then she exclaimed, "That much money would buy a lot of sausage!"

"That it would," agreed the former monk, smiling, "but a lot of the princes of the church live extremely high. Several of them have as many as three hundred servants."

As they approached the Castle Church, Luther said, "Now I must tell you about Albert. Although he was only twenty-four and already the bishop of Halberstadt and Magdeburg, he longed to be the archbishop of Mainz. Albert approached Leo through the German banking house of Fugger. He chose them because he knew many of the popes had borrowed huge amounts of money from their banks.

" 'The price will be twelve thousand ducats,' replied the spokesman for Fugger. 'Pope Leo wants a thousand ducats for each of the twelve apostles.'

" 'That's too much!' bargained Albert. 'I'll give them seven thousand ducats—a thousand for each of the deadly sins.'

"They finally compromised for ten thousand ducats, a thousand for each of the ten virgins. After he was given his new office, Albert had to think of a way to repay the house of Fugger; for, even though he now had the vast income of three bishoprics, ten thousand ducats, together with all the interest, is a lot of money.

"But the solution to Albert's problem was simple." Luther waved his rolled theses and shook his head in despair. "Pope Leo authorized him to sell indulgences! And, in order to do that effectively, Archbishop Albert hired John Tetzel, a Dominican priest, to do the actual selling. The Dominican order, as you know, was founded by St. Dominic. Dominic believed in poverty and was a close friend of Francis of Assisi. Nonetheless, Tetzel had an insatiable greed for money. Yes, human beings are full of contradictions!"

Arriving in front of the church, Luther pointed to the Ninety-five theses. "Now I'll explain indulgences," he said, "and why I nailed the theses on the door on October 31. That day is Holy Evening.[2] It is called that because it is the day before All Saints' Day.

"We will start with the history of indulgences, for it was my reaction to them that got me into trouble. The history—" Luther was interrupted by Jerome who had elbowed his way through a group of students and took his place with the girls on the top step of the church.

"Did you want something, Jerome?" asked Luther.

"I just want to listen," replied Jerome.

"All right. You can listen. But I'd appreciate it if you didn't ask any questions or make any comments. Do you understand?"

"Yes, I understand!" replied Jerome. Then stepping to Katie's side he said in a low voice, "I haven't met you personally."

"I'm Katherine von Bora."

"Katherine? I like that. How—" He stopped abruptly when he caught Luther's less than friendly glance.

"As I said," continued Luther, "the history of indulgences is long. It goes back to the Crusades—that period when the Christians tried to recapture the Holy Lands.

"During those wars, the Muslims had an advantage, for their soldiers had been taught that if they should die in battle while fighting Christians, their souls would leap immediately into Paradise. In contrast, the Crusaders feared death because they faced millions of years in the cleansing torments of purgatory. This difficulty was solved by the popes in the eleventh century. They decreed that all Christians who fell in battle while fighting Muslims automatically had all their sins forgiven and would thus escape purgatory.

"Ah, but this led to another problem." Luther began to pace back and forth and to pull nervously on his cowl. "This problem was that many Christians were physically unable to fight in the holy wars. Again the solution was child's play.

---

[2]Halloween.

The authorities in Rome agreed that an indulgence could be granted to each one who donated enough money to support a Crusader!

"In this manner, the idea was advanced that by paying money an applicant could purchase an indulgence which would pay for the forgiveness of his sins, or those of another. By the time of Pope Boniface VIII, the church was in great need of money. It was then decided to raise money by the sale of indulgences, even though this money would not be used for a holy war against the Muslims.

"Since we have now learned about indulgences, let's think of John Tetzel and the way in which he sold indulgences. Each time he approached a city, Tetzel was met by the city fathers. Then, forming a procession, he and the dignitaries solemnly headed for the town square. There he preached a sermon on hell. It was extremely dramatic; his audience could almost smell the flames, feel the heat, and hear the screams of the damned.

"Following this sermon, Tetzel led the way to the largest church or cathedral in town. There he preached on purgatory. But sometimes the crowd was too large for the sanctuary. In that case, he preached outside.

"On each occasion, a large cross was planted in the ground or stood in the church. The pope's bull granting the indulgence was displayed on an elaborate cushion embroidered with gold and fastened to the cross.

"Swinging his arms, wiping his eyes, lifting his hands, choking with emotion, Brother John was most convincing. Having described the terrible anguish of the cleansing flames, he would ask between sobs, 'Are you not willing to help them out of this terrible place?' Then he would cry, 'Listen to the voices of your dead relatives and friends, beseeching you and saying, "Pity, pity us. We are in dire torment from which you can redeem us for a pittance. Do you not wish to?" '

"Next," continued Luther, "Tetzel would add, 'Hear the father saying to his son, the mother to her daughter, "We bore you, nourished you, brought you up, left you our fortunes, and you are so cruel and hard that now you are not willing for so little to set us free. Will you let us lie here in the flames? Will you, dear children, delay our promised glory?" ' Then, his quivering hands outstretched and his face lifted heavenward, he would exhort, 'Remember that you are able to release them immediately for *as soon as a coin in the coffer rings, the soul from purgatory springs.*

" 'Will you not, then, for a quarter of a florin receive these letters of indulgence through which you are able to lead a divine and immortal soul into the fatherland of Paradise?'

"At that moment the people crowded and poured their coins into the money boxes." Luther shook his head in disgust. "Whenever I think about it my stomach churns! But this fraud never bothered Tetzel. He liked to brag that he had sent more people to heaven than St. Peter himself. He became an extremely rich man."

Luther unrolled his copy of his theses and held it high against the door. "Frauds like John Tetzel—and there are many like him—grieved me so much I finally dashed off these questions about the system. I would read you a few of them, but I have an appointment. An official is coming to discuss with me the uprising of the peasants. I'll let Jerome read them to you." As he handed the roll to Jerome, Katie said, "But, Dr. Luther, I thought you were going to tell us about relics."

"You're right." He nervously glanced at the sun again. Then he said, "I guess that official can wait a few more minutes! All of you should know about the superstitions that surround relics.

"Since most of you never specialized in Church History, you may not know that the Council of Nicaea decreed that no church should be without relics. Relics—bones of the saints, their clothing, or something they've touched—are in churches throughout Christendom. Some are authentic, most are not.

"In Rome, the authorities claim they have the bones of Peter and Paul, a coin Judas received for betraying Christ, the post from which he hanged himself, splinters of the cross, and so on.

"Across the centuries there has been an active demand for relics. There are many collectors. One of the most zealous collectors is our own ruler, Frederick the Wise.

"He began his collection when he visited the Holy Land years ago. I was told that in 1509 he had 5,005 items. Viewing these relics, it was said, would reduce one's time in purgatory by 1,443 years. Encouraged by the enthusiasm of the people to view his collection, Frederick gathered more. By 1520, he had assembled 19,013 fragments of bones."

"Human bones?" asked Katie.

"Yes, human bones! But his collections were not all bones. He also has St. Jerome's tooth and four hairs of the Virgin Mary, together with three fragments of her coat and four of her girdle. He also claims to have a strand of Jesus' beard, threads from His swaddling clothes, some of the gold brought by the Wise Men to Bethlehem, a twig of the Burning Bush, and many, many other things.

"Prince Frederick's collection is so large, it has been calculated that those who view the entire collection make the proper contribution, and utter the assigned prayers, can have 1,902,202 years plus 270 days reduced from their sentence in purgatory. Also, viewers are allowed to transfer their credit. One man transferred his credit to his widow and another to his granddaughter."

"How do they decide the value of a relic?" asked Ave.

"There are charts in Rome. Centuries ago, it was decided that viewing a certain saint's bones—I've forgotten his name—could reduce one's liability in the flames by 4,000 years.

"Since Frederick had so many relics, he has made it a custom to display them every year on All Saints' Day, November 1. That's why I displayed my theses on October 31. By doing that, the crowds were able to see them the next day.

And, my little plan worked. I heard one man say, 'Father Luther is right. Indulgences are unscriptural,' and another, 'I'm tired of sending my money to Rome to rebuild St. Peter's and to support Michaelangelo, great painter though he is.'

"I translated the theses from Latin into German and mailed them to friends and enemies. I even sent a copy to Archbishop Albert!" He scratched his head and laughed. Then he added, "I must now hurry to my appointment." He smiled at the girls and nodded toward Jerome. "He'll show you around."

With the girls about him, Jerome headed east. "His theses really stirred the world," he said. "I did a paper on them. The two that jarred Leo the most were the 82nd and 86th. They read:

> Why does not the pope liberate everyone from purgatory for the sake of love? . . . This would be morally the best of reasons. . . .

"And since the pope's income was more than the wealthiest of wealthy men, Luther's next question must have stung him. It read:

> Why does he not build this one church of St. Peter's with his own money? . . .

"Money dripped through his pudgy fingers like water in a sieve!"

Then leading the former nuns on, Jerome crossed the moat surrounding Wittenberg. He chatted with the guards, viewed the fortifications, stopped at a bakery and bought each of the young ladies a large piece of cake. Everywhere he went, he and the young ladies were greeted with smiles. Katie heard one old man exclaim, "What! Has Carlstadt finally succeeded in going back to the Old Testament and introduced polygamy?"

Alarmed, Katie demanded, "And who is Carlstadt?"

"Oh, he and Gabriel Zwilling caused Dr. Luther a lot of trouble during the time he was hiding at the Wartburg Castle," returned Jerome. "Those two almost wrecked every-thing."

"What did they do?" asked Katie, raising her voice.

"That's a long story—"

"Let's return to our rooms. I'm about to drop," interrupted Ave, sounding as if she were ready to collapse.

At the front door of the Black Cloister, Jerome suddenly beamed with new inspiration. Turning to Katie, he asked, "Would you like to go with me to the home of Lucas Cranach? He's doing my portrait."

Katie's eyes expanded. "J-just the two of us?"

"Do you mind?"

"I-I've never walked alone with a man before. Is it far?"

"No. It's between here and the Castle Church. It's a lovely place, built by Judge Kasper Treuschel who died ten years ago."

As she followed slightly behind Jerome, leaving the others behind, Katie noticed that Ave and several of the other girls looked perplexed.

Halfway down the block, Jerome stopped. "Come, walk by my side," he invited. "Conversation is easier. We're almost there."

Although she was terribly embarrassed, Katie reluctantly followed his suggestion.

8

Heartbreak

After Jerome had lifted and dropped the heavy brass knocker three times, the beautifully carved front door of Cranach's mansion swung wide. "May I help you?" asked a red-coated servant, bowing from the waist.

"Herr Cranach is doing my portrait," replied Jerome.

A moment later, Cranach appeared and motioned them through the dazzling white entrance.

"This is Katherine von Bora," announced Jerome grandly. "She's one of the escaped Nimbschen nuns."

"Yes, of course. I heard about them," he replied, nodding at Katie and displaying a wide smile. He stroked his white V-shaped beard and wide moustache. "Come up to the studio." He pointed to the top of the curved steps.

The luxurious home was beyond anything Katie had ever seen. It appeared to her like the entrance to heaven. There were thick carpets, heavy silver chandeliers fringed with tall candles, couches smothered with pillows, tall-backed chairs, polished tables.

"Your portrait is almost finished," said Cranach after he had opened the studio door.

By the light of the drooping sun shining through a colored window at the top of the stairs, Katie studied the artist out of the corners of her eyes. Cranach was ten years older than Luther, and his finely shaped skull was crowned with closely cropped gray hair, lending a mystical dimension to his dark, compassionate eyes.

The nearly finished portrait was resting on a large easel in a corner of the studio, which was littered with canvases, cans of paint, and old brushes.

"Well, how do you like it?" asked Cranach.

Jerome viewed it from several angles. "It's fine," he said at last. "Could you have it framed?"

"Certainly. But that will be extra."

"Never mind the expense. Order the best frame available."

At the door, Cranach suddenly lifted his hand. Then he said, "King Christian II of Denmark will be having dinner with us next Sunday. Would you and Fräulein von Bora like to join us? I'm sure His Majesty would enjoy meeting both of you."

"Thank you very much. We'll be there," replied Jerome. Then turning to Katie he said, "If it's all right with you."

"Yes, yes. I'd love to," she replied.

Jerome's steps slowed as they neared the Black Cloister. They had walked the long block back in silence. Finally Katie said, "Could you tell me something about the Peasants' War? It sounds ominous and Dr. Luther seems terribly concerned."

"That's a long story, Katie. It will take a long time to explain. If you don't mind, maybe we could stop at Melanchthon's house for some soup? Then I can go into some detail. It's nearly suppertime, and our cook always has something prepared this time of the evening."

Across a bowl of soup on the wide table, Jerome said, "The problems of the peasants are many. The real difficulty is that the owners of the land which the peasants farm have treated them like swine across many generations. The landowners order them around like slaves and allow them just enough grain to keep alive. Now that we have movable type, books are plentiful, and as the peasants are reading and discovering new things, they are becoming dissatisfied. Their demands for some of those good things are causing a great upheaval.

"To foster their cause, the peasants are using a peasant's boot on a pole as the rallying symbol. Sooner or later there will be pitched battles and many will die. Unfortunately, Dr. Luther will be blamed by both sides. He agrees that the peasants should have a better life, but his feet also rest securely on Romans 13."

"Romans 13?" Katie paused with her spoon halfway to her mouth.

"Yes. In the first verse, Paul wrote, 'Let every soul be subject unto the higher powers. For there is no power but of God: the powers that be are ordained of God.'

"Another problem is that Luther emphasizes there is freedom in Christ for all of us. This is a new doctrine in Germany, and anything new confuses people. When forks recently became popular, a priest objected. He said, 'If God wanted us to eat with forks, He would have made forks grow out of our fingers. Fingers are to eat with, and I'm not going to change even if I'm sent to the stake!' "

Katie and Jerome were just finishing their soup when Melanchthon stepped into the room. As he drew near the table, the light of the candle illuminated him clearly. Katie agreed with Luther: he *did* have the appearance of a shrimp!

Jerome introduced Melanchthon to Katie.

"How about more soup?" asked the Greek scholar as he sat down.

Jerome lifted his palms in a negative motion. "No thanks, Professor. But we have some interesting news to tell you!"

"Yes?"

"Fräulein von Bora and I are going to have dinner with His Majesty, King Christian II of Denmark, next Sunday in the home of Germany's greatest artist, Lucas Cranach!"

Melanchthon tilted his head to one side and shrugged his shoulder. "You do get around! King Christian is in trouble. He has been exiled from Denmark since he became a Protestant. The idea that the just shall live by faith is spreading all over the world. Dr. Luther is an inspired man."

The three visited at the table until 9 p.m. Then Melanchthon stood. "I'll escort you to the Black Cloister," he said. "We have enough gossip in this little town." He lit a lantern and led the way.

As they walked back to the cloister, Jerome turned to Katie and said, "May I call you Katie?"

"Yes, surely," she answered, overjoyed at his attention.

Katherine found it hard to sleep. So many unbelievable things had happened! She had met and walked with Jerome, a young man of apparent wealth; she and Jerome were going to have dinner with Lucas Cranach—a man whose paintings were in demand all over Europe. She pinched herself to make certain that she had not been dreaming. Then she ran her fingers slowly through her hair. If only it were longer! But, it *was* growing. Surely King Christian would understand if he was a true Protestant. Indeed, he would be proud of her for having escaped Nimbschen!

The dinner with the King and Herr Cranach was far more simple than Katie had imagined it would be. His Majesty ate and drank like any common man. It made Katie feel comfortable and at ease. During the conversation the king often referred to Dr. Luther, and seemed to have a great appreciation for him. "Yes," he affirmed, "I think his proclamation that the just shall live by faith is the greatest discovery of mankind in the last thousand years."

After they had finished the bountiful meal of vegetables, roast lamb, and various pastries and fruit, Cranach said to Katie and Jerome, "His Majesty has asked me to do his portrait. He will start sitting for it tomorrow."

"And why don't you, Fräulein von Bora, come and watch? It would be a pleasure to hear about the convent," said the king, smiling at her.

Embarrassed, Katie's face turned crimson. "I would be honored," she responded.

The next day Katie watched in amazement as King Christian's likeness grew on the canvas. Cranach studied him, painted, and turned to him again. While the painter was doing his dark beret, the king said to Katie, "How do you like the city of Wittenberg in comparison to Nimbschen?"

"That's an embarrassing question."

"I know. Just be frank."

"Well, I . . . I like the people very much. But this city is a little dirty. At Nimbschen we had acres of grass, running streams, trees, lovely gardens—"

King Christian laughed. "I've learned a little poem since I've been here. It's a good description of Wittenberg. Smiling broadly, he pushed back his head, and quoted:

> Little land, little land,
> You are but a heap of sand,
> If I dig you, the soil is light;
> If I reap you, the yield is light.

Each evening about the time Cranach was finishing his work, Jerome came to visit Katie. They were fast becoming good friends and went out to dinner, had long conversations, visited in the homes of Pastor Bugenhagen, Professor Reichenbach, and Johannes Lufft, one of Luther's publishers.

The day King Christian's portrait was completed, the king presented Katie with an expensive ring. "You have so faithfully entertained me while I've been imprisoned in this chair that you need a memento," he explained.

"Thank you. Thank you very much," replied Katie, making a curtsy.

After King Christian had gone, Katie slipped the ring on her fourth finger. The fit was perfect. Then she faced Cranach. "Have you painted many kings?" she asked.

"Oh, yes. I've done my share. The first one was our present Charles V when he was just a lad. It was a hard painting to do, for he kept squirming. But he liked the result. Indeed, he liked it so much he said to me, 'Herr Cranach, when I get to be the emperor, you may want a favor, and if you do, all you have to do is to ask.'

" 'Anything?' I inquired.

" 'Yes, anything,' he replied."

"Have you asked for a favor?"

"Not yet. But maybe someday I will," Cranach laughed.

That evening after Katie had shown Jerome the ring and while they were lingering in the shadows of the Castle Church door, Jerome held her hand. "Katie dear," he whispered, "I've wanted to ask you something rather important."

"Yes?" she answered softly as she lifted her eyes to his in the bright yellow moonlight.

"I've loved you ever since I first saw you." He ran his fingers through her short hair and kissed her eyes.

"And I've loved you too," Katie murmured.

"Will you marry me?"

"When?" Katie's heart skipped a beat.

"In the spring."

"Have you prayed about it?"

"I have."

"Do you feel it's in God's will?"

"I do."

"If you've really prayed about it, my answer is yes."

"Then let's seal our engagement with a kiss."

As the happy couple slowly walked toward the Black Cloister, Jerome said, "I'm afraid, Katie, I must tell you something."

"Yes?"

"Before our marriage can take place, I must get permission from my parents. I'm leaving for Nuremburg tomorrow, and when I receive their permission, I will return. But while I'm gone, I don't want you to think about anyone else—not even Dr. Luther."

"Dr. Luther!" Katie stared in amazement. "That would be impossible!" He's the most famous man in Germany, and I'm only an escaped nun. Besides, Dr. Luther is already forty-one!"

"Nonetheless. I don't want you even to think about anyone else." He stopped at the Melanchthon home. "Stay here in the living room; I have a present for you." Returning from upstairs, he presented her with his portrait, which Cranach had just framed. "This is to remind you of me. Remember, don't let those pretty blue eyes of yours stray onto anyone else," he reminded her, kissing her tenderly.

"I'll try not to," replied Katie. "I love you."

A week later, Katie moved into the home of Herr Reichenbach and his efficient wife. The Reichenbach home was large. He had been mayor of Wittenberg, and his wife insisted that everything be just right. A slight trace of dust was too much for her, and she was constantly testing obscure corners with a white handkerchief. "We must live as if we are civilized," she often said, speaking in the tones of a commander in chief.

Katie was given a comfortable room and assigned a long list of chores. Soon she was making beds, tending the garden, washing dishes, scrubbing floors, dusting furniture, feeding the cat, mending clothes.

Each evening as she prepared for bed, Katie cast an affectionate glance at Jerome's portrait on the dresser, and when roses were available she kept one in an exquisite vase just to the right of it. *Yes, she would soon be married and would be moving to Nuremburg!* And to be certain that she would be prepared for the customs and marvels of that city, she borrowed a copy of the *Nuremburg Chronicles* and studied it with the thoroughness with which Luther studied the book of Romans.

While daydreaming, Katie wrote her name *Frau Baumgaertner.* Then she changed it to *Frau Jerome Baumgaertner.* Both ways were attractive. But she was inclined toward the latter. The name Jerome had a lovely ring to it, even though St. Jerome's mistake in the Vulgate had caused millions of people to wear out their knees doing penance! Her mind on the ceremony, she wondered if her father would be able to attend. She also wondered what her stepmother would think when she witnessed the elaborate wedding and realized that her despised stepdaughter was marrying a man of wealth and that she would be surrounded with servants, lands, comfort. These thoughts quickened her pulse. *But is it right for me to enjoy my stepmother's coming embarrassment?* she thought guiltily.

Strangely, however, the first month dragged by, with no word from Jerome. Then another month passed, and another. Why didn't he write? Each week she sent him an affectionate letter, taking care not to sound as if she were pursuing him. To do this, she confined herself to news. Unfortunately, the news filtering into Wittenberg was alarming.

The peasants on the lands of the Count of Lupfen near Stühlingen, skirting the Black Forest, were looking forward to the harvest. But just as they were preparing to use their scythes, the count's wife decided the workers should gather snail shells and pick berries instead.

"We will do that later," replied a peasant.

"No, you will do what I say," replied the countess, her lips drawn in a firm line. "My word is *law!*"

"But if we delay, the grain will rot."

"This is *our* land. You will do what *I* say!"

This conflict became the breaking point, and soon peasants in various places were organizing, attacking landlords, and burning castles.

Katie wrote to Jerome, informing him of these events. Still there was no answer. During these months Katie had become acquainted with some of the students at the university. One of the students, learning of Katie's troubles, wrote to Jerome. But again, there was no reply.

Frustrated and anxious, Katie found it difficult to sleep. *Was it true that she was too proud?* The question presented itself to her late one Sunday night while she was trying to sleep. She lit a candle and studied herself in the mirror. Yes, her hair had grown and it was attractive! It added emphasis to the depth of her blue eyes. Wearily, she went back to bed. Again she could not sleep. In her mind she began counting the eyes in a herd of cows. It was wasted time. Again and again she changed positions, but it didn't help. Finally she got up and sat on the edge of her bed. While there, a fresh stream of accusations came to her: *You are unforgiving! You have a vengeful spirit! The Lord has forsaken you! You shouldn't have escaped from Nimbschen!*

In the midst of her agony, Katie remembered how Luther had spoken to them at the table, and how he had concluded his exposition on the words of Jesus: "Ask, and it shall be given you; seek, and ye shall find; knock, and it shall be opened unto you." His voice loud, his eyes glowing, he had said, "Ask, call out, yell, seek, thunder. You have to keep at it without respite."

Inspired, Katie knelt by her bed and followed Luther's instructions. She felt better, though she had no assurance her problem would be solved.

While Katie wrestled with this depression, word came that her father had passed away. Then in the midst of this grief, Frau Reichenbach stormed over to her. "Katie!" she shouted. "I pushed my handkerchief into the corner behind the sofa. Now look at it. It's filthy! You must do better!"

Stabbed by those words, Katie fled up the stairs two at a time and flung herself across the bed. After a long cry, she picked up Jerome's portrait. As she studied his finely cut face, smiling eyes, and dark hair topped by a blue beret worn at a rakish angle, she cried, "Jerome dear, why don't you answer my letters?" It had been over two years now since she first met him. She lingered with the portrait for a long time. Then she washed her face and went over to the Black Cloister. Previous visits with the escaped nuns had always revived her. Just an hour with them could change everything. Even Elsa's giggles were helpful! But now those days were gone. At the cloister, Katie learned that nearly all of them had found jobs or husbands or had returned to their parents. Only Margaret and Ave von Schönfeld remained in the area, having moved to the home of Lucas Cranach. But they each had a boyfriend. *What is going to happen to me? Has Jerome forgotten me?* Katie pondered as she walked back home, unhappy and depressed.

Every morning as Katie prepared for the day she had the same thought: *I'm the only one no one wants!* Utterly frustrated, she became ill and had to spend several days in bed.

To a visitor she confided, "I feel as if even God has forsaken me."

Finally Katie became so discouraged she climbed the steps to the tower and faced Luther. "I do want to amount to something. I do want to make my life count. I do want to follow God's will," she sobbed.

"Have you prayed about it?" asked Luther, leaning forward.

"Oh, yes, Dr. Luther. And I've prayed just as you suggested. I've sought; I've asked; I've cried; I've even thundered. But I get no response. It seems that God doesn't even hear me!"

"Are you willing to follow God's will?"

"Yes. I . . . I t-think so." She nervously looked out the window toward the Elbe.

Luther placed a letter in the book he had been reading and closed it. "Maybe God doesn't want you to marry Jerome. Maybe he has someone else in mind. Indeed, I know someone who desperately wants to marry you."

"Who?"

"Dr. Glatz—"

"Oh, no. No! No! I'd never marry him!"

Luther frowned. "Why not? Dr. Glatz is a fine man. I've known him for years."

"I wouldn't marry him because I'm still in love with Jerome."

"But he's forgotten you."

"Nonetheless . . ." Unconsciously she rubbed her hands together.

"All right, Katie—I mean Katherine—I'll write him a note." He spread out a sheet of paper and dipped his quill in the ink. Moments later he said, "Here's what I've written."

October 12, 1524

Dear Jerome:

If you still wish to hold your Katie von Bora, you had better act fast before she is given to another who is at hand. She still has not conquered her love for you. I would certainly be happy to see you two married.

Farewell

"Does that suit you?" he asked.

"Yes, that is fine," she said.

As Katie was stepping through the door, Luther said, "Katherine, you must ask the Lord to help you control your pride."

Katie stared. "Yes, Dr. Luther, I am proud. But why shouldn't I be? God made me, and God sent His Son to die for me, so why shouldn't I be proud?"

Luther laughed. "You are quite right," he said. "I shall be praying for you!" He studied her for a long moment and then his mood changed. "Katherine, you and the other girls who escaped from Nimbschen were extemely fortunate. About a month ago I received a letter from Brussels that contained terrible news. On July 1, last year, two young men, Heinrich Voes and Johannes Esch, were condemned to be burned alive!"

"What had they done?"

"They had denied the power of the pope."

"And so?"

"They were led to the stake. When they refused to recant, the straw surrounding their feet was lit. Ah, but they died with such courage their confessors burst into tears. As the flames swept over them, they recited the Apostles' Creed and sang *Te Deum Laudamus*, Thee God we praise, Thy name we bless.

"Those two were our first martyrs! Sometimes I envy them and wish the Lord would also bless me with martyrdom."

As Katie descended the stairs, she was so overcome she almost stumbled on the third step.

Less than a week after this, Luther invited all the former nuns to a special breakfast. While they were eating, he said, "Today is one of the happiest days of my life. And the reason is that my translation of the New Testament just came from the press. I've brought a copy for each of you."

9

He Is Our Wartburg Castle!

Just before the first snows whitened Wittenberg, Katie moved into the home of Lucas Cranach. Her room at the top of the stairs was twice as large as her cell at Nimbschen, it had a fine view of the Elbe, and Frau Cranach was most understanding.

Katie's chores included dusting the studio, mixing paints, cleaning brushes, making beds, helping with the cooking, and working in the garden. Having never cooked, she put her heart into this occupation. There was a modest shelf of cookbooks, and both the cook and Frau Cranach taught her how to produce appetizing meals.

Cranach owned four houses in Wittenberg, along with an apothecary. Sometimes Katie worked in the drugstore, helping customers as they came to purchase drugs, paper, wax—and the current almanac. She soon discovered that almanacs were extremely popular. Indeed, most customers were more concerned with the statements and diagrams of astrologers than with the directives from Rome. Astrologers governed their lives, instructing them when to plant, when to harvest, when to marry. A noted surgeon, Guy de Chauliac, had written in 1363: "If anyone is wounded in the neck while the moon is in Taurus, the affliction will be dangerous." This dogma was accepted by almost everyone; and so whenever a person suffered a neck wound, the almanac was always consulted.

Bloodletting, performed by barbers, was accepted as *the* cure of most diseases. But potential patients felt better if they had checked with the almanac before submitting themselves to the procedure. The almanac listed the best time and the worst time for this operation.

As customers came to the store, Katie began to hear more and more about the Peasants' War. The stories were grim. One afternoon a peasant and his wife came for an almanac. "The men from our village burned a castle," said the man, stoop-shouldered and wearing low boots. "Last week the nobles sought revenge. They came to our village, killed every man, woman and child. Then they burned all the houses. Me and my wife escaped because we was away visitin' our children. If this killin' don't stop, Germany will be ruined!"

Katie kept an eye open for Jerome, always hoping, always wondering why he didn't write. But he never appeared, nor did she hear anything about him until a Nuremberg student returned from vacation. "I met Jerome recently," he said.

"Oh! Did he say anything about Dr. Luther's letter?" Katie asked hopefully.

"Yes, he did receive it. But he said that his parents didn't want him to marry you. He's now going with a girl from the south."

"He should have let me know!" she sputtered, exasperated and hurt. "How could he be so heartless?"

"That's the way with some people." The student shrugged. "I've been told that the girl from the south is rich."

Feeling as if she had come to an abrupt turn in her life, Katie climbed the steps of the tower to consult with Martin Luther. Her one desire was to find the will of the Lord and to remain within that will.

Luther listened carefully as she emptied her heart. Then,

after glancing at the clock, he said, "Katie, I mean Katherine, God works in mysterious ways; and the more experience we have with Him, the more we find this to be true. Pastor Bugenhagen is teaching my class this morning, so I'm going to take the time to relate to you the darkest days of my life. It might help you.

"After I had nailed my theses to the door of the church, I was amazed to discover that I had set Europe on fire. Pope Leo X was so shocked he didn't know what to do. As indolent as he was, however, he had the wisdom to know that if I were martyred, it would hinder his cause. Tertullian wrote, 'The blood of martyrs is seed,' and His Holiness knew that statement was true. So he decided his best method was to get me to recant. With this in mind, he asked me to go to Augsburg and meet with Cardinal Cajetan.

"I must tell you, Katherine, I was afraid to make that trip! To me, it was like stepping into a dungeon filled with lions. I was almost certain I would be burned at the stake. Still, after much prayer, I was convinced God wanted me to go, and deep inside I was convinced that He would protect me. Nonetheless, I asked Frederick the Wise to secure for me a safe-conduct letter from Emperor Maximilian. And, in time, he secured one."

"And what was that?" asked Katie.

"It was a letter that guaranteed I would not be arrested while on the trip. That journey was a difficult one, especially since I did not feel well, suffering from acute stomach trouble. Finally, I arrived and faced Cardinal Cajetan. The date was October 12, 1518.

"As all priests are supposed to do, I prostrated myself on the floor before the cardinal. He then took my hand and, after pulling me to my feet, informed me in a firm voice that I should recant.

"Cajetan insisted that my main trouble was that in my ninety-five theses, I had denied that there existed a bank of merit filled with the righteousness of the saints from which, through an indulgence issued by the pope, a sinner could draw and have his sins forgiven.

"Again and again I insisted that the Scriptures stand higher than the words of any pope. This made Cajetan very angry. It was like pouring bits of glass into his eyes. Soon he was so angry he literally shouted that I should leave unless I was prepared to say humbly, *revoco*, or I recant.

"I now heard it rumored that in spite of my letter of safe conduct, Cardinal Cajetan had been empowered to have me arrested if I didn't recant. I also learned that the gates of the city were being guarded to prevent my escape. Friends, however, provided me with a horse. But in my hurry to escape, I fled without my sword or breeches. I was dressed only in a cowl. By God's help I evaded the guards.

"Things got worse. I was challenged to go to Leipzig and openly debate John Eck, a professor at the University of Ingolstadt. By the time I arrived, the whole country was stirred. The streets were crowded with armed men carrying banners. Since the town council feared that Eck might be harmed— there were about two hundred students from the University of Wittenberg present—he was provided with a guard of seventy-six men.

"Katie, I mean Katherine, you should have been there! The debate was held between July 4 and 14, 1519, and the weather was scorching hot. I had to keep wiping my face.

"As I debated before the crowds, I felt very humble, for within each assembly there were distinguished scholars, knights, and princes. Some honored me. Others, like Duke George, wanted to burn me at the stake. We debated all sorts of subjects: original sin, purgatory, the power of the pope, the worthiness of councils—and especially indulgences.

"At one place, I spoke in German so that even the laymen could understand me. I said: 'A simple layman armed with Scripture is to be believed above a pope or a council without it.' By the end of the debate, my conflict with Rome was being discussed all over Europe.

"In the summer of 1520, Pope Leo issued his *Exsurge Domine* bull against me. That bull ended with these words."

He picked up a document and read . . .

> Now therefore we give Martin sixty days in which to submit, dating from the time of the publication of this bull in his district. Anyone who presumes to infringe our excommunication and anathema will stand under the wrath of Almighty God and of the apostles Peter and Paul.

"That bull was dated June 15, 1520. For one reason or another, I did not receive it until October 10. In the meantime, my books were being burned in Rome and other places. This, too, caused a problem. At Mainz my books were tossed into a pile, and the executioner, whose job it was to burn them, stepped forward. But before he applied his torch, he had a question: 'Have these books been *legally* condemned?' When a voice in the crowd cried no, he walked away."

"Was that the end of the matter?" asked Katie, her eyes wide.

"Oh, no. My enemies were determined, and so on November 29, a smaller pile of books was made. When the executioner refused to burn them, they were burned by a *grave-digger*! Only a few old women could be enticed to stay and watch." Luther chuckled.

"Not all of your works were completely burned," put in Katie. "The copy of *The Babylonian Captivity* that reached Nimbschen had only been scorched. It was that tract which persuaded many of us to escape."

Luther rubbed his hands. "That proves that God's truth cannot be destroyed. But let's hurry on. On January 3, 1521, the pope issued another bull: *Decet Romanum Pontificem*. That one excommunicated me!

"Perhaps His Holiness believed this would end the problem. It didn't, for now there was a war of pamphlets, and the issues were debated by all classes of people—even beggars. I finally decided to end my persecutions by appealing directly to our new emperor, Charles V. In this, I was following the example of the Apostle Paul.

"In time, as the world knows, I was invited to defend myself at the Diet of Worms. Fearing for my safety, I demanded, and received, a safe-conduct letter from the emperor, Charles V. I was warned that the safe-conduct letter might be ignored just as it was ignored in the case of John Huss."

"The John Huss who was burned at Constance?" asked Katie.

"Yes, I mean the Bohemian reformer who preached that the communion wine was intended for all. When Huss was summoned to trial at Constance, Emperor Sigismund granted him a safe-conduct document for his journey both ways. But that document was ignored, and he was burned at the stake. The date was July 6, 1415.

"Since I worried that this might happen to me, I made a study of Charles V to see what kind of a man he was. Was it possible that he, too, would break his word and that I would be burned at a stake?

"At the time, Emperor Charles was just a little over 21, and all kinds of contradicting influences were within him. The pope had not favored his election and refused to crown him, yet he was a loyal Catholic. Also, although he was the grandson of Emperor Maximilian, his mother, Joanna, had gone insane. When her husband, Philip the Handsome, died, she refused to have him buried. Indeed, she kept the casket in the palace, and when she went on trips, insisted that the casket be taken along. She even demanded that it be opened from time to time!

"In order to help me understand this new emperor, one of the university students made a chart of his ancestors and handed it to me. Let me see if I can find it." Luther got up and searched through his books. Then, exclaiming, "Ah, here it is." He spread it out on the desk in front of Katie.

"There, you can see that he was a grandson of Queen Isabella, who financed Christopher Columbus, and a nephew of Catherine of Aragon, who married England's Henry VIII.

"I must admit, Katie, that I was frightened. But through prayer I was strengthened. Yes, I knocked, sought, pleaded, waited, and pleaded some more. On April 2, Doctor Amsdorf, three others, and myself set out for Worms." He paused and

GENEALOGY OF CHARLES V

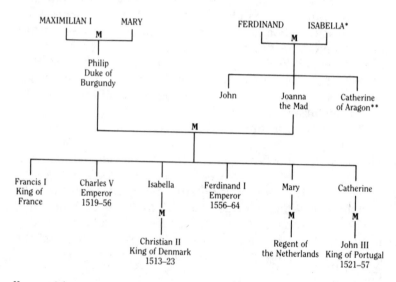

M = married
* She financed Christopher Columbus's voyages
** Wife of Henry VIII

smiled. "Mentioning Dr. Amsdorf reminds me that he wants to see you this afternoon. He said it's important. Do you know him?"

"Of course! I've heard him preach many times, and I enjoy him very much, for he's not as long-winded as Pastor Bugenhagen. But, Dr. Luther, why would he want to speak to me?" She frowned.

"I think he wants to make a suggestion to you. Now don't be frightened. You'll survive. But back to our journey to Worms. As we traveled, throngs of people came out to see us and to shake my hand. At one place, however, I was handed a note from Spalatin—chaplain to Frederick the Wise. That note warned me that I was in grave danger. I already knew that. But as God was helping me, I suddenly had a surge of new strength. I replied: 'Even though there should be as many devils in Worms as shingles on the roof, I would still enter.'

"On April 16, at ten in the morning, a watchman on the walls noticed that we were coming. He then climbed up on the spire of the cathedral and blew his trumpet, announcing that we were about to arrive. Then a hundred horsemen rode out and escorted us in. When we entered the city, the streets were lined with people; the trees and windows were also full. Indeed, the crowds were so great it was hard to get our carriage through the gate. Some two thousand well-wishers escorted us to our lodgings. On the 17th the *Reichmarshall* came to my room and informed me that I was to appear before the Diet that afternoon at four." He got up and began to pace. "Those next hours of waiting, Katie, were tense. Finally, it was time to go. Since the streets were black with the curious, I was led to the hall by a roundabout way and ushered inside through a back door.

"After more delay, during which my nerves were about to snap, I was summoned upstairs to face my judges. There in front of me were Emperor Charles V, several bishops, other high dignitaries—and many armed men. As I looked around, I saw a bench piled high with my books. This gave me a clue about what would take place.

"While I stood and waited like a prisoner in the dock, the names of the dignitaries were read, each with his proper title. Then Johann von Eck, an official from the court of the Archbishop of Trier, pointed to the books and asked me a double question: 'Did you write them, and are you ready to recant?' That question was a two-edged sword, and I needed time to think. Fortunately, my friend, Dr. Jerome Schurff, a professor at Wittenberg and an expert in Canon Law, had been allowed to act as my defense lawyer. He gave me time by asking that the names of the books be read.

"As the titles to the twenty-five books were read, I prayed earnestly that God would give me the right answers. And He did. I acknowledged that I was the author of the books. Then I said that since the next part of the question concerned faith and the salvation of the soul, I would need time to think before I gave my answer. It was then agreed that I could return to my lodgings and confront them again the next day.

"This delay displeased my bitterest enemies. But I am convinced that it was in the will of the Lord. Back in my room I prayed, studied, made notes. I knew that the great test of my life was just ahead, and, Katie, as I prayed I felt the strengthening arms of Christ about me. Believe me, those arms are real. Yes, real!

"The next day, that is the 18th of April, I was not summoned upstairs until six o'clock. By that time it was dark. Again, I faced the glitter of power. As I glanced at the emperor, I wondered what he might do. He had a habit of sitting with his mouth slightly ajar. I feared a touch of his mother's insanity might influence him. Safe-conduct letter or not, one twitch of his lips could send me to the stake.

"Soon Eck—not the Eck I faced at Leipzig—began his prosecution. I don't have time to repeat all he had to say as we discussed my books. During his questioning, his anger kept increasing until he finally cried: 'I ask you, Martin—answer candidly and without horns—do you or do you not repudiate your books and the errors which they contain?'

"At that moment, Katie, I felt another surge of strength

from the Lord. Facing him, I replied: 'Since Your Majesty and your lordships desire a simple reply, I will answer without horns and without teeth. Unless I am convinced by Scripture and plain reason—I do not accept the authority of popes and councils, for they have contradicted each other—my conscience is captive to the Word of God! I *cannot* and I *will not* recant anything, for to go against conscience is neither right nor safe! Here I stand, I cannot do otherwise. God help me. Amen.'

"I remained in Worms for several days after this while scholars tried to convince me that I was wrong. I remember that the Elector of Brandenburg inquired, 'Do you mean that you will not submit unless convinced by Holy Scriptures?' To this I replied, 'Yes, Most Gracious Lord, or by clear reason.'

"On April 26 our group left the city. I had not recanted, and I had not changed my mind. During our trip back to Wittenberg, we were suddenly stopped while passing through the forest of Waltershausen. One of the brigands grabbed the bridle of a horse and then knocked the driver to the ground with a blow of his fist. Next, another demanded our names, and when I acknowledged that I was Martin Luther, he pointed a crossbow at me.

"Dr. Amsdorf was really frightened. But knowing the secret, I whispered in his ear, 'Do not become excited. We are among friends.' Next, when we were in a dark spot, I was dressed as a knight and told that I was now *Junker Joerg*. We traveled a long way until we reached Wartburg Castle. There I was locked in a cell.

"After hours in that cell, I was moved to a more pleasant room. Here I was kept until my hair and beard were full length. As my hair grew, I was taught the words and manners of knighthood."

"And who arranged this fake kidnapping?" asked Katie.

"Frederick the Wise!"

"Why?"

"Because my safe-conduct period was running out, and I

102

knew that the emperor was determined that I be arrested."[1]

Katie's eyes were wide. "Were you frightened?"

"Of course. After all, I was under the sentence of death. But mostly, I was bored. Hours seemed terribly long. Then the Lord assigned me work. He requested that I translate the New Testament into German.

"While I labored, trying to make my version so simple any lay person could understand it, I was inflicted with bad dreams, feelings of insecurity, and stomach trouble. And sometimes it seemed the room was full of devils. Nonetheless, the Lord helped me. I completed the translation in eleven weeks.

"Katie, all of God's children have to pass through dark times. But God will always help us. Always! He is our Wartburg Castle! Today, my *Das Newe Testament Deutzsch* is read all over Germany." He glanced at the clock. "Now don't forget to see Dr. Amsdorf! He was teaching here at Wittenberg nine years before I came. Trust him. He's dependable." Luther held out his hand. "You must excuse me. I have a class."

[1] His edict, presented to the diet on the sixth of May, concluded: "We have given him twenty-one days, dating from April 25th. . . . *Luther is to be regarded as a convicted heretic. When the time is up, no one is to harbor him. His followers also are to be condemned. His books are to be eradicated from the memory of man.*"

10

Romance

Alone at the kitchen table, Katie found it hard to eat—even though she was facing a favorite food: cabbage and curls of sausage. Her mind kept whirling. *What did Dr. Amsdorf want? And why was Dr. Luther in on the secret?*

She took a small bite of sausage. It was tasteless even though when she had butchered the pig and made the sausage, she had laced it with spices. Forcing herself to chew, her mind returned to the career of the man she was about to encounter. Like herself, Dr. Nicholas von Amsdorf had noble blood. He was a mere three weeks younger than Luther, and Luther had complete confidence in him. Indeed, he was one of the few who knew when Luther was hiding at the Wartburg Castle.

Katie returned to her room in the Cranach home and forced herself to lie down. Instinct convinced her that she should not go too soon. Too much hurry could frighten the cat! As long minutes trickled by, she studied herself in the mirror at least a dozen times. Yes, her braided hair was just right. Yes, her wide white collar was spotless and had been properly starched. Yes, her shoes were a glistening black.

After stepping out the door, she bowed her head and silently asked for the Lord's guidance.

With throbbing heart and an air of excitement, Katie ascended the lower section of steps leading to Amsdorf's study two at a time. Then, after pausing for breath, she mounted the remaining steps one at a time.

"I've been waiting to tell you something for a long time," said Amsdorf, leaning forward from behind his enormous desk.

"Yes?" Katie held her breath.

"All of the nuns who escaped from Nimbschen have gone, with the exception of yourself. Correct?"

"That's right. The Schönfelds left last week."

"Mmm. Mmm." Amsdorf drummed his right fingers on his cheek. "Mmm. Did you know that there's a fine gentleman who's in love with you?"

"Who?" Katie's blue eyes lit up. She studied him carefully.

"Dr. Glatz."

"Dr. Glatz! Oh, not him." Katie stared.

"He's a fine man, Fräulein von Bora," Amsdorf interrupted. "He was a former rector of the University of Wittenberg. Now he's the dedicated pastor at Orlamuende."

"No! No! Dr. Amsdorf, I would never marry him. Never!" Breaking the silence that followed, she had a question. "Did Dr. Luther suggest that you ask me to marry Dr. Glatz?"

Amsdorf smiled. "He and I have discussed it many times. Yes, he made the suggestion. He would even perform the ceremony!"

"Well, there will never be such a ceremony!"

"Why not?"

"Because I don't love him. And, and b-besides, I've heard that he's tight with his money."

Amsdorf laughed. Then he tapped his fingers on his cheek. With one eyebrow lifted, he inquired, "Is there anyone in Wittenberg you would marry?"

"Yes, there are two," replied Katie promptly.

"Two! And who are they?" His eyes had widened.

"They are both distinguished men," she teased.

"Who?"

"Either you or Dr. Luther!"

Amsdorf slapped the desk with both hands and roared with laughter. While still shaking his head, he exclaimed, "Katie von Bora, you're as proud as a peacock! But I like you anyway. However, I'm going to remain a celibate, and Dr. Luther has assured me he will never marry."

Back in her room, Katie wondered if she had done the right thing. She considered opening her heart to Frau Cranach, but after a week of thought decided against it. Soon chores and current events turned her mind to other things.

Astrologers had warned that peasant uprisings would occur in 1524. Katie had read the predictions in old almanacs and had shuddered when they came true. Now she was praying that a way of peace would be discovered and that the bloodshed would cease.

But the bloodshed continued and was increasing daily.

On Good Friday three groups of peasants laid seige to Weinsberg, a town near Heilbronn in southwestern Germany. The confident peasants sent a delegation to negotiate with Count Ludwig Helfenstein. The count ordered them murdered.

That Easter Sunday, the infuriated peasants smashed through the city walls and slaughtered those who resisted. Next they captured the count, his wife and sixteen knights.

Then, in spite of the fact that the countess was the daughter of the late Holy Roman Emperor Maximilian and thus an aunt of Holy Roman Emperor Charles V, the peasants decided that the seventeen men would have to run the gauntlet.

The count shuddered. "Have mercy. Free us. I will give you my entire fortune."

"You have not had mercy on us, and we will not have mercy on you!" snapped a spokesman for the peasants. The man beneath the pole bearing a peasant's boot nodded to his men. "Form two rows."

Overwhelmed, the countess begged that her husband be

spared. Her tears were ignored. Having collapsed, she was held up and forced to watch the grim spectacle. As the prisoners walked through the two rows and were methodically cut down with daggers and pikes, those who struck the blows snarled their complaints.

"You thrust my brother into a dungeon." "You harnessed us like oxen to a yoke!" "You cut off my father's hands because he killed a rabbit in one of your fields!" "Your horses and dogs and hunters tramped down our crops!"[1]

The countess alone was spared and placed in a convent.

This outrage chilled fair-minded people throughout Germany. Luther himself was dazed. Something had to be done to stop the bloodshed. But what?

In April 1525, Luther supported the peasants, praising them for being willing to be corrected by Scripture. His tract, *Ermabung zum Frieden* (Admonition of Peace), was filled with strong words:

> We have no one on earth to thank for this mischievous rebellion except you, princes and lords, and especially you blind bishops and mad priests and monks, whose hearts are hardened against the Holy Gospel, though you know that it is true. . . . The peasants are mustering, and this must result in the ruin, destruction, and desolation of Germany by cruel murder and bloodshed unless God shall be moved by our repentance to prevent it.

As stories of new horrors filtered into Wittenberg, Katie discovered a new tract by Luther which took the side of the nobles and landlords. Utterly shocked, she read:

> Any man against whom sedition can be proved is outside the law of God and the empire, so that the first who can slay him is doing right and well. . . . Therefore let everyone who can, smite, slay and stab, secretly or openly, remembering that nothing can be more poisonous, hurtful, or devilish than a rebel. It is just when one must kill a mad dog.[2]

---

[1] *The Reformation* by Will Durant, p. 388.
[2] About the time this tract was issued, the landlords were gaining the upper hand. Luther is blamed for his harsh words. Still, most historians do not believe they changed the course of events.

Almost in tears, Katie showed the tract to Frau Cranach. "We live in terrible times," said Cranach's wife. "Let's pray that God will spread love on both sides. I saw Dr. Luther yesterday. His shoulders droop like those of a condemned man. Both the nobility and the peasants are saying hard things against him. I just received a letter from an old friend. She said that the peasants have named him 'Dr. Lügner' (Dr. Liar). That's a pity, for he has already given the world the blessing of knowing that the just shall live by faith. His great trouble is that he is the best writer in Germany and likes to use strong words. Katie, we must continue to pray for him!"

Frederick the Wise died on May 5 of that year. Cautious to the end, he took the sacraments during the last hours in both the Catholic and Protestant manner. Making peace with God, he asked his servants' forgiveness and commented: "We princes one way or another do a lot of things that are not good."

Frederick's position as elector was taken over by his brother, Duke John—a Protestant. John felt that Frederick was too lenient with the peasants. He joined forces with other princes to defeat them utterly.

Not seeing Luther at church or on the streets for several days, Katie approached Frau Cranach. "Where is Dr. Luther?" she asked. "Oh, he's gone to visit with his parents. These uprisings have shaken him and he needs a change of atmosphere."

That spring, Katie was in the kitchen when Luther strode in. He was like a new man. His eyes had a fresh glow, his shoulders were straight, his step firm.

"Where have you been?" asked Katie.

"I've been visiting with my parents."

"And how are they?" Katie laid down a pewter cup she had been drying.

"They're fine." He stepped closer and held her hand in both of his. "Do you remember what you said to Dr. Amsdorf?" he asked, tilting his head.

"About what?"

"About whom you would be willing to marry."

"I do." Katie studied him curiously.

"When I first heard that, I laughed until my sides ached. I laughed because I'm a monk and you're a nun, and you're twenty-six and I'm forty-two. I could almost be your father! When I repeated your words to my father, he thought it was a good idea. He said, 'Martin, why don't you marry her? I need grandsons to carry on the Luther name.' "

After squeezing her hand a little more tightly, Luther said, "I think my father was right. Do you agree?"

Katie handed him some pewter to shelve in the cupboard.

"Well, do you agree?" he asked, his eyes glowing, drawing near to her face.

"I do. Hans Luther is a wise man."

"Then will you marry me?"

She handed him some more pewter. "Put this on the lower shelf of that cupboard over there." She pointed to the tall cupboard by the chimney.

"Well, what is your answer?" he asked, after he had completed his task.

"My answer is—I will!"

"Oh, Katie, that's great!" he exclaimed, hugging her ecstatically.

Luther lingered in the kitchen until the candles were lit. Just before he left he kissed her and said, "Katie, we must be married soon. Let's not delay. Remember, Hannibal lost Rome because he delayed, and we wasted too much time. I shall contact Pastor Bugenhagen at once."

So on June 13, 1525, before a handful of people, Luther and Katie exchanged vows in a simple ceremony in the Black Cloister. Lucas Cranach and his wife substituted for Luther's parents. A number of guests were invited to the special breakfast the next morning.

Now that she was a bride, Katie's quick eyes noted things that would have to be done. Bachelor Luther knew nothing about housekeeping. He confessed, "Before I was married the bed was not made for a whole year and became foul with sweat. But I worked so hard and was so weary, I tumbled in without noticing it."

While Katie kept her broom swinging, Martin wrote to friends. The note to Leonard Koppe, referring to the "public" wedding which was scheduled for the 27th, read: "I am going to get married. God likes to work miracles and to make a fool of the world. You must come." The letter to Spalatin had a twinge of humor. "You must come. . . . I have made the angels laugh and the devils weep." Amsdorf learned, "The rumor of my marriage is correct. I cannot deny my father the hope of progeny, and I had to confirm my teaching at a time when many are so timid. I hope you will come."

Were Katie and Martin deeply in love? The answer is a definite no. In 1538, Luther was brutally frank. He said, "Had I wished to marry fourteen years ago, I would have chosen Ave von Schönfeld, now the wife of Basil Axt. I never loved my wife but suspected her of being proud, as she is, but God willed me to take pity on the poor, abandoned girl."

The public ceremonies on the 27th began at ten o'clock in the morning. While church bells sounded, Martin, now dressed in a robe made from cloth provided by the elector, led Katie down the streets to the parish church. This time Hans and Margaretta Luther, Martin's parents, were present, along with other distinguished guests.

The new elector had indicated his warm approval by donating the Black Cloister to Luther and by having it repaired. City records show that two tons of plaster were used. He also provided the couple with one hundred guldens for new furnishings. And, realizing the importance of the occasion, Lucas Cranach painted portraits of both the bride and groom. He also did portraits of Martin's parents.

Katie and Martin were greeting the people and accepting congratulations when John Rühel stepped up. "I have a present for Frau Luther," he announced. "It is from Archbishop

Albert of Mayence." He then presented Katie with twenty gulden.

"I'm sorry," said Luther. "We can't accept it," handing it back.

His face shadowed with disappointment, Rühel left.

Moments later, Katie excused herself and stepped through the door. "Dr. Rühel," she said, "it was generous of the Archbishop to send the twenty gulden. Since it was for me, I will accept it."

"Thank you very much. Here it is. The Archbishop will be very pleased. He's on the verge of becoming a Protestant."

Katie had just returned inside when she saw another gift. It was a silver pitcher decorated with gold. What luxury! Yes, being married to a man like Dr. Luther was an unusual experience.

The celebrations continued until eleven o'clock that night. Wearied by the excitement, Katie forced herself to ascend to their room. Each foot aching, she managed only one step at a time. She had just braided her hair into pigtails when there was a series of thundering thumps on the downstairs front door. "Herr Doctor, will you help your exhausted wife and see who it is?" asked Katie.

Minutes later, Luther returned. "It's Professor Bodenstein von Carlstadt! He's fleeing the uprising. At one time he and Gabriel Zwilling almost made me pull my hair out by the roots. He was heartless then." Luther shook his head. "But now that he's afraid, he seeks my help!"

"And what shall we do?" Katie's eyes widened.

"Prepare a room. No one will ever be turned away from my house!"

After Katie had dressed, provided food and prepared a room, she collapsed into bed. She had just closed her eyes when there was another knock. This time Luther returned with a box.

"What could that be?" yawned Katie.

"Read the letter."

Katie read:

Dear Niece Katherine:

Congratulations! We miss you at Nimbschen. We're praying for you. Here's a present. God bless you!

The Abbess

"Look, Luther," Katie cried, "the box is alive!"

As Luther was removing the lid, there was a low whimper. "Oh, Katie!" he exclaimed. "Your aunt has sent us a dog!" He held the black puppy close to the candle. He wasn't quite as large as Methuselah, the convent cat, Katie noted. Except for three white paws, the puppy was completely black.

"Maybe I'd better get him something to eat," suggested Katie.

Candle in one hand and the dog in the other, Katie went to the kitchen. She found a piece of leftover meat and poured some milk. As the dog was eating, Luther appeared with the box. "We'd better keep him in this," he suggested.

"And what shall we call him?" asked Katie.

"Tolpel," replied Luther promptly.

11
Problems

Awakened by the loud crowing of a rooster, Katie yawned, sat up, stretched and stared out the window. Dawn was breaking, and slowly her eyes focused on the reddening horizon. As usual, Martin was gone. She had just donned her robe when the door opened and he stepped in.

"I was in the study having morning devotions," he explained. "Each year I read the Bible through twice, and the more I read it the more refreshing it becomes." He sat close to her and batted one of her pigtails playfully.

As she held his hand in both of hers, Katie said, "Now you must tell me about Gabriel Zwilling and Professor Carlstadt."

"Ah, yes. As I told you yesterday, both of them almost caused me to pull my hair out by the roots. Basically, both are good men. Their problem is that they're too much in a hurry; they want to change the world in one day.

"While I was hiding at the Wartburg Castle, Zwilling and Carlstadt launched an attack on the Catholic mass, images, priests, and music in the church. On Christmas Day, Carlstadt led the services in the Castle Church where he was archdeacon. That service, at least to the two thousand who squeezed in, was the most shocking spectacle any of them had ever observed. Carlstadt stood before them without his customary robes. That alone caused eyes to bulge. And although he sang the mass in Latin, he carefully omitted all passages about sacrifice. Next, he blessed the bread and wine in German! Doing that inspired gasps all over the building. Some almost fainted.

"Those departures from tradition, however, didn't satisfy Carlstadt. Oh, no! He also told them that all images are devilish, that it is a sin to partake only of the communion bread—and that organs are only for the theater. Following that, he asked the people to come forward on their own and help themselves to both the bread and the wine." Luther shook his head.

"Many of the communicants were almost paralyzed by fear. One man accidentally dropped his bread. When Carlstadt told him to pick it up, he refused. To him, it was the *very* body of Christ!

"About two weeks after this, Zwilling and Carlstadt and some monks burned the holy oil Roman Catholic priests use for Extreme Unction. Then they smashed images taken from the churches and even desecrated gravestones.

"Katie, it was terrible!" He glanced at the clock.

"It had taken years of prayer and study to learn the correct meaning of 'the just shall live by faith.' Now these two men wanted everyone to swallow these freshly revealed truths in one mighty gulp. But that isn't all!

"While Zwilling and Carlstadt were smashing images, and their followers were actually stoning priests at the altars, three self-appointed prophets arrived from Zwickau. That's near the Bohemian border. These men declared they didn't need the Bible. No, they relied on the Holy Spirit! According to them, the Kingdom of God was about to come, and that to speed its coming, all unbelievers should be slaughtered.

"Their message even ruffled our normally calm friend, Melanchthon!

"The town council became so horrified it invited me to return to Wittenberg. This was against the wishes of Frederick the Wise, who feared I might be burned at the stake.

What did I do? Still in disguise as Junker Joerg, I headed for Wittenberg. On the way, I sent him a letter. Let me go to the study and get a copy."

While Luther was gone, Katie let down her hair, combing and rebraiding it, then wrapping it around the top of her head.

"Here's a copy of that letter," said Luther when he returned. "I'll just read portions of it:

> Most serene, highborn Prince, most gracious Lord. I have obeyed your Grace this year by staying at Wartburg to please you. The devil knows I did not hide out of cowardice, for he saw my heart when I entered Worms. Had I then believed that there were as many devils as tiles on the roof, I would have leaped into their midst with joy. . . . I am fully persuaded that had I been called to Leipzig instead of Wittenberg, I should have gone there even . . . if it had rained Duke Georges nine days and every duke nine times as furious as this one. . . .

> I have written this to your Grace to inform you that I am going to Wittenberg under a far higher protection than the elector. . . . The sword ought not and cannot decide a matter of this kind. God alone must rule.

"As I was traveling, I knew I might be recognized in spite of my beard. But I also knew the Lord was protecting me. The Reformation, Katie, was hanging by a thread!

"Accompanied by several knights, I arrived here on Friday, March 6, 1522. That Sunday I began a series of sermons dealing with what should be done. Each time I spoke, the church was so crowded one could hardly move. In one sermon I said, 'I will preach it, teach it, write it, but I will constrain no man by force, for faith must come freely without compulsion.' Then I pointed out that Paul had not even spoken against the images on Mars' Hill.

"Those eight sermons settled the problem! Zwilling acknowledged that he had been wrong and promised that he would never again offer mass with feathers in his beret. Carlstadt, however, refused to change. He moved away, and peace returned to Wittenberg." Luther glanced at a clock. "But we'd better get our friend something to eat. Carlstadt's always hungry. Eats like a bear!"

"How long will he stay?"

"I don't know. As long as he likes." Luther shrugged.

Basket in hand, Katie went to Helmut Schmidt's butcher shop to buy some meat. As she was standing by the counter, she overheard a conversation.

"I cannot believe that Dr. Luther has gotten married," said a wide-hipped lady in peasant boots.

"Don't you know the reason?" asked another, this one a young woman with a basket of herring hanging from her arm.

"Why?" asked the lady in the boots.

"Because she was expecting a baby! And do you know what happens to a nun who has a baby by a monk?"

"I have no idea."

"She has a demon!"

Horrified, Katie's eyes misted until she could barely see as she rushed home to the Black Cloister. After storing the meat in the kitchen, she hurried up the steps two at a time to their room. Martin was away teaching a class and would not be back until just before the evening meal.

Before leaving Nimbschen, Katie had been encouraged by believing that the Lord could use her to inspire others just as He had inspired St. Bernard of Clairvaux. That intuition had been like a puff of fresh air on a humid day. *But how could she inspire anyone if she was being accused of misconduct?* As she considered this, her eyes overflowed.

This thought led to others. Had Dr. Luther married her because he loved her, or was it merely to raise children to please his father and to make the devils weep? In his letter to Dr. Amsdorf inviting him to the "public" wedding, Luther had been candid. He had written: "I was not carried away by passion, for I do not love my wife that way, but esteem her as a friend."

A glance at the clock reminded her that if they were to have their evening meal on time, she would have to get busy.

Apron around her waist, she worked out a menu. Frau Cranach's teachings were most helpful. Soon, the meat was cut, the fire was blown into a blaze, vegetables were sliced, drinks were prepared, dishes were placed.

"Tell me about the war," said Luther to Carlstadt, speaking across the table. "How is it going?"

"Bloodshed continues, and it will increase. There have been fearful executions on both sides. Our new elector is inflexible. Still, there are hopeful signs. When Elector Ludwig of the Palitinate was surrounded by eight thousand peasants, he invited their leaders to dinner. Then across mugs of beer he agreed to all their demands." Carlstadt spoke with modest enthusiasm.

"The whole affair breaks my heart," said Luther. "Each side has grievances; each side has truths. But, Carlstadt, God did provide rulers! And in Romans 13 Brother Paul tells us that we should obey them. Every day I pray for both sides, just as I pray, and often weep, for Duke George."

As the conversation retreated to the old days in the university, Katie's mind drifted to other things. She wondered how long Carlstadt was going to stay, how many more "boarders" were going to descend upon them, and how she was going to do all the required work. But even though she was only half listening, she heard her husband say, "I'll never forget the time when you presided over the graduation ceremonies at the Castle Church. My spine still tingles when I remember how you placed the doctoral beret on my head and slipped the silver doctor's ring on my finger." He held up his hand to display the ring. "Those were happy days, even though they were anxious ones."

"I wish you and I could work together again," said Carlstadt.

Luther laughed. "We can. All you have to do is to submit to the truth!"

Later, standing with his arms around her in the privacy

of their bedroom, Luther listened as Katie related what the women had said at the butcher shop. "Don't let that bother you," he replied. "In time, the real truth will be known."

"True, but it hurts."

"You must keep in mind, Katie, that Satan hates us. Why does he hate us? Because we—you and I—are spreading the truth to the whole world." He kissed her on both cheeks and smoothed her hair.

"I am spreading truth? I've never published a word in my life."

"True, but your love and affection inspire me."

She held him tight. "How do you fight the devil?" she asked, a little playfully.

"Oh, that's simple. I use sarcasm. When I go to bed, the devil is always waiting for me. When he begins to plague me, I give him the answer, 'Devil, I must sleep. That's God's command, "Work by day. Sleep by night." So go away.' If that doesn't work and he brings out a catalog of sins, I say, 'Yes, old fellow, I know all about it. And I know some more you have overlooked. Here are few extra. Put them down.' If he still won't quit and presses me hard and accuses me as a sinner, I scorn him and say, 'Satan, pray for me. Of course you have never done anything wrong in your life. You alone are holy. Go to God and get grace for yourself. If you want to get me all straightened out, I say, "Physician, heal thyself." ' "

Katie laughed. "Does that send him away?"

"For a time. Satan is persistent and hates the truth as much as Duke George!"

Katie tried to follow Luther's advice. But it seemed that she was Satan's choice target. Morning and evening and in-between he would say, "Look at all those empty rooms! They'll soon be filled with boarders who won't pay their way. Martin Luther doesn't really love you. He would have preferred Ave von Schönfeld to you. You're just a housekeeper like one of those who work in a monastery. Think of all the work that has to be done: the cowshed needs repairs, the pigsty is filthy, the orchard needs trimming, the fishponds are empty. How are you going to do all the work? Luther won't help. He's too busy preaching, writing books, advising people. Duke George will have him burned at the stake. You're wasting your life!"

Emerging from one of these battles, she approached Luther. "Herr Doctor," she said, "Satan is tormenting me night and day."

"Have you tried sarcasm?" he asked after he had kissed her.

"I have, and it worked for a time. But now Satan merely chuckles, and attacks me in other ways."

"Then you must hurl Scripture at him."

"Like what? When I was at Nimbschen we never even read the Vulgate."

"Give me the New Testament I presented to you a few months after you escaped, and I'll mark some passages you will find extremely useful." As he was searching for them, he said, "Satan loved to tempt Jesus. You can read the story here in the fourth chapter of the Gospel according to Luke." He showed her the place and marked the passage. "On this occasion, Jesus got rid of Satan by hurling Scripture at him. Listen! 'And Jesus answering said unto him, It is said, Thou shalt not tempt the Lord thy God.' That, Katie, was just a short statement, but it was so effective Satan 'departed for a season.'

"Don't make the mistake of arguing with the devil. Why? Because he has had 5,000 years of experience, and he will defeat you! The best way, as I said, is to quote Scripture." He leafed through her New Testament and marked a dozen passages. "And please keep in mind that Brother Paul told us, 'There hath no temptation taken you but such as is common to man: but God is faithful, who will not suffer you to be tempted above that ye are able; but will with the temptation also make a way to escape, that ye may be able to bear it.' That passage is found in the tenth chapter of Paul's first letter to the Corinthians."

Summer continued hot in Wittenberg; then the cool

winds of fall began to blow. As leaves turned crimson, Katie began to experience morning sickness, and she had to stop going up the steps two at a time. Overjoyed by what was happening, Luther wrote to a friend, "My Katherine is fulfilling Genesis 1:28."

As the months passed and the child within her grew, Katie worked harder to make the adjustments necessary to live with the former monk. Stumbling on the steps, she exclaimed, "Hail, Mary!"

"Oh, Katie," corrected Luther who was just behind her, "you must complete your prayer. Always add, 'and Christ!'"

Sometimes Katie found herself arguing with her husband. On such occasions he would admonish, "Katie, before you preach you must always quote the Lord's Prayer. All of it! That will shorten your sermons."

Katie learned that she had two new names: *Kette* (chain) and *My Rib*. Her husband frequently concluded a letter, "My Rib sends greetings to your Rib"; or, if the man's wife was named Katherine, "My Chain sends greetings to your chain."

As time for her confinement drew near, Katie's worries increased. Permanent moneyless guests kept coming, and Martin kept saying, "Stay as long as you like." Money was becoming extremely short. In the privacy of their room, she tearfully confronted him. "Herr Doctor, we now have eighteen guests! Even Helmut won't extend any more credit; we'll be out of flour on Thursday, and I'm so low on energy I can hardly climb the steps."

"What do you suggest?"

"Why don't you make your publishers pay you so much for each of your books which they sell? They're getting rich at your expense!"

"Oh, but then they would have to raise the price of my books."

"So?"

"Then the poor people couldn't buy them."

Katie shook her head. "You're the most popular writer in Germany. You're even more popular than Erasmus! You should be adequately paid."

"No, Katie. God will take care of us. I'll hire another servant tomorrow."

"And how will you pay him?"

"I don't know. God hasn't told me. But He will." Five minutes later he was sound asleep.

12

A Mighty Fortress

Their food reserves were gone. Their credit was depleted. Their bills were unpaid. Schmidt's butcher shop was insisting on cash. Even worse, Lucas Cranach had refused to sign a note for them. Nonetheless, new boarders kept moving in. "These two girls and four boys are my sister's children," said the doctor. "Find them a good room and see that they are fed."

"How long will they stay?" asked Katie when she and Martin were alone.

"As long as they like."

"But Herr Doctor, we don't have any food, and Aunt Lena moved in last week—"

"God will take care of us. Excuse me, I have a class."

One by one their wedding presents had been pawned in order to raise money for food. "How are we going to redeem them?" demanded Katie. She rubbed her hands together and stared.

"Don't worry about bills. As soon as one is paid we have another. Bills are like the Elbe. They keep coming and always will. Bills are a fact of life."

Pondering what to do to get sufficient meat from Helmut Schmidt, Katie's eyes rested on a gold-rimmed silver vase that had been presented to them at their wedding. She picked it up, admiring its fine craftsmanship. Miraculously, it had escaped the greedy hands of the pawnbroker, and she was determined he would never see it. But what was she to do? If her husband didn't pawn it, he would give it away. There was only one logical answer: She'd hide it!

Later that night, while Luther was asleep, Katie tiptoed out of the room and hid the vase in a secret place.

Still, hiding the vase didn't solve their economic problems. In desperation, Katie uncovered the twenty gulden the archbishop had sent her. Reluctantly, she divided it between the butcher and the flour dealer. That evening as Luther surveyed the table loaded with food, he remarked, "Notice, Kette, God has provided!"

Katie forced a smile.

Katie's first child was born on June 7, 1526. Joyfully, Luther wrote a friend: "My dear Katie brought into the world yesterday by God's grace at two o'clock a little son, Hans Luther. I must stop. Katie calls me."

Bending over Hans, who was named after Martin's father and was bound in swaddling clothes, Luther had a word of advice. "Kick, little fellow. That's what the pope did to me. But I got loose."

Later, Luther made another observation. "Hans is cutting his teeth and beginning to make a general nuisance of himself. These are the joys of marriage of which the pope is not worthy."

The progress of this product of a monk and a nun was noted throughout Germany. The news produced letters and occasional gifts—gifts which Katie accepted at once and carefully hid to keep them from being returned or given to others. To a happy couple, Luther wrote: "I am sending you a vase as a wedding present. P.S. Katie had hidden it."

In spite of the gifts, it was hard for Katie to pay the bills and keep the table supplied. "We must be careful with our money," she admonished. In reply, Luther laughed and spread his fingers. "Money flows through them like water through a sieve," he confessed.

The elector had doubled Luther's salary at the time of his marriage. But it was now insufficient to feed all the mouths that gathered at his tables.

Katie kept her eyes focused on both her husband and little Hans. From the time Martin had discarded his cowl, just before their marriage, he had been gaining weight. It was with joy that Katie watched the outline of his ribs disappear. He had an uncanny way of lifting his pen and writing words that shouted to be read. Her duty, Katie was convinced, was to remove all distractions from his life in order that he might produce commentary after commentary. Toward the end of the year he had started on his *Exposition of Jonah*. Often she sat next to him as he studied, made notes in the margins of his books, and then left a trail of ink on manuscript paper—a trail she was convinced would influence the world for centuries to come.

Then on July 6, 1527, Katie's world was shaken.

Luther had just emptied his plate and was headed for the bedroom when he fainted and fell. Quickly Katie summoned help and carried him to his bed. The sudden illness lasted only two days, but its effect refused to leave. On August 21, Luther wrote to his friend, Agricola: "Satan rages against me with his whole might, and the Lord has put me in his power like another Job. The devil tempts me with great infirmity of spirit."

As Katie brought food, placed cool cloths on Luther's forehead, and fanned him, he made word pictures of his troubles. They were all dark. "Every night," he groaned, "devils come into this place. They make noises, rattle chains. I can hear them."

"They shouldn't frighten you," admonished Katie. "You know better than I the words of John, 'Greater is he that is in you, than he that is in the world.' "

"Thank you, Katie. Thank you." He patted her wrist. But his assurance didn't last. "Bring me the map that includes eastern Europe and Turkey," he ordered. "You'll find it on my desk."

124

With his finger on Constantinople, Luther said, "All this area used to be Christian. Luke and Paul preached here. Then in the third century the people started arguing about the Trinity and gathering holy bones. Now it's Muslim." He shuddered. "But, Katie, that's not the worst of it. Last year as you were struggling to bring little Hans into the world, Suleiman the Magnificent, Sultan of Turkey, was encamped before Buda in Hungary.[1] And Buda is closer to us than Rome!" He pointed to the map. "The Hungarians were confident. Louis II, their king, had been born before he was due; they had kept him alive by placing his body in the warm carcasses of animals slaughtered for his benefit.

"Indeed, they were so confident that when Suleiman sent his ambassador to them they dragged him around their streets, cut off his ears and nose, and then sent him back to Constantinople. This insult was one of the reasons that inspired the sultan's attack.

"Utterly confident, Louis led his army of 25,000 out to face Suleiman's army of 100,000. It was a mad thing to do. Louis was drowned and most of his men were killed. Next, the Turks marched 100,000 Hungarians back to Turkey."

"What will happen to them?" asked Katie, thoroughly alarmed.

Luther shook his head. "If the Muslims are as cruel to the Christians as some of the Christians were to the Muslims during the Crusades, it will be terrible." He threw up his hands and shuddered. "If we're not careful, all our churches will be destroyed and replaced by Muslim mosques! Oh, Katie, we must pray! Christianity is in peril both from within and without."

Political facts often inspired Luther to pace the floor. But he was also tormented by other problems. Sometimes he cried out, "Oh, Katie, my teeth are aching until I can't stand it." Likewise, he suffered from earache, dizzy spells, piles,

[1]Buda and Pest, now joined by bridges across the Danube, are known as Budapest.

rheumatism, vertigo, and stones. Sometimes his pain was so intense he longed to die.

Frequently when he couldn't sleep he went to his study and read, worked on manuscripts, and prayed.

Katie learned how to cater to him. She made simple medicines, listened to his troubles, quoted Scripture, rubbed his feet. Then even her world fell apart. The plague had descended on Wittenberg, leaving many dead bodies in the streets. Frantic victims pounded at the doors of the Black Cloister, crying to get in.

"We must take them in," said Luther.

Soon the Luther home resembled a hospital.

Then the elector ordered that the university be moved to Jena.

"Will we be leaving Wittenberg?" asked Katie, her eyes wide.

Luther rubbed his jaw, swollen from a toothache. "Certainly not! A shepherd never forsakes his sheep."

Katie slipped her arms around his neck. "Herr Doctor," she whispered softly, "I have a secret."

"Yes?" He studied her, eyebrow uplifted.

"Little Hans is scheduled to have either a brother or a sister in December."

"Oh, Katie, that's wonderful!"

She ran her fingers through his hair. "Are we going to remain in Wittenberg?" she asked again. There was a hopeful note in her voice.

"Of course!" He pulled her onto his lap and kissed her.

Most professors left for Jena. Nonetheless, George Rörer and his wife remained. "That is most agreeable to me," said Luther. Rörer, a deacon in the City Church, had worked as his secretary and had been most helpful with his translation of the Bible—especially the Old Testament, which was far from being completed.

As Katie treated plague victims, more and more bad news filtered into Wittenberg. During January 1526, Luther had learned that Michael Gasmaier, a leader of the Peasants' War in Austria, had decreed that all "godless" [non-Lutherans!] in that land be put to death; that all pictures and images in Catholic churches be destroyed; and that the saying of mass be forbidden.

"This makes me sick," groaned Luther, pacing the floor. "The only sword I accept is the sword of the Spirit—the one used by Paul. In time truth will win, but it takes time—lots of time."

The Peasants' War continued, and the idea circulated that Luther advocated communism. Sickened by the idea, Luther dragged himself into his study and, using his pen like an ax, wrote some unforgettable words:

> The Gospel does not make goods common, except in the case of those who do of their own free will what the Apostles and disciples did in Acts 4. They did not demand, as do our insane peasants in their raging, that the goods of others— of a Pilate or a Herod—should be common, but only their own goods. Our peasants, however, would have other men's goods common and keep their own goods for themselves. Fine Christians these! I think there is not a devil left in hell; they have all gone into the peasants.

By the end of the revolt, 130,000 peasants had been killed. Of these, 10,000 were executed, and one executioner boasted that he alone had executed 1,200. Luther was nauseated by all this bloodshed, and he had become so unpopular with the peasants he feared leaving Wittenberg.

The plague continued. Rörer's wife succumbed to the disease and died. Little Hans was confined to his room. Sorrowfully, Luther wrote to Justus Jonas:

> I am anxious about the delivery of my wife, so much has the example of Rörer's wife terrified me. . . . My little Hans cannot send you greetings on account of illness. . . . It is twelve days since he has eaten any solid food. . . .
>
> Margaret Moch was operated on yesterday and, having at last thrown off the plague, begins to convalesce. She is lodged in our usual winter room; we live in the lecture hall; little Hans has my bedroom and Schurf's wife his room. We hope the pestilence is passing. . . .

While Luther's world was crumbling, Suleiman the Magnificent was slicing into Europe. The only person who could stop his fanatical, Allah-shouting hordes was Charles V. But instead of fighting Muslims, Charles, with the help of German mercenaries—many of them Lutheran—was attacking Rome! Not having been paid, the troops mutinied, sacked the Eternal City and imprisoned the pope, Clement VII. At the time, Charles V was in Spain. But although he deplored the excesses of his hired troops, he approved the conquest of the city and the imprisonment of the pope.

The attitude of the Protestant mercenaries was that since the Roman church had robbed them, they would rob the Roman church! Consequently, they looted, raped, burned, murdered, and ridiculed. "On Holy Thursday [April 8], when Clement was giving his blessing to a crowd of 10,000 before St. Peter's, a fanatic, clad only in a leather apron, mounted the statue of St. Paul and shouted to the pope: 'Thou bastard of Sodom! For thy sins Rome shall be destroyed. Repent . . . !²

Almost every house in Rome was burned, hostages were taken, and enormous ransoms were demanded. "In the whole city," says one "there was not a soul above three years of age who had not been forced to purchase his safety."³

Mad with hysteria, the looting troops pillaged the churches. They stole the gold crosses, gold vessels, and other valuables. The "holy bones" taken from beneath the altars were scattered across the floors. Cardinals were seized, tortured, put up for ransom, and forced to ride backward on the scrawniest animals that could be found. One imaginative soldier dressed up like the pope while other soldiers, wearing the red cardinal hats, formed a long line and mockingly kissed his toe.

By a voice vote, Martin Luther was proclaimed the new pope!

Books and entire libraries were destroyed. At least two thousand corpses were thrown into the Tiber. Thousands of

---

²*The Renaissance* by Will Durant, pp. 630–631.
³Ibid.

other bodies were left to rot in the streets.

Pope Clement remained imprisoned in Sant' Angelo Castle from May 6 to December 7, 1527. During that period he hoped that Francis I or Henry VIII would rescue him. Neither even made the attempt. Finally Clement was forced to sign an almost impossible peace treaty. In that document, he agreed to turn over a number of cities, castles, and 400,000 ducats to Charles. Moreover, it was agreed that he would remain a prisoner until 150,000 ducats of the agreed amount had been paid.

Horrified, Erasmus exclaimed, "This is not the ruin of one city, but of the whole world!"

After learning all of this and being utterly heartsick, Luther concluded his letter to Justus Jonas:

> I am sorry Rome was sacked, for it is a great portent. I hope it may yet be inhabited and have its pontiff before we die.
>
> He signed it "Martin Luther, *Christi lutum*" (Christ's mud).

One evening while alone with Katie, Luther sat on the edge of their bed and rehearsed his troubles. This time he had an additional one. "People wonder why Frederick the Wise defended me. Realistically, he should have been my enemy. Why? I ridiculed his collection of relics, I disagreed with his doctrine, and I was a sharp thorn in his flesh. Why did he stand up for me? Because I attracted students to the university—the great project of his life. In 1518, the year after I posted my ninety-five theses, there were almost six hundred students. My lectures were crowded. The students were eager. This year we have only about fifty. Why? One reason is that Duke George has forbidden his subjects to attend. But, Katie, that may not be the worst problem. The worst problem may be that God is through with me." He wiped his eyes and rubbed his jaws. "My teeth. *Akh! Akh!* My teeth."

"Sit still. I'll get you a hot pad," said Katie, patting him on the shoulder.

Luther pressed the pad to his jaw. "With only fifty students the elector may forsake us."

"Nonsense. He's a Protestant, and he's called John the Steadfast. Isn't that true?"

"I guess so."

"The attendance is down because of the plague. Last year we had more than a hundred students."

"Yes, that's true. Nonetheless, Katie, you must remember that I've been excommunicated, that I'm under the emperor's sentence of death, that the nobles hate me, and the peasants hate me. One of them even called me Dr. Liar to my face! Should my parents become ill, I'd be afraid to visit them. I might be killed on the way."

Katie listened intently. Then her face lit up. "I'm puzzled about something."

"Yes?"

"What did you say when you were on the way to Worms?"

Luther smiled. "I said, 'Even though there should be as many devils in Worms as shingles on the roof, I would still enter.' "

"And what did you say when you faced the emperor?"

"I said, 'I cannot and I will not recant anything, for to go against conscience is neither right nor safe. Here I stand, I cannot do otherwise. God help me. Amen.' "

"Now, Herr Doctor, if you were so determined and brave then, why aren't you just as determined and brave now?"

"Today things are different."

"So? Is God's Word different? Is Jesus Christ different? Are the just still being saved by faith?"

"What do you mean by all this questioning?" He cocked his head, a smile lighting his face.

"One more question. Were you bored at Wartburg?"

"At first. I was so bored I almost died."

"Were you bored when you were translating the New Testament?"

"Certainly not. I completed it in a few weeks."

"Could it be that you were doing something then that you aren't doing now?" She studied him carefully.

"Yes, I was. I was active. I was busy." His eyes began to

glow. "Katie, you've preached long enough. I've gotten the point! I've moped long enough. Now I am going to my study. A new inspiration has gripped me."

Katie smiled as she watched him head for the study. Each step was firmer than the last. For three days he left the table early and almost ran to his task. At the end of the third day he appeared before Katie with his lute and a page of manuscript. "I have been writing a hymn," he announced. "It's titled *Ein feste Burg ist unser Gott* [A Mighty Fortress Is Our God]. Listen while I sing it."

Accompanying himself, he sang in his rich baritone voice:

> A mighty Fortress is our God,
>   A Bulwark never failing;
> Our helper He amid the flood
>   Of mortal ills prevailing:
> For still our ancient foe
>   Doth seek to work us woe;
> His craft and power are great,
>   And, armed with cruel hate,
> On earth is not his equal.[4]

Before he was finished, Katie was in tears. After the last verse she exclaimed, "That's great! Where did you get the inspiration to write it?"

"From you! From Christ! From Duke George! From my diseases! From the Wartburg Castle! And from the 46th psalm in the Vulgate!"

Arms tight around his neck, Katie sobbed, "Herr Doctor, that hymn will live!"[5]

Luther smiled. "Any more questions?"

"Yes, Herr Doctor. One question. Did you really throw a pot of ink at the devil when you were hiding at Wartburg Castle?"

Luther smiled. "The ink, I'm told, is still on the wall. Make up your own mind!"

---

[4]The melody is by Martin Luther. This translation by Frederick H. Hedge was made in 1852.

[5]That was an understatement. A century ago Heinrich Heine declared it to be "The *Marseillaise* of the Reformation."

13

The Coburg Fortress

Late in the fall, as Wittenberg's trees began to face the world without leaves, the plague disappeared as mysteriously as it had come. Those who had fled, returned and once again crowded the streets. Little Hans recovered, and Katie's second baby arrived on December 10, 1527.

"Her name is Elizabeth," announced Luther, rocking her in his arms by the window.

When Elizabeth began to cry, he quickly handed her over to Katie, who was still lying in bed. "It's her breakfast time," he said. He started to leave and then hesitated. "History will remember me as the one who defied both the emperor and the pope, and who explained to the world the meaning of Paul's words, 'The just shall live by faith.' But Katie, you and I will be remembered for something else—something equally as important."

"And what could that be?" Katie studied him curiously.

"For establishing the parsonage!"

"Pastor Bugenhagen was married before we were married."

"True. But we're better known. When Hans cut his first teeth, it was known all over Germany. And, Katie, founding the parsonage is a major accomplishment."

"What do you mean?"

"Many of the finest minds have entered the priesthood. Unfortunately, from about the third century on, priests were—and still are—forbidden to marry. That means that such truly remarkable and saintly men as Thomas Aquinas and Bernard of Clairvaux were unable to bequeath their brilliance to future generations. This is a pity. The rabbis didn't make that mistake! That's one of the reasons we have so many gifted Jews."

"Did the apostles marry?"

"Of course! Brother Paul wrote: 'Have we not power to lead about a sister, a wife, as well as other apostles, and as the brethren of the Lord, and Cephas?'[1] Katie, we have a duty! We must raise and train an excellent family. This is the will of the Lord."

Raising two children, keeping Martin happy, providing food for the often-not-paying boarders, supervising servants and paying bills were difficult tasks. And, although Martin was good to her, she kept wondering if he really loved her.

Night and day Luther's mind was on those things which he considered to be of the greatest importance: the growth of the church, his classes, the activities of the Turks, the moves of Charles V—and especially his translation of the Old Testament.

"Herr Doctor, I need money to buy meat for the guests who are coming tomorrow," said Katie.

As she spoke, Luther seemed to be listening, but he didn't reply. "We need money to buy meat for the guests," she repeated.

"Oh, I'm sorry, I was thinking about Isaiah. I have some money due this afternoon. In the meantime, just go ahead with your preparations."

Katie went ahead with her preparations. She had an inner confidence because she had hidden a dozen gulden to buy cloth for a new dress, and if Martin's money didn't come in

---

[1] 1 Corinthians 9:5.

she could use that. As she worked, her husband went to his study. There were open books all over the floor; the desk was piled high with papers, pots of ink, quills, maps, letters, proofs from a new book, and stacks of fresh parchment. Selecting a new quill, he addressed a letter to Wenceslaus Link, one of the men who helped him in his translation work. He wrote:

> We are now sweating over the translation of the prophets into German. . . . What a great and hard toil it requires to compel the writers against their will to speak German. They do not want to give up their Hebrew.

On August 3, sorrow came into the Luther home. Elizabeth, less than a year old, succumbed to an unknown disease. Brokenhearted, Luther wrote to his friend Hausmann:

> Little Hans thanks you for the rattle. . . . My little daughter Elizabeth is dead. She has left me wonderfully sick at heart. . . . I am so moved by pity for her. I could never believe how a father's heart could soften for his child.

On May 4, 1529, Katie had a new daughter: Magdalena. Peering down at her feeding at Katie's breast, Luther exclaimed, "She's a special gift from heaven!" Although he never neglected Hans, Luther enjoyed rocking his daughter in his arms and singing little songs to her, some of which he composed on the spot. Within weeks her name had shrunk to Lena, and then, especially on important occasions, it became Sweet Lenniken. Frail as she was, Luther enjoyed taking her around his study. Pointing to pictures on the wall, he would say, "That's your Grandma Luther, and that's your Grandpa Luther."

Magdalena was almost her mother's duplicate. She had similar facial features, including the same almond-shaped eyes and the same slender hands.

"Do you think she really understands German?" asked Katie one morning after Martin had been naming Magdalena's toes.

"Not yet. But she will. She'll even speak Latin. Sweet Lenniken is my little scholar. Just look at those eyes!"

Katie laughed. "What will you do if she says, 'Ave Maria'?"

"I'll tell her to complete her prayer by adding, 'and Jesus Christ,' just as I told you." He laughed and pulled Katie onto his lap.

Katie's ecstatic happiness didn't last.

One evening as Luther was preparing for bed he said, "Katie, I have sensational news."

"Yes?"

"Pope Clement VII and Charles V have become friends!"

"F-friends?"

"Yes, they've become friends, and Charles has publicly kissed his toe. In return, the pope crowned him emperor of the Holy Roman Empire!"

"When did all of this take place?"

"At Bologna on February 24, 1530."

"Why?"

"Because Suleiman the Magnificent is at the gates of Vienna, and if he succeeds Europe will become Muslim. Until now, the emperor has almost ignored Germany. But now, because of the Turkish threat, he has humiliated himself in order to smooth out our religious differences in order to strengthen his hand in fighting the Turks. As a result of this, he's ordered a special diet to meet at Augsburg."

"Like the Diet of Worms?"

"Correct. I've a copy of the theme right here. The purpose is that 'true religion may be accepted and held by us all, and that we live in one common church and unity.' "

"Are you going?"

"Certainly."

"But, Herr Doctor, you're an outlaw! You'll be burned like Huss."

"Perhaps. Still, God has called. Jesus didn't flinch, nor will I."

"And leave Hans and Lenniken with me?" She bit her lip and struggled unsuccessfully with her tears.

"Yes, I'll have to leave you. You manage everything while I'm here, and you can do the same when I'm gone."

"Protestants have already been burned in Holland." She held his hand and looked imploringly into his face.

"Nonetheless, I must go. The just shall live by faith!"

Katie kissed Martin good-bye in early April. Then she watched as he joined Melanchthon and other theologians while they seated themselves in the carriage that would take them to Coburg, a city in southwestern Ernestine Saxony. As the carriage disappeared and the clipclop of the horses faded, she flung herself across the bed.

"Oh, God!" she sobbed, "keep them from harm. Don't let them be arrested." In her heart she was all but convinced that she would never see her husband again. In her mind's eye she saw the hungry flames as they consumed his body, chained to a stake in a public square.

While feeling sorry for herself, Katie remembered how she had snapped Martin out of his depression by urging him to go to work. Now she decided to do the same.

While Luther and his theologian friends, along with the elector, waited at Coburg, an imperial herald thundered upon his lavishly arrayed horse and handed an official pouch to the elector. After opening the thick envelope bright with seals, the elector announced, "Along with instructions, it contains our safe-conduct letters."

"Is there one for me?" asked Luther anxiously.

The elector thumbed through the papers several times. "I'm sorry, Dr. Luther; you've not been included."

"That means I'll be arrested!" he exclaimed, turning white.

"It probably does. You'd better remain in the fortress. Germany and the world need you—alive! I'll meet the expenses."

Feste Coburg, the formal name of the sprawling fortress, occupies the top of a hill and frowns down on the lower areas for many miles. Here, together with his nephew and secretary, Veit Dietrich, along with thirty of the elector's men, Luther remained for nearly six months.

Tense for her husband's safety, Katie listened for news

and kept her eyes on the mails. Like Martin, she knew that Protestantism was in an acute state of crisis. As she sought news about the activities of Charles V and the Turks, she learned that her husband's father, Hans, had passed away on May 29. Hoping to comfort Martin, she mailed him a box along with a painting of Magdalena.

Luther replied:

Dear Katie:

I believe I have received all your letters. This is my fourth. . . . I have Lena's picture and the box you sent. . . . At first I didn't know the little minx; she seemed so dark. I think it would be a proper thing if you weaned her; do it little by little. . . .

Our friends at Nuremberg and Augsburg are beginning to wonder if anything will happen at the Diet, for the emperor still tarries at Innsbruck. . . . I must hurry as the messenger will not wait. Greet, kiss, hug, and be kind to each according to his degree.

Martin Luther

While Katie was busy with the children and household duties, whiffs of what was taking place at Augsburg kept coming to her. "I never before saw such pageantry!" exclaimed a former Wittenberg student. "Crimson, white, purple robes embroidered with gold were everywhere. I had never even imagined such color. It hurt my eyes. The electors were there, including our own John the Steadfast. Elector John was entrusted with the emperor's naked sword. Frau Luther, you should have seen the way it flashed in the sun.

"When the Cardinal of Campeggio pronounced the benediction, all of the dignitaries, with the exception of John, bared their heads and knelt. Standing with his head covered, Elector John was as conspicuous as a tower. I was proud of him!

"At the cathedral, the emperor, together with the princes and all the other dignitaries, knelt at the high altar. As they were kneeling, my eyes were attracted to our elector, Philip of Hesse, and the Archbishop of Mainz—the one who sent you the twenty gulden. Again I was proud. Neither of them knelt."

Katie's eyes widened. "Weren't they risking their lives?"

"Of course. A twitch of the emperor's lips would have meant their deaths."

Katie sighed. "And to think that my husband missed all of that! It would have been one of the greatest experiences of his life."

"Yes, he would have been overwhelmed. Then the next day," continued the former student, "His Majesty summoned the Lutheran princes and informed them that they were not to allow their ministers to preach at Augsburg.

" 'We can't agree to that,' replied an elector.

" 'Then forbid them to preach on anything controversial!' snapped the emperor, raising his voice. He then stated that he fully expected each of them to march in the *Corpus Christi* procession the next day.

"At that moment, the *margrave*—governor of Brandenburg—stepped forward. As you know, he's now a stooped old man. His hair is like snow and his face is eroded like a hill after a storm. Marveling at his courage, I listened closely."

"And what did he say?" Katie's mouth was slightly ajar.

"In clear tones the brave old man said, 'Before I let anyone take from me the Word of God and ask me to deny my God, I will kneel and let him strike off my head!' "

Katie blew her nose. Wiping her eyes, she exclaimed, "Oh, I wish Dr. Luther had been there! To have heard that would have meant more to him than his doctor's beret."

Suddenly their conversation was interrupted by the shrill crying of Magdalena. "She's hungry," said Katie, taking quick steps to the door. "Poor thing. She doesn't like being weaned." Over her shoulder, she added, "We'll talk some other time. In the meantime, we must pray for Dr. Luther."

Each morning and evening Katie lingered by her bed as she prayed for her husband. "Lord, don't let him get depressed," she pleaded, "and if he is depressed, put new songs in his heart." She also organized the boarders and servants. "We're going to make the Black Cloister a model building," she said.

Having handed a hoe to a former monk who couldn't get a church and who was famous for the number of sausages he consumed, she said, "Clean out the pigsty."

"Oh, but I have to pray."

"You can pray while you work," she replied, glancing severely at his ample middle. "In order to have sausages we have to raise pigs."

Then she approached a hanger-on who hadn't paid a gulden in the five months he had been there. "Take this shovel and clean out the cowshed."

"I don't know how."

"Come, I'll show you. And when you get it all cleaned out, I'll teach you how to milk."

"Oh, but Frau Luther I—I—"

"Never mind. Get busy. A little work will make the milk and cheese taste better."

Others were assigned to clean out the fishponds so that more fish could be raised for the table. To those who complained about their assignments, Katie had a simple sermon: "We rejoice that Brother Paul taught us that 'the just shall live by faith.' But we must also remember that he explained to the Thessalonians that 'if any would not work, neither should he eat.' "[2]

Toward midsummer, Katie's heart became heavy with a special burden for Luther. An inward something impressed her that he had special needs. Having summoned Aunt Lena to her room, she said, "I have an almost unbearable burden for my husband. I feel impressed to ask you to join me in praying for him. She opened her New Testament to Matthew 18. "Listen to this," she began. "Jesus said, 'Again I say unto you, That if two of you shall agree on earth as touching any

---

[2] Thessalonians 3:10.

thing that they shall ask, it shall be done for them of my Father which is in heaven.' "

"That passage is true, and I believe it," replied her aunt. "But Katie, tell me, what are the specific things for which we should pray?"

"That he not get depressed. Dr. Luther has a brilliant mind, but like other gifted men he gets extremely discouraged. Sometimes he even longs to die."

Day after day, Katie and Lena met in Katie's room and prayed, and each continued to pray even as they continued their work.

The Coburg Fortress was a dreary place. Still, Luther refused to be idle. On May 12 he wrote to Melanchthon:

> I have completed my warning to the prelates and sent it off to the Wittenberg press. I have also translated two chapters of Ezekiel about Gog. . . . Then I took the Prophets in hand and attacked the labor with such ardor that I hope to finish it before Pentecost. . . . But the old outer man cannot keep up with the ardor of the new inner man; my head has begun to suffer from ringing, or rather thundering, and this has forced me to stop work. Yesterday . . . I narrowly escaped fainting, and this is the third day on which I am unable to look at a letter of the alphabet. . . . Satan was busy occupying my attention. . . . I was alone . . . and Satan conquered me so far that he forced me to leave my room and seek the society of men.

Luther worried about what would happen at the diet. It was possible it would end in civil war, that Charles V would join with the pope to crush the Protestants. His fears were augmented by the dreary sounds within the fortress: the moaning of the wind, the shift of squeaking timbers, the scramble of rats. And from outside he could hear the cries of birds in nearby trees and the haunting hoots of owls as their big eyes searched for food.

Also, he was extremely lonely. Katie and the children were on his mind day and night.

Then on August 5 he felt an unusual surge of strength. It was as if the Spirit of the Lord had descended upon him in the same way in which He had descended on Samson when he was surrounded by the Philistines. Only instead of picking up a jawbone, Luther reached for his quill.

Addressing a letter to Dr. Gregory Brück, prime minister of Electoral Saxony, he wrote:

> . . . I have recently seen two miracles. The first was that as I looked out my window, I saw the stars and the whole vault of heaven, with no pillars to support it; and the sky did not fall and the vault remained fast. But there are some who want to see the pillars and would like to clasp them and feel them. And when they are unable to do so they fidget and tremble as if the sky would certainly fall in, simply because they cannot feel and see the pillars under it. . . .
>
> Again I saw great, thick clouds roll above us, so heavy they looked like great seas, and I saw no ground on which they could rest nor any barrels to hold them and yet they fell not on us, but threatened us and floated on. When they passed by, the rainbow shone forth, the rainbow which was the floor that held them up. . . . But some people look at the thickness of the clouds and the thinness of the ray, and they fear and worry. They would like to feel how strong the rainbow is, and when they cannot do so they think the clouds will bring another deluge.

Luther laid aside his quill and folded the letter. As he awaited the messenger, he had no way of knowing that he had just composed one of the world's great letters, a letter which would inspire the depressed for half a millennium. Nor did he realize that his inspiration had been triggered by his wife's persistent prayers knocking at the gates of heaven—even though those prayers were originating from the other side of Germany.

14

God Is Dead!

In the fall of 1530, Katie was supervising a handful of boarders at the rear of the Black Cloister when Luther suddenly rode up. Eyes wide, heart thumping, Katie rushed to the carriage. Pulling him into her arms as he was dismounting, she exclaimed, "Welcome home, Dr. Luther! Welcome home!"

Katie's quick eyes noticed that he had lost weight. "I'll hurry into the kitchen and get you something to eat," she said. An hour later, with Hans sitting on one side and Magdalena squirming in the cradle of his left arm, Martin said, "Katie, I knew you were praying for me. Every day I was aware of a mysterious source of strength. And when the devil assaulted me, I assured him that you were on your knees."

"And what did he say?"

"He didn't like it!"

During the weeks that followed, Luther confided bits of information to Katie. "Our evangelical faith is in great danger," he confessed in the privacy of their room. "The emperor wanted a statement of faith from us, and since I was confined to the fortress, I left the final presentation of such a statement, or confession, to Melanchthon. He, of course, had a detailed statement in his possession on which several of us had labored at Torgau. Still, I feared that our diplomatic friend might compromise. Rumor had it that he might even recognize the pope!" Luther frowned. "Melanchthon, brilliant scholar though he is, has a touch of Erasmus in him. He can almost walk on rotten eggs without breaking them. I'm the wild boar." He laughed.

"Our princes, however, were firm in their faith and helped to strengthen his hand. Finally, on June 24, the Protestants were ready to present their document. They had two copies, one in Latin and the other in German. Like the princes, Melanchthon wanted the work read before as many as possible— and to be read in German.

"During the morning and afternoon of that fateful day, some Catholic delegates wasted valuable time making long speeches in regard to the Turkish menace. About the time the sun began to sink, there was time for the reading of the confession. At this juncture the weary emperor declared that it was too late. He also suggested that instead of being read publicly, it be merely handed to him for private study!

"The Protestants strongly objected to this. A spokesman even reminded his Imperial Majesty that we had been promised a public reading. After some argument, it was agreed that the confession be read the next day—June 25. Ah, but the emperor and his friends were determined! Unable to stop the public reading, they shifted the place for the reading from the city hall, where there was plenty of room, to a cramped lower room in the Episcopal Palace, where a mere two hundred could be seated. Satan, Katie, is a clever strategist!

"The emperor entered the room at three in the afternoon. At the last moment, the emperor's brother, Ferdinand, suggested that since there were delegates present from other countries, the confession be read in Latin. To this the Protestants objected. They contended that since they were in Germany, the confession should be presented in German.

"Every inch of space in the room was crowded, and there were throngs in the hallways and yard. When Dr. Beyer stepped forward to read the manuscript, every Protestant delegate rose to his feet to indicate his respect." Luther's eyes misted.

"My, Katie, I wish I could have been there!

"The reading of the Augsburg Confession[1] required two full hours, and as Dr. Beyer read it, his trumpet voice was so clear even those outside could understand it."

"And what did the emperor do as he read the confession?" asked Katie.

"There are several reports. One delegate said that he went to sleep; another insisted that he commented, 'I would that such doctrine were preached throughout the whole world.' Charles V, of course, does not know German well, and so he asked his secretary to translate the Latin version into French so that he could study it in private."

"And did the emperor accept the confession?"

"I think he was impressed. But his advisors suggested that a reply be written against it. The reply was written by John Eck—all 351 pages of it—and was ready to be presented by July 8. This rebuttal—it has been named the *Confutation*—is so sarcastic I've been told that His Majesty isn't too happy with it. Nonetheless, his ancestors are Catholic, he is Catholic, his subjects are Catholic, his advisors are Catholic, and, in order to confront the Turks, he needs the backing of Pope Clement VII."

"So?" Magdalena had started to cry. Katie gently lifted her onto her lap.

"So the emperor issued the following statement." Luther withdrew it from his pocket and began to read:

> Therefore His Imperial Majesty, for the benefit and prosperity of the Holy Empire, for the restoration of peace and unity, and for the purpose of manifesting His Majesty's leniency and special grace, has granted the Elector of Saxony, the five Princes, and the six cities a time of grace from now until the 15th of April next year in which to consider whether or not they will confess the other articles together with the Christian Church, His Holiness the Pope, His Imperial Majesty, the other Electors, Princes, and Estates of the Holy Roman Empire, and other Christian rulers and the

---

[1]The Augsburg Confession is a cornerstone of Lutheran doctrine and has had monumental influence on all evangelical Christianity.

members of universal Christendom until a general council shall be convoked.

As Katie listened, she nervously rubbed her hands together. "The document is an ultimatum," she said the moment Luther had finished reading it.

"Correct."

"What will happen if you and the other evangelicals don't submit?"

"There will be civil war, and if we're defeated many of us will be burned at the stake. Duke George is already licking his lips!"

Katie's eyes widened. Starting with October, she counted the months on her fingers. "That means you have only seven months in which to submit."

"Correct. And the odds against us will be enormous. Imagine pitting the few Protestants in Germany and Holland and Denmark and a few other places against the entire Holy Roman Empire! It will be an impossible contest. Our only refuge is in God."

"And what are you doing now?"

"Melanchthon is writing a book against the *Confutation*. He's calling it the *Apology*."

As the months hurried by, Katie made full use of every minute of the day. Her husband's study was his throne room, and she saw to it that he was never disturbed. He was always busy working on his translation of the Bible and revising his translation of the New Testament.

Late one Saturday night, Katie found Luther patching his pants. "You shouldn't be doing that!" she exclaimed.

"Why not? Frederick the Wise always mended his own pants. Am I better than the elector?"

"No, but the world needs every minute of your time. Besides, mending your clothes is my job."

The next morning as Katie was dressing little Hans for church, she suddenly gasped. A large section had been cut out of his leather breeches. Showing them to her husband, she said, "What do you suppose happened to them? Surely he didn't do that by just sliding down the staircase rail."

Luther hung his head. "Don't blame Hans. I needed a patch and his pants matched mine. Besides, Jesus taught us that we shouldn't put new patches on old clothes! I'm sorry. I'll buy him a new pair."

"Oh, Martin, Martin!" she groaned helplessly.

As the brown and gold leaves of Wittenberg's oaks and elms slowly fluttered to the ground and the weather chilled, Luther's shoulders continued to droop. The dreaded April 15 deadline of the emperor was only a few months away. True, John the Steadfast and the other Protestant princes stood firm. Likewise the *Schmalkald League*, composed of Lutheran cities and Lutheran princes, had solidified into an alliance. Even so, the future seemed bleak.

"Unless God performs a miracle, there will be a bloodbath," said Luther while sitting at the table. He shook his head.

"Do you think the emperor will compromise?" asked Katie.

"Never! If he allows the Protestants to retain their faith, it will be the end of the Holy Roman Empire."

Two weeks after this exchange, word came that Luther's mother was seriously ill. "You must go and visit her," said Katie.

"Oh, but I can't. Remember, I'm still an outlaw."

"It would do her a lot of good."

"Of course. Nonetheless, I must not risk my life."

Reluctantly, Luther contented himself by writing his mother a letter. He pointed out to her that Jesus had said, "I have overcome the world." Then he concluded, "All my children and Katie pray for you. Some cry. Some say, while eating, 'Grandmother is very ill.' "

Having just lost his father, this was a time of great turmoil for Luther.

Melanchthon spent every spare moment working on the

Page 146

Apology.[2] He enlarged, rewrote, corrected, started over again, tightened sentence structure, studied the Church Fathers, researched Erasmus, consulted with Luther. He dug up scriptural proof that "the just shall live by faith." He checked the alleged mistakes in the Vulgate. He worked on Sundays, wrote during meals and late at night. He had the compulsion of an army fortifying a position with the enemy in sight and approaching on the double. Luther suffered with him, and on one occasion snatched the quill from him. "Philip," he chided, "God has called us not only to work, but also to rest."

The former monk, however, didn't heed his own advice. He got up early and worked late. He was always writing, composing, teaching, preaching, settling disputes. And when he wasn't physically working, he was fighting the devil by hurling scripture, calling him names, resorting to sarcasm. His shoulders continued to sag, his eyes to dim, his memory to lapse. Once, after having to expel two of his relatives from the Black Cloister for repeated drunkenness, he became limp as a rag.

Nothing cheered him.

The emperor's April 15 deadline came and passed. Nothing happened. Still, Luther's shoulders continued to sag. In May Katie told him that she was expecting another baby. His only response was, "When's it due?"

"In December," she replied. But instead of commenting, he headed toward his study without making a sign that he had even heard.

Distressed, Katie went to Pastor Bugenhagen. "What am I to do?" she asked, her voice husky with concern.

"Pray."

"Oh, but I am praying."

"Pray some more."

She then approached Dr. Augustine Schurf, a distinguished professor of medicine at the university.

"He's working too hard," said Schurf.

---

[2] Published in 1531 with the title, *Apology of the Augsburg Confession.*

"But I can't get him to stop."

"Insist that he take a vacation. He likes to hunt rabbits."

"He won't agree."

"Then, Frau Luther, you must pray. Ask, knock, thunder, keep everlastingly at it."

Desperate, and even fearing for Martin's life, Katie decided on bold measures. She searched her New Testament, placed bookmarks in key passages, and then ransacked her wardrobe for every garment that was black. Next, she dressed in these mourning clothes.

"And what's the matter with you?" demanded Luther, staring in astonishment from behind the mountain of books and papers on his desk.

"Can't you see that I'm in mourning?" asked Katie, forcing a sob.

"Who's dead?"

"A very important person." She blew her nose and wiped her eyes.

"Tell me. Who is it?"

"God!"

"You mean the heavenly Father?"

"That's right." She nodded. "Yes, God is dead. D-E-A-D!"

Luther frowned. "Who told you that?"

"You!"

"When?"

"Because of the way you've been dragging around for the last few weeks, I've decided that God is dead."

"Oh, Katie!"

"And I've also found a lot of mistakes in your translation of the New Testament."

"Name one!" A shadow of horror smudged his face.

"That favorite passage of yours in the first chapter of Romans which you translated 'the just shall live by faith' should be translated *the just shall live by faith if they do lots of penance.*"

Luther stared. "Any more?"

"Yes, you have another favorite verse in the eighth chapter of the same book. I've heard you quote it a thousand times. You say, 'All things work together for good.' That is wrong. The correct translation is *few things work together for good.*"

"And who is your authority?"

"A brilliant man by the name of Dr. Martin Luther!"

Luther leaped to his feet, his eyes flashed, his lips expanded into a smile, and he held out his arms. "Oh, Katie," he said, "that was a brilliant sermon. Where did you get the idea?"

"From you. You said I should always repeat the Lord's Prayer before I preached, and that is what I've been doing ever since you've been so depressed."

Katie's new baby was born on November 9, 1531. "And now *I'm* going to name him," announced Katie. Her voice was as firm as Luther's had been at the Diet of Worms.

Luther laughed. "And what's his name?"

"Martin!"

While little Martin was nursing, being burped, and cutting his teeth, Luther often paced the floor. "God only knows when the emperor will attack us," he said. "Charles V is a good strategist. He's just awaiting the right moment."

"But hasn't the Schmalkald League signed a mutual assistance pact with him?" asked Katie.

"Yes. It was signed last March. Nonetheless . . ." He shook his head. "I'm afraid some of our princes cannot be trusted!"

The emperor's eyes were on the Turks. Many had said that Suleiman's followers were a fresh incarnation of the Saracens, who had wrested Jerusalem from the Crusaders. As the emperor's spies sent him reports about the Turks, Suleiman's spies sent him reports about the Europeans. Even Luther held his breath.

Thoroughly frightened, Charles V agreed to a treaty with the Lutherans. This treaty, signed on August 2, 1532, is known as the *Peace of Nuremberg.*

Feeling certain that Suleiman would attack Vienna, Charles V packed the city with troops and armor. The troops came from Spain, Italy, the Netherlands, Germany—and included among them were many Lutherans. This army, historians say, was the largest mobilized army in Europe during that generation.

But this enormous concentration of power faced only a phantom army—one that has puzzled men of history for centuries.

Believing that Jesus was inferior to Mohammed, and zealous to replace Europe's churches with mosques, Suleiman mobilized a fierce army that included the finest horses and a vast array of Tartars—the most skillful horsemen in the world.

Then, jewels flashing on his turban, Suleiman headed north.

Reports of Suleiman's progress filtered into Vienna. "They've already burned villages north of here," reported a messenger. This was a mystery, for none had seen the main Turkish army. It was later learned that the areas north of Vienna were being ravished by the Tartars. It was also discovered that Suleiman's main army—the Phantom Army—was besieging the little town of Güns, sixty miles to the south.

Strangely, Güns was being defended by a garrison of only seven hundred!

Suleiman's Phantom Army remained at Güns for twenty days. When the garrison surrendered, Suleiman merely demanded the keys of the already demolished gates. He then astonished the defenders by granting them total immunity.

Soon after this, without even approaching Vienna, Suleiman and his undefeated followers returned by a winding route to Turkey. That November, Suleiman went shopping in the bazaars of Constantinople!

Charles V was mystified.

"Why didn't he attack?" asked a commander.

"Perhaps it was because he feared our cannon," replied his friend. "Suleiman didn't have cannon in the quantities we have. If he could have lured us to the plains between here and Güns, his horsemen would have cut us to pieces."

Katie Luther had a different version. Speaking across the table, she said, "Herr Doctor, I think God used Suleiman the Magnificent to divert the emperor's attention and thus avoid civil war in Germany."

"You may be right, Katie," replied Luther. "Now we have the time to become solidified and to show the world that 'the just shall live by faith.' "

On January 28, 1533, Katie presented her husband with his third son. "What shall we name him?" asked Katie.

"Paul."

"And why Paul?"

"Because Paul believed in God's providence!"

15

The Rich Lady of Zulsdorf

After the retreat of undefeated Suleiman the Magnificent, Emperor Charles V tabled his determination to crush the Lutherans into conformity with Rome. From Germany he returned to Spain. There he busied himself with other wars. He attacked North Africa by sea, captured Halq al-Wādī and Tunis. Next he turned his rudders toward Naples and in 1536 spoke before Pope Paul III and his College of Cardinals. (It was in this speech that he challenged the King of France to a personal duel.)

While the emperor was thus occupied, Luther was busy with his quill, and Katie with her task of raising the family, paying the bills—and keeping sufficient food on the many tables. As the family had increased, so had the number of boarders.

"How will we feed them if they don't pay?" pleaded Katie.

"God will supply our needs," shrugged Luther in his usual manner.

God did supply their needs. Unexpected gifts arrived from princes and kings. Even friendly-for-a-time Henry VIII sent fifty gulden, and the King of Denmark remitted a similar amount each year. Still there was not enough money. In despair, Katie confronted her husband. This time she was desperate.

"Herr Doctor," she said in her most affectionate manner, "my brother Hans owns a little farm at Zulsdorf."

"So?" He lifted an eyebrow suspiciously.

"The soil there is much more fertile than this sandy stuff here in Wittenberg."

"So?" He cocked his head to one side.

"It belonged to my father and we could buy it for a mere six hundred ten gulden."

Luther blinked. "And where would we get six hundred ten gulden?"

"God will supply them!"

Reluctantly Luther replied, "I'll agree, if the money can be raised."

Hearing about the proposition, Elector John put up six hundred gulden, leaving a mere ten for Luther to provide. After the deed had been prepared, Luther had a question: "Now, how are you going to farm it?"

"Zulsdorf is only twenty miles south of Leipzig. I'll commute."

Luther shook his head, amazed.

In order to commute, Katie had to rise before sunup. This inspired Luther to call her "The Bright and Morning Star of Wittenberg." But since the land was fertile, Katie loved the place and frequently stayed for days at a time. She improved and repaired the buildings. And soon she was raising vegetables, pigs, sheep, cattle, and grain. Needing grazing land, she approached the elector and rented the Boos farm. Its wide meadow was just what she needed for the livestock.

Watching his wife bring in vegetables, slaughter pigs, prepare sausages, cure hams, milk cows, and persuade former monks to work, Luther was overwhelmed. In a letter, he addressed her: "To the rich lady of Zulsdorf, Mrs. Doctor Katherine Luther, who lives in the flesh in Wittenberg but in the spirit in Zulsdorf." And on another occasion he was even more dramatic. This time Katie's astonished eyes read: "To my beloved wife, Katherine, Mrs. Doctor Luther, mistress of the pig market, lady of Zulsdorf, and whatsoever titles may befit thy Grace."

Often as Katie worked to exhaustion—plowing the soil, supervising the painting of her barns, raising pigs, looking after the cattle—she wondered if Martin really loved her. The faraway look in his eyes was frequently exasperating.

On one occasion she said, "Herr Doctor, I just sold three cows for three gulden each. What do you think of that?"

Instead of answering, he continued to stare out the window.

"I asked you a question," she said, speaking a little severely.

"Oh, yes. Will you please repeat it. I was thinking about my next lecture on Genesis. Those lectures are becoming quite popular, and I'm convinced they're doing a lot of good."

Katie repeated the news about the sale of the cows and asked what he thought about the price she had received. Still his mind remained on something else.

But Katie need not have worried about the doctor's affection toward her. To a friend, he wrote:

> I would not swap Katie for France with Venice thrown in. Now, in the first place, God gave her to me and me to her. In the second place, I often notice that there are more faults in other women than in my Katie—although she has some all right, she has much greater virtues to balance them. In the third place, she is faithful to me.

Occasionally Katie and Martin exchanged sharp words, even at the table and in the presence of guests. Once, after he had made a typically coarse remark which involved the digestive system, she snapped, "Herr Doctor, that's too raw!" Often when there was a distinguished guest at the table, Luther would speak to him in Latin. Then, when it became evident that Katie was following them, they would switch to Greek.

The lack of money to pay the household bills was a constant source of irritation. When Katie learned that her husband's publishers had offered to pay him four hundred gulden a year for his manuscripts and he had refused it, she confronted him.

"Herr Doctor," she said, "why did you not accept the money your publishers offered you? That money would pay some of our debts!"

"But, Katie, if I accepted that money, they would have to charge more for my books and that would hinder their distribution."

"Well, then, why don't you accept a fee from each of your students like the other professors?"

"Katie, I am determined not to charge for my teaching."

"But we must pay our bills!" she replied a little angrily.

"True, but the good Lord looks after the sparrows, and He will look after us. He owns the cattle on a thousand hills . . ."

Katie shrugged and walked away. Sometimes Martin could be so exasperating!

After an unusually bitter argument with Katie, Luther exclaimed to a friend, "What a lot of trouble marriage is. Adam made a mess of our nature. Think of the squabbles Adam and Eve must have had in the course of their nine hundred years. Eve would say, 'You ate the apple,' and Adam would retort, 'You gave it to me!' "

One afternoon as she was dusting near the doctor's study, she overheard him say, "You know, Albert, Paul's letter to the Galatians is one of my favorite books. I cherish it very much. It's my Katie von Bora!"

Curious, Katie decided to study Galatians and learn which portions of her portrait the doctor had read into that epistle. So after milking the cows and feeding the pigs, Katie sat on a stump near the henhouse and opened the copy of the New Testament which Martin had given her. Soon her eyes were riveted on the eleventh verse in the second chapter. Out loud she read:

> But when Peter was come to Antioch, I withstood him to the face, because he was to be blamed.

Katie smiled and then she almost laughed. Yes, it took a lot of courage for a newcomer like Paul to withstand Peter, the chief of the apostles. Had the doctor been thinking of her in connection with this passage when he made his remark? *Well, if he had, it was perfectly all right, for both she and Paul had been absolutely correct!*

Another passage also caught her attention:

> And let us not be weary in well doing: for in due seaon
> we shall reap, if we faint not.

She marked those words in the sixth chapter and the ninth verse and was reading them aloud when a shadow darkened her New Testament. Looking up, she saw her hired man, Leonard Wolf.

"Frau Luther, are you a modern Francis of Assisi?" he asked.

"What do you mean?"

"Francis preached to the birds, and you're reading the Bible to the chickens!" Katie laughed and explained her purpose.

"Well," replied Leonard after he had laid down his hoe, "you've probably just read the scripture Dr. Luther had in mind. You have sown, and now you're going to reap. Look at all those cabbages and all that wheat, and notice how fat your pigs are becoming."

Katie was singing to herself on the way back to Wittenberg when she discovered that her skirt was checkered with burrs. While her horse guided himself, she slowly picked them off. But their stubborn tenacity squeezed the joy out of her heart. *Why,* she wondered, *did the heavenly Father make burrs?*

Having alighted from the wagon, Katie noticed that Martin and Hans were romping with the dog. "It's all quite scriptural," explained her husband. "The Bible teaches that people will rule over the beasts of the field. And look at Tolpel; he's really happy."

"Do you think there will be animals in God's kingdom?" Katie frowned.

"Certainly. Peter says that there will be a time when all things will be restored. Then, as is said elsewhere, God will create a new heaven and a new earth. He will also create new Tolpels with a skin of gold and hair of pearls. Then and there God will be all in all. No animal will eat another. Snakes and toads and other beasts which are poisonous because of original sin will then be . . . pleasing and nice to play with. Why is it that we cannot believe that all things will happen as the Bible says? Original sin is at fault!"

As Katie stepped into the house, Luther strode up from behind. "Where have you been?" he demanded. "The back of your coat is covered with burrs."

On December 17, 1534, Katie had her last living child, Margaretha, her sixth child in just a little more than eight years. When the children reached school age, tutors were employed. And in the Black Cloister, fresh tables were required, for including a dozen of Luther's relatives—aunts, nieces, nephews—there were often as many as one hundred and twenty to be fed.

Viewing this sea of mouths that required food twice a day—10 a.m. and 5 p.m.—Katie had to think of additional ways to either produce more food or buy more food. As a result of her sharp eyes and efficient management, the Luther holdings gradually increased. In addition to the Zulsdorf property, they owned a large house and lots that had belonged to Claus Bildenhauer, a small garden for the use of a servant, a cottage and lots next to the cloister, and some acreage where they raised hops for the beer Katie brewed.

A potential source of income gradually showed up in the dining room. Since he was the most famous man in Germany, Luther's opinions on any subject were highly valued. And since his speech was always extremely colorful, everything he said at the table was recorded by numerous scribes. This *Table Talk* was all duly published by them and for their own profit. This annoyed Katie.

"Why don't you make them pay?" she asked him more than once.

"Because I don't want to make a material profit from what God has given me."

Although dismayed at his refusal to earn money from his comments, Katie was an ardent listener. The daily routines were almost identical. At the beginning of each meal there was always a respectful silence as each "guest" ate what had been set before him. Then Luther would throw out a question: "What's new?"

Generally, this first question passed unnoticed. But after the former monk had repeated the question, there would be smiles and shining eyes throughout the room, and the shorthand reporters would reach for their quills.

Asked about relics, Luther beamed. This was a favorite target. "What lies there are about relics!" he said. "One claims to have a feather from the wing of Gabriel, and the Bishop of Mainz has a flame from Moses' burning bush. And how does it happen that eighteen apostles are buried in Germany when Christ had only twelve?"

"Why do you speak and write with such harsh words?" asked a student.

Rocking on his bench, Luther replied, "A twig can be cut with a bread knife, but an oak calls for an ax." This reply lifted numerous eyebrows since everyone knew that he was adept at swinging his ax. Many of his statements were so coarse that sensitive writers are reluctant to reprint them. But the reason for his crude statements was that he lived in a crude era. To him, the functions of the digestive system were understood by everyone and were, to him, a colorful source of material for illustration.

"What do you think of monks?" ventured a guest.

"The monks are the fleas on God Almighty's fur coat!" he snapped.

Most of his comments were answers to questions. But not all. With his attention on his dog, Tolpel, whose eyes were fixed on him, Luther exclaimed, "Oh, if I could pray the way this dog watches the meat!" And referring to a guest's dog, he commented, "If I were as devoted to prayer as Peter's dog is to food, I could get anything from God. The beast thinks of nothing all day but licking the platter."

In the winter of 1536 while inflation was soaring, the pastors and ministerial students were unusually attentive as Luther addressed the problem. "Master Philip Melanchthon spoke about the high cost of living in this town and said that a student requires twice as much money now as ten years ago. We see by experience. When farmers hear the pastors complaining about the shortage of food, they [the farmers] say, 'Oho, but they were able to make out before!' To this I have responded, 'Yes, when one could buy fifteen eggs for four pieces of copper and a bushel of rye for two pieces of silver, they were able to manage. But now everything is three times as much . . .' "[1]

During the winter of 1539–40, Katie had a miscarriage and was prostrate for weeks. All over Germany the devout remembered her in prayer, and Luther spent every spare moment by her bedside. But to Katie it was a period of utter frustration. She felt as if she had been seized with cramps while swimming against a rising tide.

"I keep worrying about the children and about you and about the farms and about the boarders," she confessed to her husband.

"Don't you believe in the heavenly Father?" asked Luther as he laid a cool cloth on her forehead.

"I do, but . . ."

One of her worries was little Hans. He was a bit slow, and each day she pleaded with the Father for him. She was also concerned with her husband. When she was well she frequently sat in his study while he worked, and she was confident that her presence minimized his continual war with depression. At this time he was busy with his commentary on Genesis, which was based on lectures he had started to deliver in 1535.

---

[1]The published *Table Talk* became very popular and still is. Altogether, 6596 statements were recorded. Unedited by Luther himself, the exact wording in many of his alleged comments has been questioned.

At Nimbschen, Katie dreamed of being a help to mankind in the same manner as Bernard of Clairvaux had been. Then, after her marriage, she had been convinced that she would do this best by being a special help to her husband. Now, unable to leave her bed, it seemed that those dreams would never be fulfilled.

Sometimes she wept herself to sleep.

In time, Katie's fever lessened and her general health improved. Still, her physical body was not as strong as her will. Nonetheless, goaded by a desire to keep her husband writing at his best and to keep the household running smoothly, she forced herself to move about the house on her hands and knees.

On May 4, 1542, Katie arranged a special birthday party for Magdalena who had just turned thirteen.[2] The Luthers were extremely fond of children, and numerous letters from Dr. Luther to his children have been preserved. Each evening the entire family, along with the guests, worshiped together. They also sang and played games together. There was a bowling alley in the Black Cloister yard, and Luther often relaxed by rolling balls with Katie and the children. A favorite indoor game was chess.

Magdalena had blossomed into an extremely attractive young lady and, being the daughter of the Luthers, was the center of attention. Already the attentions of many young men were beginning to focus on her. With dark eyes, attractive lashes, long, slightly curly hair, curved lips, artistic hands, and a sharp mind, she had increasingly become a printer's proof of her mother.

Then in the summer of 1542 Magdalena was stricken.

The Luthers prayed, lingered at her bedside, called in the best doctors. But she continued to fail. Since she had been very close to Hans, they summoned him home from his school at Torgau. It didn't help. Convinced that she would not live,

---

[2] In the sixteenth century this was an important milestone, for it was at this age betrothals were often made.

her father leaned over her wasted form and gently asked, "Lenniken, little daughter, you'd like to stay here with me, your earthly father, but you are willing to go to your other Father, are you not?"

After shifting slightly in the narrow bed and painfully moistening her lips, Magdalena murmured, "Yes, darling father, whatever God wants."

Overwhelmed, and not wanting Magdalena to understand, the man who had defied the emperor at Worms, resorted to Latin. Between sobs which shook his entire being, he muttered, "You dear little daughter! The spirit indeed is willing, but the flesh is weak. Oh, I love her."

On September 20, Magdalena passed away in her father's arms. As she was being laid in the coffin, Luther commented, "The bed is not big enough for her." When the carpenter appeared with hammer and nails to fasten the lid, he was stricken by a fresh flood of tears. He fled to the door. Then he stopped and turned. Addressing the carpenter, he said, "Hammer away! On Resurrection Day she'll rise again."

Later, his eyes on the closed coffin, Luther added, "You will rise and shine like a star, yea, like the sun. . . . I am happy in the spirit, but the flesh is sorrowful and will not be content; the parting grieves me beyond measure. . . . I have sent a saint to heaven."

As Katie watched her grieving husband, she realized that he, too, was failing. No longer did he walk with his shoulders back and his head high. In her heart she felt that she had a new assignment from the Lord: to cheer the doctor so that his literary projects could be adequately finished. Each evening she prayed, "Lord, help me to brighten his eyes, to give him strength, to help him finish his task."

She was especially concerned with his lectures on Genesis, which were now being transformed into a monumental commentary.

16

Decline

As snow fell, and carts formed and followed ruts, Katie watched with increasing anxiety the changes that were slowly altering and weakening her husband. It was like viewing the death of a landmark oak. He continued to be in agony from stones, vertigo, earaches, dizziness, acute uremia—and a weakening heart. Days passed in which he could not produce a drop of urine. A cataract blinded one eye. Likewise, he became alarmed at the changing times. When Copernicus declared that the earth moves around the sun, he exclaimed, "That is blasphemy!"

The return of houses of ill-fame to Wittenberg, the increased drunkenness among the citizens, and the finery worn by some church members disgusted him. "The way these modern girls whirl their skirts and prance about with plunging necklines is an abomination!" he stormed. Almost daily he pounded the table and, raising his voice, assured Katie that the Second Coming of Christ was near.

In the midst of an evening meal, he complained of a severe headache. "My head is about to burst," he groaned, wiping his eyes.

"Are you sure, Herr Doctor, that you're not imagining things?"

Luther held his head. "No, Katie, this is not imagination." He sucked in his breath and the marks of severe pain crossed his eyes. Thoughtfully, he said, "I won't die so suddenly. I'll first lie down and be sick, but I won't be there very long." He groaned and closed his eyes until a stab of pain had lessened. "I'm fed up with the world, and it's fed up with me. I'm quite content with that. The world thinks that if it is rid of me everything will be fine."

The changes in his world had not all been negative. Although Duke George had remained intolerant until his death in April 1539, he had never put a Lutheran to death as had other princes. All his sons having died, he left his domains to his brother Henry on condition that he become Catholic. Henry, however, took the position but remained Lutheran. He was able to do this because the vast majority of his subjects had agreed with Luther for years.

Henry was so zealous history dubbed him "Henry the Pious."

Luther's illnesses continued. Each depression was followed by another. He prayed to die. While preaching in June 1545, he exclaimed, "If you would but mumble and grumble, then go and join the cattle and swine! You can converse with them and leave the church in peace." The next Sunday he strode out the door in the midst of the service.

Adding to his depression was the scandal that whirled around his secret advice to Philip of Hesse. Philip's marriage to the daughter of Duke George had been "arranged" for him at the age of nineteen. It was obviously a political match, and, although he had several children by Christina, there had not been nor was there any romance in the union. This unhappiness inspired him to have several affairs for which he felt so condemned he refrained from partaking of the Lord's Supper.

What was he to do?

The easiest solution was to return to the Catholic church and have his marriage annulled. This was a common procedure and one that would not have caused the slightest comment. But he refused to consider this way out, for he was an avowed Lutheran. His problem became acute when he met and fell in love with the charming seventeen-year-old Margaret von der Saale. After winning the girl's approval, he approached her mother.

Anna was thoughtful. "Before I agree to your marriage," she replied, "I must be given several opinions. We must not break any of God's laws!"

Philip approached Martin Bucer, and Bucer consulted with Melanchthon and Luther. Finally Melanchthon sent him an extremely long letter in which he pointed out that God's will was, "They two shall be one flesh." But at the end of the letter, he said, "If, however, your Grace should at length resolve to take another wife, we think this should be kept secret."

This letter was signed by Luther and Melanchthon, together with seven other prominent men.

Philip accepted this document as consent and proceeded to marry his new love and to continue living with Christina. Moreover, he had several additional children by each spouse! Soon the secret was out and the Reformation was placed in severe jeopardy.

Because the penalty for bigamy in the Holy Roman Empire was death, Prince Philip was forced to prostrate himself before Charles V and beg his forgiveness. (The irony of this was that the emperor himself had illegitimate children all over Europe and the pope had legitimatized each one in order that they all might inherit titles and attain high office.)

As news of the scandal darkened and spread, a minister in Philip's court published a pamphlet justifying polygamy. Melanchthon became so distraught he was unable to eat or drink, lost his memory and could not speak. To a friend, he wrote: "I cannot describe the pain I suffered. . . . I witnessed at the time the deep sympathy of Luther. . . . If he had not come to me I should certainly have died."

Luther himself was so upset over the affair he exploded, "Let the devil bless future bigamists with a bath in hell!"

Katie's heart ached as she watched her husband grow old. And she became heartsick over the way his spirit was hardening against those who had opposed him. Andreas von Carlstadt, whom they had sheltered on their wedding night, died of the plague in Basel on Christmas Eve 1541. At the time, even though the doctor was certain that Carlstadt had suffered the judgment of the Lord, he and Melanchthon had used their influence to persuade the Basel Council to support his family.

That spirit of generosity was now leaving him. His quill, always sharp, became a surgeon's scalpel. In 1545 he denounced the Roman church in the darkest words that seeped into his mind.

He also carved a few Protestants, especially those who disagreed with him about the presence of Christ in the communion bread and wine.

These statements, which have caused Luther's enemies to gloat, were viewed by Katie with more understanding eyes. She knew her husband better than anyone else, and she knew his heart was right even though his speech and writings smoked with brimstone. That Luther was living under excruciating strain is indicated by a letter he wrote to James Probst on January 17, 1546.

> I am writing, my James, as an old man, decrepit, sluggish, tired, cold, and now one-eyed. . . . I am now overloaded with matters on which I have to write, speak, negotiate, and act. Yet Christ is all in all; he is capable of doing all things, and he does them; blessed be he in eternity. Amen.

Understanding and even feeling his strain, Katie used all her highly developed skills to put light back into his face. She labored long in procuring and preparing the delicacies he especially loved. Likewise, she nudged him into repeating the great moments of his life even though she had heard each story repeated many times.

Finding him slumped in his study and staring out the window with lackluster eyes, Katie said, "Herr Doctor, please tell me about the time you confronted Ulrich Zwingli."

"Ah, yes," he replied, leaping at the request. "That was an occasion I'll never forget. Never! Philip of Hesse arranged the meeting. That was before he became a bigamist! He arranged for our discussions to be held in a magnificent castle overlooking Marburg. The purpose of the meeting, of course, was to see if we could not come to an agreement on the true meaning and nature of the Lord's Supper." Thoroughly aroused, he got up and began to pace back and forth.

"The New Testament clearly teaches that Christ is *present* in both the bread and the wine. Zwingli and that scamp Oecolampadius and several others were teaching that the bread and wine merely *represent* the blood and the body of Christ!" He shuddered.

"Our confrontation took place on the second and third day of October 1529. Since Philip wanted us to come to some definite conclusions in order to heal the several divisions which were developing, each of us came with a group of our most able helpers. Mine included Melanchthon, George Röerer, and several others.

"The meeting opened at 6 a.m. When I first shook hands with Zwingli, his eyes moistened when he told me how my writings had changed his life. That made me feel good. Nonetheless, Katie, I knew that if I were to be obedient, I would have to state the truth; and so, wild boar that I am, I took a piece of chalk, drew a circle on the table and wrote within that circle *Hoc est corpus meum.* Those Latin words, as you know, mean in German, 'This is my body.' They are fully explained in the sixth chapter of John.

"Those chalked words sharpened our teeth. Each of us tried not to be sarcastic. But it was hard to restrain our tongues. Zwingli attempted to show that Jesus' words should be spiritualized. Our arguments were long and sometimes heated. There were about fifty spectators who came to listen. Those who had not been trained in theology found it difficult to understand either of us.

"At the end of the two days, Zwingli and I found that we could not agree on the subject of the Lord's Supper. He remained convinced that the words of Jesus in the sixth chapter of John should be spiritualized, while I remained convinced that they should be taken literally—that the presence of Christ is in both the bread and the wine.

"Zwingli's party wanted to have us consider them as Christian brethren. But, Katie, that was impossible!" He shook his head. "I told them plainly that they had our charity, but that we could not consider them as our brothers within the body of Christ."

Exhausted from his explanations, he slumped back into his seat.

As she held his hand in both of hers, Katie said, "Now, Herr Doctor, please explain one thing to me. How does your doctrine of the presence of the blood and body of Christ within the bread and wine differ from what the Roman Catholic Church teaches?"

Luther stared. Then the hardness of his face softened and his lips opened into a smile. "There is a wide, wide distance between those two points of view. Papists believe in *transubstantiation*. The Latin word *trans* means across. To them, when the priest elevates the elements, the wine becomes the *actual* blood of Christ even though it still resembles wine, and the bread becomes the *actual* flesh of Christ even though it still resembles bread.

"In my view, the *presence* of Christ is in the wine and it is also in the bread. Nonetheless, the wine *remains* wine and the bread *remains* bread. Some of our enemies have accused us of being cannibals. They say that we eat the flesh of Christ in the manner in which a wolf gobbles up a sheep and that we drink his blood just as a cow guzzles water. That is a lie! But I'd better go to bed, for I'm getting dizzy."[1]

With her arm around him, Katie gently led him into their bedroom. Having made him comfortable, she secured a cool

---

[1]Today, transubstantiation is the accepted doctrine of the Roman Catholic and Eastern Orthodox churches. Consubstantiation, Martin Luther's view, is the recognized view of all Lutheran bodies. Zwingli's view remains that of the Reformed and many other groups.

cloth from deep in the well and placed it on his forehead. Then she rubbed his feet and legs until some of the pain was gone. While patting his hand, she said, "Remain here and be quiet while I get you a bowl of soup."

But Katie had barely closed the door when he shuffled into his study. There was work to be done! He made room for himself at the desk by reshelving some of his books, shoving others to the side, and making a neat pile of the letters that required answers. Then he dipped his pen and went to work. A letter which he wrote on December 2, 1544, indicates some of the pressures surrounding him at all hours of the day.

> You often urge me to write a book on Christian discipline, but you do not say where I, a weary old man, can get the leisure and health to do it. I am pressed by writing letters without end; I have promised our young princes a sermon on drunkenness; I have promised certain persons and my-self a book on secret engagements, to others one against the sacramentarians; still others beg that I shall omit all to write a comprehensive and final commentary on the whole Bible. One thing hinders another so that I am able to accomplish nothing. Yet I believe that I ought to have rest, as an emer-itus, to live and die in peace and quietness, but I am forced to live in restless action. . . .

Katie placed the soup on his desk and rubbed his shoulders. He thanked her with a kiss. But when she came back an hour later, she found that the soup had not been touched. The desk, however, was all but smothered by several stacks of opened books, many with notes in their margins; and in front of him and slightly to the right there was a fresh pile of manuscript all ready for the printer.

In between typhoons of depression and life-threatening illnesses, Luther often wrote breathtaking tracts or paced back and forth while he denounced those who disagreed with him. At such times his brain provided him with sizzling in-vective.

Sometimes Katie was so disturbed by the products of his pen or his tongue that she unconsciously washed her hands in the air. Luther deplored anger, and yet he claimed it could be useful. He candidly admitted, "Anger refreshes all my blood, sharpens my mind and drives away temptation."

Once, after being admonished for his uncouth remarks, he replied, "I must root out the stumps and trunks, hew away the thorns and briar, fill in the puddles. I am the coarse woodsman who must pioneer and hew a path."

During his final years, the Jews and Anabaptists were among his favorite targets. Although shocked by her husband's language, Katie remembered that he had written fine things about both the Jews and the Anabaptists. Some of his early writings concerning the Jews had been compassionate:

> If we wish to help them, we must practice on them not the papal law but rather the Christian law of love, and accept them in a friendly fashion, allowing them to work and make a living. . . .
> If some are obstinate, what does it matter? After all, we too are not all good Christians. . . .

Likewise he showed a generous spirit toward the Anabaptists, even though he rejected their idea that infant baptism was wrong and their insistence that those who had been baptized as infants should be rebaptized. Moved by the dedicated way they worked among the poor, he wrote:

> It is not right, and I am deeply troubled that the poor people are so pitifully put to death, burned, and cruelly slain. Let everyone believe what he likes. If he is wrong he will be punished enough in hellfire. Unless there is sedition, one would oppose them with scripture and God's Word. With fire you won't get anywhere.

These past statements by her husband helped balance the fact that he had suggested that the Jews should be deported to Palestine and that the Anabaptists should be exiled.

As the icicles melted and the snow disappeared from the streets of Wittenberg, workers streamed into the city. While Katie and the doctor were watching from a window, he said, "I do wish they were constructing buildings for the university instead of turning Wittenberg into a fortress!" He closed his eyes for a long moment. Then he added, "I'm going to talk to the elector about it this afternoon."

Elector John Frederick listened with concern as Luther explained to him his doubts about spending so much money on fortifications while neglecting the intense needs of the university.

"Dr. Luther," replied the enormously fat ruler, "I know exactly how you feel and I sympathize with you. Nonetheless, the emperor is determined to crush us and make us give up our faith."

"But even if our city is fortified, can we withstand the armies that will attack us?" A shadow of doubt smudged Luther's face.

"If the Schmalkaldic League hangs together we have a chance—"

"But will it hang together?"

"It had better hang together!" The elector shook his head. "I will be depending on you to pray that it *will* hang together."

Early in the summer, the doctor approached Katie. "If I don't get away from Wittenberg, I'll explode!" he stated tersely.

"And where will you go?"

"To Zeitz. Amsdorf wants me to come to settle an argument between two of our pastors at Naumburg."

"But are you feeling well enough to make such a trip?"

Luther shrugged. "I don't feel as well as I did ten years ago. But the change will do me a lot of good. Moreover, I'm needed. If the emperor attacks us, we'll all have to be united; maybe I can get those two pastors to love one another again."

Katie looked doubtful. "I'm worried about your health. What will you do if you have an attack of stones?"

"God will take care of me. And besides, I've asked Hans to be my companion. He has always been a good helper."

Standing within her husband's arms, Katie looked up into his eyes and said, "I'll be on my knees praying for both you and Hans."

"I know you will, and I know how effective your prayers

are," he replied. His voice trembled with emotion. Holding her close, he stroked her hair tenderly. "Katie, I never could get along without you. You are the Queen of the Reformation! Your prayers are what kept me going when I was at Coburg."

During the three days before Luther and Hans left, Katie washed and mended their clothes. And as she packed them, she also included several of the doctor's favorite books. Before kissing him good-bye as he prepared to step into the carriage, she repeated her former promise, "Remember, Herr Doctor, you can depend on my prayers."

She watched and waved until the carriage had disappeared, and then she returned to the house. Keeping the boarders fed required every minute of her time.

Katie was cleaning the fishponds when Professor Cruciger approached. "Frau Luther," he said, "I've just returned from Zeitz—"

"How's the doctor?" she interrupted eagerly.

Cruciger shrugged. "He's fair. You'd better keep praying for him. When he learned I was returning to Wittenberg, he dashed off a letter and asked me to deliver it. Here it is."

Alone on a stump, Katie broke the seal. The letter was marked Zeitz and was dated July 28, 1545. Fearing the worst, her heart raced as she read:

> Dear Katie, Hans will tell you about our journey, unless, indeed, I decide to keep him with us. . . . I should like to arrange not to have to go back to Wittenberg. My heart has grown cold so that I do not care to live there, but wish you would sell the garden and the farm, house and buildings, except the big house, which I would like to give back to my gracious lord.

Frightened by what she had read, Katie stared. Then she gulped down the opening lines again and continued to peruse the rest of the epistle:

> Your best course would be to go to Zulsdorf; while I am alive you could improve the little estate with my salary, for I hope my gracious lord will let my salary go on, at least during the last year of my life. . . . It looks as if Wittenberg and her

government would catch, not St. Vitus' dance, but the beggar's dance and Beelzebub's dance; the women and girls have begun to go bare before and behind, and there is no one to punish or correct them, and God's Word is mocked. Away with this Sodom. . . .

Shocked, Katie folded the letter. Dazed, she shuffled around the largest pond. But although she was terrified about what would follow, she returned to the stump and continued to read:

I hear more of these scandals in the country than I did at Wittenberg, and am therefore tired of that city and do not wish to return. . . . I will wander around here and eat the bread of charity before I will martyr and soil my poor old last days with the disordered life of Wittenberg. . . . You may tell Melanchthon and Bugenhagen this, if you will, and ask the latter to give Wittenberg my blessing, for I can no longer bear its wrath and displeasure. God bless you. Amen.

Martin Luther

Although stunned by the new responsibilities dropped on her shoulders, Katie, by force of habit, returned to the big house. After giving orders to the servants for the preparation of the evening meal, she sank into a chair and reread the entire letter. Then, having quoted the Lord's Prayer to herself, she got up, freshened her face and headed toward the office of Pastor Bugenhagen.

17

Sorrow

Katie unconsciously rubbed her hands together as she studied the varied expressions that crossed Pastor Bugenhagen's face as he read her husband's letter. Finally after a nervous cough he put the letter down and said, "Frau Luther, the doctor is suffering from another storm of depression. Someone has filled his ears with gossip! But don't worry, the sun will shine again. I'll call on Melanchthon right away. You have my promise that we'll do something. In the meantime we must all continue to pray for the dear man."

Within hours, Bugenhagen, Melanchthon, the mayor of Wittenberg, along with the elector's personal physician, were on their way to see Luther. As their carriage bounced over the road, each agreed that Wittenberg needed Luther. Melanchthon was quite definite. "If the doctor leaves, I, too, will leave."

Although pleased that these distinguished men were on their way, Katie spent hours on her knees praying for her husband; and even as she worked, she kept a silent prayer churning within her heart.

Pastor Bugenhagen and his friends found Luther busy at work in Meresburg. His depression had almost cleared, and they had little difficulty in persuading him to return to Wittenburg. Indeed, Katie welcomed him home on August 16.

Knowing that work was the best cure for his depression, she made subtle suggestions that he finish his commentary on the book of Genesis. In time, she succeeded. As she watched him study and fill the manuscript, she noticed that his health kept improving. Within a few weeks they were back to old routines.

Soon opened books were stacked on the desk, over the floor, on all the chairs—even in their bedroom. The meals at the table were also filled with laughter and the questions of reporters seeking colorful quotes from the doctor.

But although routines were reestablished in the Luther home and the university, workers continued to fortify the city. They built walls, mounted cannon, stored ammunition. Elector John, now dubbed the Magnanimous, was confident in his belief that Charles V was going to attack. "It will be a bloody war," affirmed this nephew of Frederick the Wise.

On November 10 Luther celebrated his sixty-second birthday. On Tuesday, seven days later, his eyes were sparkling again as he drew Katie close. "This is a great day for me," he said joyously.

"Why?"

"Because today I will give my last lecture on Genesis and I already have the manuscript ready for the printer. I started the lectures and commentary in 1535. That was ten years ago! At that time I predicted I would not live to complete it. But here I am, and, as you can see, I'm still alive." He kissed her resoundingly, laughing with triumph. Then, after picking up the manuscript, he said, "Now I'll read you my last paragraph."

His voice was slightly husky as he read:

> This is now the book of Genesis. God grant that others after me will do better. I can do no more. I am weak. Pray God for me that He may grant me a good and blessed last hour.

"Well, what do you think of my ending?" he inquired as he wiped his eyes.

"Herr Doctor, it's great!" she exclaimed as she kissed him soundly on the cheek. "How could anyone do better? You've worked so hard!" She threw her arms around him, holding him close. Then after a long hesitation, she asked, "Why is it you keep thinking about your last hour? Maybe—maybe you're not feeling well."

"I'm feeling fine," he assured quickly. "But you must notice that the last verse in this final chapter says, 'So Joseph died, being an hundred and ten years old; and they embalmed him, and he was put in a coffin in Egypt.' That statement reminded me of my own life. Remember the author of Ecclesiastes said: 'To every thing there is a season, and a time to every purpose under the heaven: a time to be born, and a time to die.' "

Katie had almost forgotten that talk about his final hour when, while listening to him preach, she heard him say, "I have finished my commentary on Genesis, and now I want you all to pray that God will grant me a gracious final hour."

In spite of her prayers, it seemed the doctor was convinced that his time to die was fast approaching. But, although deeply troubled, she kept her worries to herself.

During the Christmas season, Luther announced that he would have to leave for Mansfeld.

"Why?" asked Katie.

"An argument has erupted between the brother counts in that area."

"About what?" Katie's voice was edged with a slight note of anger.

"It's about their territories. Both want me to come and help settle the argument."

"Oh, Martin! It's so bitterly cold, and you should be with your family at Christmas!"

"Yes, I know." He took her in his arms and just stood holding her, trying to reassure her. He loved his Katie and the children and would love to be with them. "But the work of the Lord comes first; and, Katie, with Charles V planning to crush us, we need unity. Melanchthon will accompany me."

Again Katie kissed him good-bye and arranged a special time to linger on her knees and storm the gates of heaven on his behalf.

Luther and Melanchthon stayed in Mansfeld over Christmas and negotiated with the brothers, but without success. Then, when Melanchthon became ill, both returned to Wittenberg.

"Did you accomplish anything?" asked Katie.

Luther shrugged. "We didn't settle everything completely. But each brother agreed to some compromise." He made a face and shook his head. "Some of these princes are as stubborn as the pope. The apple Adam and Eve ate must have been a sour one!"

Katie hoped that the doctor's interest in reconciling the stubborn counts had ended. It hadn't. During the third week of January, while roads were high with snow, he said, "Katie, I've again been summoned to help those counts. Since I'll be in the area where I was raised, I'll take the boys along. This might be my last chance to show them the places I knew in my youth."

"Aren't you afraid of the cold?" asked Katie.

"I am. But God has called. I must obey."

Along with his secretary, John Aurifaber, and his sons, Hans, Paul, and Martin, Luther departed on January 23, 1546. After three days of difficult travel, their carriage reached Halle. Here they were joined by Justus Jonas. This city was considerably less than fifty miles southwest of Wittenberg. Before proceeding, Luther wrote to Katie:

> Grace and peace in the Lord. Dear Katie, we arrived this morning at eight o'clock, but have not journeyed on to Eisleben because a great lady of the Anabaptist persuasion met us, covering the land with waves of water and threatening to baptize us. . . . I did not think the Saale could make such broth. . . . Pray for us, and be good. . . . God bless you.

> Martin Luther

On February 1, he mailed Katie another letter. This one was from Eisleben:

I wish you grace and peace in Christ and send you my poor, old, infirm love. Dear Katie, I was weak on the road to Eisleben, but that was my own fault. Had you been with me you would have said it was the fault of the Jews or of their God. . . . As I drove through the village, such a cold wind blew from behind through my cap on my head that it was like to turn my brain to ice. This may have helped my vertigo, but now, thank God, I am so well I am tempted by fair women. . . .

Your little sons went to Mansfeld day before yesterday. . . . God bless you with all my household and remember me to my table companions.

Your old lover,
M.L.

Reading between those lines, Katie was alarmed about his health. And if Melanchthon shared with her the letter he had received from Luther, which was written on the same day that Katie's letter was written, she had even more reason to be alarmed. In that letter, Luther had written: "A fainting fit overtook me on the journey and also that disease which you are wont to call palpitation of the heart. I went on foot, overtaxed my strength and perspired; later . . . my shirt became cold with sweat; this made my left arm stiff. My age is to blame for the heart trouble and the shortness of breath. . . . When even youth is not safe, age can little be trusted."

Thoroughly disturbed, Katie immediately mailed a letter to her husband. (That letter is not available, but his answer gives us a clue as to what she may have written. His salutation to her even hints at the contents of her letter.) Posted at Eisleben, Luther's answer was dated February 10. Katie's eyes misted as she read:

Grace and peace in Christ. Most holy lady doctoress! I thank you kindly for your great anxiety which keeps you awake. Since you began to worry, we've had a fire at the inn . . . and yesterday, due to your anxiety no doubt, a stone nearly fell on my head which would have squeezed it . . . as a trap does a mouse. . . . I fear that unless you stop worrying, the earth will swallow me up. . . . Do you not know the catechism . . . ? Pray and let God take thought as it is written: "Cast thy burden on the Lord, and he shall sustain thee," both in Psalm 55 and in other places. . . .

God bless you. I would willingly be free of this place and return home if God will. Amen. Amen. Amen.

Martin Luther

The next week Katie received what was to be her last letter from Martin. Dated February 14 and written at Eisleben, the terse message was short. (This was also his final letter.)

Grace and peace in the Lord. Dear Katie, we hope to come home this week. . . . God has shown great grace to the lords who have been reconciled in all but two or three points. It still remains to make the brothers Count Albert and Count Gebhard real brothers; this I shall undertake today and shall invite both to visit me, that they may see each other, for hitherto they have not spoken but have embittered each other by writing. . . .

Your little sons are at Mansfeld.[1] James Luther[2] will take care of them. We eat and drink like lords. . . . I am no more troubled with stones. . . .

Some say the emperor is thirty miles from here at Soest in Westphalia, some that the French and the Landgrave of Hesse are raising troops. Let them say and sing; we will wait on God. God bless you.

Dr. Martin Luther

Although alarmed about the news concerning the likelihood of war, Katie felt a surge of optimism when she learned about the possibility of the near return of her husband. Paper in hand, she wrote special menus for the days ahead. Each meal had to feature those items the doctor especially loved. Then she ordered the servants to clean all the rooms until they were spotless. When she found a servant who was a little lax, she said, "The doctor is coming! We must give him a fine welcome." She picked up the broom and gave her a demonstration about how the floor should be swept. "My husband

---

[1]Hans was 19, Martin 14, and Paul had just celebrated his 13th birthday on January 29.

[2]Luther's brother.

deserves the best," she exhorted.

The approach of every carriage drew her eyes to the street outside. Each day the traffic was unusually heavy with wagons loaded down with stones and other materials for the fortification of the city. Then on the 19th, she recognized the carriage her husband had used when he left on January 23. Even before it stopped, she hastened toward it with such speed she narrowly escaped tripping over her ankle-length black skirt. After a frantic glance at the pale faces of her sons, she gasped, "And w-where is Papa?"

"We have bad news," replied Hans.

"I-is s-something wrong?"

"We'll tell you when we get to the house," he managed.

After they had all been seated, Katie said, "Now let's hear the bad news. I . . ."

"I-I think Margarethe should be here," interrupted Paul.

"Yes, our sister should be here," agreed Martin.

After their twelve-year-old sister had been located in the basement where she was washing a dress, Hans began to relate what had happened. "On the 17th Papa persuaded the counts to shake hands and be brothers again. He was extremely happy that he had helped settle their dispute. But he was very tired. You see, he had preached four times, helped serve communion, and had taken part in the ordination of two pastors. He was so tired he could hardly see.

"But now, since Paul wants to be a doctor, I'll let him tell the rest of the story."

"In the afternoon," said Paul, "Papa began to complain about sharp pains around his heart. I was a little frightened, but I managed to keep still. After dinner that evening, we went with him to his rooms. When he continued to complain about pains in his chest, he lay down on the couch. We then rubbed his legs and warmed them with cloths which had been soaked in hot water. We also warmed pillows and placed them around him."

"Why?" asked Katie.

"Because his pulse had become a little thready and we

wanted to stimulate his circulation. Soon he fell into a light sleep. This was encouraging. But he awakened at about nine o'clock and asked us to help him get into the bed in the next room. There he slept a little better. But at about two o'clock in the morning be began to moan out loud. He then asked us to help him get back to the couch.

"His face became so pale we were all frightened. Two doctors were summoned. But they could do very little. While they watched, he suffered another attack. Knowing that he was about to leave us, we all listened closely for any word he might say—"

"And did you hear any?" interrupted Katie. Her voice was eager.

"Yes, slowly but surely he quoted that passage from the third chapter of John which he loved so much. Haltingly and yet clearly he said, 'For God so loved the world, that he gave his only begotten Son, that whosoever believeth in him should not perish, but have everlasting life.'

"He repeated those words three times. While this was taking place, the doctors injected a stimulus into his veins to strengthen him. It had no effect. Then I heard him commit his soul to God. A moment later his eyes opened wide and he seemed to rally. At this point, Jonas, directing his voice toward him, asked, 'Reverend Father, are you willing to die in the name of the Christ and the doctrine which you have preached?'

"To that Papa replied in a very distinct voice, 'Yes.' He then closed his eyes. The doctors tried to stimulate him. He did not respond. Minutes later, the doctors agreed that he was gone."[3]

"And what are the plans for the funeral?" Katie's face was drawn. But she was still dry-eyed.

"His body was placed in a tin coffin as it awaited preparation. By early dawn hundreds began to come to view the

---

[3]One doctor believed he died of a stroke. But since strokes were considered God's punishment, the official statement was that he had succumbed to a heart attack.

body. Today at two o'clock, they had a memorial service for him at St. Andrews. We could not attend because we left the day before."

"And where is St. Andrews?" Katie began to wipe her eyes.

"It's across the street from the house where Papa died," explained Hans. "Strangely, it's only a few blocks from the place where he was born, and it's also the church where Papa preached his last sermon."

Following moments of quiet, Katie said slowly, "He was born in Eisleben and he passed away in Eisleben." Then, as if she were speaking to herself, she murmured, "It's just as Ecclesiastes says: 'To every thing there is a season, and a time to every purpose under heaven: A time to be born, and a time to die; a time to plant, and a time to pluck up that which is planted.' " She wiped her eyes. "God never makes mistakes. Never!"

Paul spoke up. "On our way home we learned that John Frederick has requested that Papa's funeral be here in the Castle Church on Monday, February 22."

"That means we'd better get busy," said Katie matter-of-factly. She stood up and stepped out of the room, still finding it difficult to believe that her Martin was dead.

The funeral entourage, accompanied by uniformed officials, left Eisleben on the 20th and headed for Wittenberg. In every city throngs turned out to pay their last respects. At Kemberg, a short distance from Wittenberg, the casket was placed in the church where Luther had first introduced his new church liturgy. Here, hundreds streamed through the sanctuary to honor their spiritual leader.

The final procession was assembled in Wittenberg. Katie, dressed in mourning, together with several distinguished ladies, rode in a carriage just behind the hearse. The mournful boom, boom, boom of the large tower bell pounded at her brain. She had heard it boom for Elizabeth and Magdalena, and now it was booming for her husband. The casket was carried through the doors of the Castle Church where Luther had nailed his Ninety-five Theses nearly twenty-nine years before.

As Katie sat with her children and listened, her mind overflowed with long thoughts of the past. She could still see the doctor as he stood behind the pulpit and laced his sermons with the common expressions of the day so that everyone could understand him. And everyone did!

Katie's eyes remained dry as Philip Melanchthon mounted the pulpit. She knew that, other than herself and her children, no one loved her husband more than this man whom the doctor had described as resembling a shrimp. He was like a member of the family.

In his scholarly and yet energetic way, Melanchthon compared Luther to Moses, Isaiah, John the Baptist, Paul, and Augustine. Likewise, he mentioned his virtues: "No lewd passions were ever detected in him. . . . He was the advocate of peace. . . . Often have I found him weeping and praying for the whole church. He spent a part of almost every day reading the Psalms, with which he mixed his own supplications amid tears and groans."

Melanchthon was quite aware of Luther's coarseness and numerous faults. In his eulogy he made it plain that his hero lacked the perfection of Christ. Said he, "I do not deny that the most ardent characters sometimes make mistakes, for amid the weakness of human nature no one is without fault. But we may say of such a one what the ancients said of Hercules, Cimon, and others: 'Rough indeed, but worthy of all praise.' "

Katie remained dry-eyed and composed until she was alone with her children at home. Then, along with them, she burst into tears. But while she was shaking with emotion, she inadvertently glanced in the mirror and noticed the black garments of mourning which she was wearing. The sight of her black clothes brought back a memory, and that memory dried her eyes and formed a tiny smile on her face.

Noticing the change that had gripped their mother, the

children stared. Then Paul said, "Mama, what are you smiling about?"

"I was just remembering another time I put on these same black clothes."

"Tell us about it," urged Hans.

"Your father had been so discouraged I almost feared for his life. I tried to cheer him up. Nothing worked. In desperation, I put on these clothes and went sobbing into his study."

" 'Who's dead?' he asked.

"I replied, 'A very important person.'

" 'Who?' he demanded.

"Struggling to keep my sobs going, I replied, 'God.'

" 'God!' he exclaimed.

" 'Yes, God,' I answered. Then I added, 'I also discovered that you were mistaken when you translated the famous passage in the eighth chapter of Romans. You wrote, 'All things work together for good.' That should read, 'Few things work together for good.'

"All at once he realized that I was trying to tell him something. He then threw his arms around me and squeezed me until I was gasping for breath. And do you know what? His depression vanished! Maybe we, too, in this dark hour should realize that God is not dead and that 'all things work together for good.' "

Soon Katie and all the children were laughing. But that evening, while she was lighting room candles, she faced a new anxiety. "Mama," asked Hans, "did Papa leave a will?"

"Of course, and I know where it is."

"Was it written by a lawyer?"

"No, the doctor didn't believe in lawyers."

"Then, I'm afraid the courts will not accept it."

"But it was witnessed. Melanchthon, Cruciger, and Pastor Bugenhagen all signed it."

"Nonetheless, I don't believe it will be considered valid."

"What will happen?" Katie stared.

"It will be broken."

"Are you sure?"

"Yes, Mama, I'm sure."

18
War!

As she twisted and turned in bed, the one thing Katie desired was sleep. But sleep would not come. Each sound seemed many times louder than usual. From a distance came the mournful barking of a dog, the voices of drunks singing on their way home from the taverns, the snarls of tomcats fighting for supremacy; and from nearby, the opening and closing of doors, faint whispers, the dropping of a shoe, the sigh of the wind, the crashing of an icicle falling from the roof to the ground. In addition, the stench of a brewery tainted the air.

After what seemed an eternity, she got up and glanced at the clock. It was only eleven. An eternity later, it seemed, she shuffled toward it again. Now it was eleven-thirty. After numerous additional eternities, a deep quiet settled over the city. But even though it was quiet on the outside, inner thoughts thundered from the inside. The mocking ticks of the clock in the background, tormented her.

You are now a widow . . . God has forsaken you . . . The doctor's salary will be stopped . . . War will come . . . Wittenberg will fall . . . The Black Cloister will be burned . . . You and your children will starve . . . Your husband's grave will be opened in the Castle Church and his remains will be desecrated . . .

Haunted by these fears and accusations pouring into her mind, Katie began to plead with the Lord for enough peace of mind to fall asleep. As she prayed, she remembered the occasion when she, along with the other recently escaped nuns, asked Dr. Luther to explain the way to apply the words of Jesus as expressed in Matthew 7:7.

"What do those words mean?" he asked. "First, we are to *ask*. When we begin to ask, He slinks off somewhere and doesn't want to listen, or to be found. So we have to *seek* Him out—that is, keep on praying. Now when you seek Him, He shuts himself up in a closet. If you want to get in, you have to *knock*. When the knocking becomes excessive, He'll open up and say, 'Well, what do you want?' And you'll say, 'Lord, I want this, or I want that.' And He'll say, 'Well, go ahead and have it!' The verse 'Ask and ye shall receive' means nothing else than, Ask, call out, yell, seek, knock, thunder. You have to keep on and at it, without respite."[1]

Relying on this memory, Katie asked, sought, and knocked; and soon a sense of well-being settled over her. Remembering that God took care of the sparrows, she was soon asleep.

After the ten o'clock meal, which she and the children shared with the boarders, Katie said to Hans, "Now, let's take the will over to Chancellor Brüeck and see if it will be accepted. Also, I'm a little worried because the doctor never mentioned the Black Cloister in his will."

"That's nothing to worry about," assured Hans. "I've just read a book on wills. I know the law. The Black Cloister belonged to both you and Papa. I do hope the will is accepted as legal."

While the chancellor was reading the document, Katie noticed that his face became somber. "Is . . . is the Black Cloister mine?" she asked hesitatingly.

---

[1] Beginning with the word "first" and ending with the word "respite," this is an exact quote from Luther. See *Luther, and Experiment in Biography* by H. G. Haile, p. 278.

"Yes, yes, of course. But it's not yours because of the will. It's yours, Frau Luther, because you are the doctor's widow." He scratched the end of his nose. "The will is illegal—"

"Illegal!" exploded Katie. "The doctor wrote it with his own hand, and all three of the witnesses live right here in Wittenberg."

"True, but it was not written by an attorney, and—"

"What are the consequences of its not being legal?" Katie interrupted, leaning forward.

"One consequence is that I, not you, am now responsible for the education of Dr. Luther's sons," he stated.

Katie stared. "B-but that's impossible!" she exclaimed, incredulous at the thought. "Give me the will and let me read one of the paragraphs," she demanded. Making a strong effort to control both her nerves and anger, Katie snatched it from him and read with emphasis:

> Thirdly and chiefly, because I want her not to look to the children, but the children to hold her in honor and submit to her as God has commanded. . . . Moreover I think a mother is the best guardian for her children, who will not use her property and portion to their injury and disadvantage, as they are her flesh and blood and she has carried them under her heart. . . .

"Yes, I read that," replied Brüeck. "But, as I told you, the will is illegal."

"In what way?"

Brüeck shrugged. "The doctor's own words near the end of this document show that it's illegal. Listen: 'Finally, I beg every one, that as in this bequest I do not use legal forms and words (for which I have good cause), they will recognize me to be what I am in truth . . . and who may be trusted and believed more than a notary . . .'

"Your husband, Frau Luther, may have been an authority on the Bible and morals, but he was not an authority on German law. I'm sorry. The will is not legal." He stood and held out his hand. "I'll do all I can to help. Nonetheless, I have to obey the law."

Katie's knees felt wobbly as she stumbled down the steps and out into the street. Stopped by a wagon filled with ammunition near the Black Cloister, she had to wait until a group of men pushed it out of the way. As she waited she said, "Hans, I'm not going to worry. God helped your father and He will help us. He will find a way for you to complete your education and be a lawyer. Don't worry."

"I won't," he replied, giving her a reassuring hug.

The next few weeks were difficult for Katie. She worked hard supervising the kitchen and providing for the boarders. But her heart wasn't in it. She missed her husband terribly. She missed the sound of his voice, the scratch of his pen, his answers to the reporters at the table, his explosive statements.

The boarders were kind; most were prompt with their payments, but Katie's heart was no longer in this work. She remembered the letter in which the doctor had suggested that she sell everything except the Black Cloister and move to Zulsdorf. Some of the happiest moments of her life had been spent on that little farm which had previously belonged to her father. A favorite letter from her husband had been addressed: "To the rich lady of Zulsdorf, Mrs. Doctor Katherine Luther, who lives in the flesh in Wittenberg but in the spirit at Zulsdorf." But realistically she knew that the little place could not possibly support both her and her children. The solution was to purchase Wachsdorf, a parcel of land joining Zulsdorf.

Unfortunately, such a transaction required the approval of Chancellor Brüeck, and this self-appointed guardian did not approve. "That land, Frau Luther," he said, "is no good. It is much too sandy for crops. As a friend of your husband and a guardian of his children, it is my duty to say no." He stood, indicating that she had heard his final word.

Katie stopped at the door. "Would it not be possible for me to discuss it with you at another time?" she asked.

"Certainly, and in the meantime I'll pray about it."

All the doors at which Katie knocked did not remain closed however. Elector John Frederick assured her that she was free to make use of the Black Cloister the rest of her life. He also banked one thousand gulden with the understanding that she could use the interest for the benefit of her children. The Counts of Mansfeld were likewise generous, promising two thousand gulden.

With the coming of spring, the snows melted and the trees blossomed, and Katie found her blessings multiplying. The King of Denmark forwarded his annual gift of fifty thaler, the Duke of Prussia agreed to support Hans while he attended the University of Köenigsberg, and the chancellor finally agreed that she could buy the Wachsdorf farm. And better yet, Elector John Frederick enabled her to raise the twenty-two hundred gulden purchase price.

That spring, while she went around humming a tune as she prepared to move to Zulsdorf, everything seemed to be perfect. Then a disturbing document written by Melanchthon fell into her hands. With deep concern she read:

> As regards myself it were easier for me to suffer and die than to encourage a vague suspicion; but if it be true that the Emperor intends to fall upon these states on account of religion, then undoubtedly it is the duty of these states by the help of God to protect themselves and their subjects, as St. Paul says: "The magistrate beareth not the sword in vain, for he is the minister of God to punish those who do evil, as murderers." Such resistance is as when a man repels a band of murderers, be he commanded by the Emperor or by others. This is a public tyranny. . . . As to how the Spaniards, Italians, and Begundians will act in these lands, we know by what they have done in Julichs. *Hence every father should offer his body and his life to repel this huge tyranny.*

Facing John Frederick, Katie's face was pale and drawn. "Your Grace," she asked anxiously, "what does this mean?"

"It means there will be war," replied the elector. "Charles is determined to crush all the Protestants in the Holy Roman Empire."

"Can we withstand him?"

"If all the princes work together, we have a chance. But I'm worried about my cousin Maurice, the ruler of Albertine Saxony. He is a Protestant. But he is an admiring nephew of Duke George! Also, he helped Charles fight the Turks in 1542 and the French in 1545. That was only last year! Maurice is ambitious. He would like to take my position as elector." Frederick got up and paced back and forth without saying a word for a long moment. Then he added, "I don't know what he'd do if the emperor offered to make him the elector in my place. If that happened, he might, just might, turn traitor to the Schmalkald League."

"What do you think I should do?"

"Remain here in Wittenberg until we see how things develop. A special meeting has been called with the emperor on June 16. If that meeting succeeds, there will be peace. Otherwise there will be war. If war breaks out, you will have to flee for safety."

While Katie remained in Wittenberg, daily rumors reached her. The most alarming rumor was repeated to her by the son of a pastor.

"Frau Luther," he confided, "I've just come from the Danube where the emperor is concentrating troops. He has gathered thousands of Spaniards and thousands of Italians. Those men are fully armed and they loathe Protestants. Moreover, the emperor has appointed the Duke of Alba to be his top general."

"The Duke of Alba?" Katie frowned.

"Some call him the Duke of Alva. He's from Spain and he commanded troops for the emperor in his war against Tunis." He studied Katie, hesitated, and then continued: "Maybe I shouldn't repeat this, but a deserter told me that the duke has publicly vowed he will dig up your husband's remains, burn them, reduce them to ashes, grind them into powder—and scatter them in the Elbe."

Katie blanched as white as her discarded wimple. "That's terrible!" She stared and then shuddered. "W-why would he d-do that?"

"Because he considers the doctor to have been the vilest heretic who ever lived."

"Nonetheless, he's dead."

"Have you ever heard of John Wycliffe?"

"You mean the reformer called The Bright and Morning Star?"

"That's right."

Katie managed a smile. "That's what Dr. Luther used to call me. He called me that because I got up so early to go to Zulsdorf."

"Wycliffe died of a stroke in 1384. I remember the date because he was one of Father's heroes. But even though he was dead, his enemies were unwilling to let his body rest in peace. They claimed he was a heretic because he didn't believe in transubstantiation, and so they dug up his body in 1428, burned it, and threw the ashes in the Swift River."

"Let's pray there will be no war," groaned Katie. "The elector thinks there is still a chance for peace. It will depend on the outcome of the meeting scheduled with the emperor on June 16."

The youth shook his head. "Both the Duke and Charles are extremely determined. War is inevitable!"

As the weather warmed, Katie became more and more nervous. Rumors kept sifting into Wittenberg. And as the boarders listened they began to leave. "Me and wife are leaving while we have a chance," explained an old man who, with his wife, had lived in the Black Cloister for the past seven years.

With the boarders leaving, Katie was hard pressed to pay the bills. While awaiting news about the results of the meeting with the emperor, she became so nervous she dropped a huge tray piled high with dishes. During every spare moment she went to her room and sank to her knees. "Guide me, dear Lord, guide me," she sobbed. "Help me to do that which is right for the sake of the children." But pray as she would, she received no assurance that her prayers had been heard. Then on June 17 she was summoned to the office of the elector.

"I am sorry, Frau Luther," said John Frederick, "but you will have to flee. Our meeting with the emperor failed. His troops are already moving in our direction."

"Should I go to Zulsdorf?"

"Never! Zulsdorf is southwest of here and that's where much of the fighting will take place. Go north. Melanchthon left yesterday for Magdeburg. If I were you, that's where I would go."

"When do you think I should leave?"

"By tomorrow morning at the latest."

"Tomorrow?" She gasped.

"Yes, tomorrow."

"But . . ." Katie's mouth had gone dry.

"Frau Luther, you must not delay. God entrusted you with the doctor's children. You must protect them!"

Having gathered her children, Katie said, "We're leaving for Magdeburg tomorrow. Choose your necessities and pack them in that trunk over there. We don't have much room, so you must bring only the absolute essentials. While you're doing that, I'll hire a wagon."

Drivers with wagons were difficult to find. But Katie finally located one, and by offering double the usual rate got the driver to agree to leave the next morning at nine. "You must be ready on time," the fierce-looking man stated as she was leaving. "Magdeburg is at least fifty miles from here. The roads will be choked with refugees, and I won't be able to change horses. You must not be even one minute late. Not even *one*!"

Her mind working fast, Katie went over to Helmut Schmidt's place of business. "We're leaving tomorrow, and I'll need some food to eat on the way," she explained to the broad-shouldered man. As he was cutting it, she said, "Are you and your family leaving?"

"No, Frau Luther. I cannot leave. The elector needs my

help and I will be going to the front." He pointed to his gun.

"How are the twins?"

"Oh, fine. Both John and Peter will be one year old next month."

"They are good boys. The doctor told me he really enjoyed baptizing them. He said that they were great lads and he hoped they would become ministers of the gospel."

Schmidt laughed and rubbed his well-trimmed, sharply-pointed beard. "That would please their mother and me. Of course we want God to have His way."

"And how's your wife?" Katie placed two gulden on the counter.

"Esther is not well. We've changed doctors. You must pray for her. She insists on remaining in the city." He shook his head.

Addressing the cook, Katie said, "Here's some meat. Prepare a lot of food for our journey. Magdeburg is a long way from here, and we may have trouble on the way." She then slipped into the garden and cut a dozen roses.

While lingering at the graves of Elizabeth and Magdalena, she placed a selection of roses by each marker. As she did so, the high points of their lives loomed before her. Elizabeth had been plucked by her Maker just prior to her eighth month, while Magdalena had remained with them until her fourteenth year. Katie could still hear her brokenhearted husband say to the carpenter as he nailed her coffin shut, "Hammer away! On Resurrection Day she'll rise again."

From the graves of her daughters, Katie entered the Castle Church and sat in the nearest pew to Luther's burial place under the pulpit. As she meditated and prayed, she was startled by a shadow.

"Oh, Pastor Bugenhagen!" she exclaimed. Then looking up, she added, "We are leaving for Magdeburg tomorrow, and I wanted to pay my last respects to my dear husband. As you know, we were married nearly twenty-one years."

"Frau Luther, you've been a very fortunate woman," replied Bugenhagen, speaking in a gentle whisper. "He did more to change the world than anyone else in the last one thousand years."

"Pastor, do you think our city will be able to repel the armies of the emperor?"

"If the Schmalkald League sticks together, we have a chance. At least we're well fortified." A grim smile brightened his face.

"Should Wittenberg fall, do you think they'll disturb the doctor's remains?" She studied his face with damp, anxious eyes.

Bugenhagen shook his head and thoughtfully rubbed his heavy cheeks. "I hope not. But the Duke of Alba is a hateful man. If he had his way, he'd kill every one of us. But, Frau Luther, God still reigns, and should they burn your husband's bones, it will not damage his soul, for he has already gone to be with the Lord. Remember Paul's words: 'We are confident, I say, and willing rather to be absent from the body, and to be present with the Lord.'[2] Our task right now is to pray."

After the pastor had gone, Katie laid the remaining roses on her husband's grave. Then, choking back her tears, she stepped through the main entrance doors. There she paused while she studied the place where Martin had nailed his Ninety-five Theses. While her eyes were focused on the various papers tacked to the door, she closed her eyes and asked the Lord to help her promote the work her husband had started.

While Katie and the children awaited the driver and his wagon, Lucas Cranach strode over to her side. "I see you are leaving," said the famous painter and her former employer.

"Yes, the elector suggested that we should go to Magdeburg," replied Katie. "How about you; are you going to remain here?"

---

[2] 2 Corinthians 5:8.

"Of course! I've lived here for more than forty years, my home is here, I've been the mayor, and I'm not going to forsake the city in its time of trial."

"But aren't you afraid?"

Cranach laughed. "Katie, I mean Frau Luther, I'm in my seventy-fifth year. God has been good to me, and deep in my heart I have a feeling that He has one remaining task for me to perform. I have no idea what it is, but I have His assurance that it is important." As he spoke, he nodded his head in confidence. Then he put his arm around Hans. "Remember, I was your godfather," he said.

Hans smiled. "Yes, I know; and I'm proud that you were."

As they were visiting, the wagon pulled up. "We'd better get started," barked the driver.

After they had gone through the gate and had passed over the moat, Katie spoke to the driver. "Do you think Wittenberg can withstand the emperor?"

"Never!"

"Why not?"

"Maurice has already left the League and joined the armies of Charles V."

"But Maurice is a Protestant!" exclaimed Katie.

"True. Nonetheless, the emperor offered him John Frederick's position as the elector. That offer changed him. Position means more to some than righteousness."

By noon the two teams of horses that were pulling the wagon were covered by sweat. "Don't you think they need some rest?" asked Katie.

"Magdeburg is still a long way," replied the driver impatiently.

After another hour Katie spoke again. "Those horses are tired. They need water and rest."

"Are they yours or mine?" snarled the man, lacing his reply with a series of oaths.

"They're yours. But they're tired. Besides, all of us need to stop."

Reluctantly, the driver pulled up under a tree near a stream of water. While the animals rested, Katie got out the lunch the cook had prepared. "Come and dine with us," she said, motioning to the man.

"I'm only a driver," he replied.

"No, you're not just a driver; you are our friend and you are helping us escape. What is ours is yours."

Although still complaining, the wagon owner shared their food.

Within half an hour they were on their way again. The road was now getting crowded with refugees. When they passed an elderly woman whose carriage had lost a wheel, Katie suggested that they stop and help her. "Ain't got time," replied the driver in vulgar German. "Look at the sun! It's already halfway down."

When they were only a few miles from Magdeburg, the driver acted as if he were possessed by a demon. While lashing the horses he cursed and yelled at them. "Get a move on you, you lazy, good-for-nothing, ungrateful critters!"

Katie shuddered as she watched the sweat pour from the animals. She complained, but the more she begged him to slow down, the wilder he became. Over and over again he screamed at the horses, called them unprintable names, and sliced their backs with his whip. He was trying to speed them over a small incline when the lead horse on the right made a loud whimper and fell to the ground. A quick examination indicated that it was dead.

"Now what will we do?" asked Margarethe.

"We'll divide the contents of the trunk between ourselves and walk," replied Katie.

"But what about the trunk?" asked Paul.

Katie shrugged. "We'll leave it with the driver," she said.

19

Fugitive!

Their arms overflowing with clothes, shoes, food, and other necessities, Katie and her family trudged northward on the narrow, dusty road. After a long period of silence, broken only by the crunch of their feet, Martin asked: "Mama, how do we know that we're walking in the right direction?"

"We don't. But since all these carriages and wagons are moving in this direction, we must assume that we're right."

"If eventually we ever get there, where will we stay?" asked Margarethe.

"I don't know. But since Magdeburg was one of your father's favorite cities, someone ought to know us. Every time he preached there he always had crowded congregations. He called it the Lord's Chancery." Katie was silent for the next forty or fifty steps. Then she added, "Like Abraham, we must walk by faith."

"But Abraham didn't just walk," replied Hans. "Abraham had camels and servants! I'm afraid I don't have very much faith, and this load is getting heavy. My back is about to break."

"My feet are killing me," added Paul dejectedly. "When we get there, if we ever do, I hope we can have some soup."

"We have a lot of food left," said Katie. "But I think we'd

better forget about eating until we find a place to stay. It's already getting dark, and we forgot to bring a lantern."

Shortly after the sun had disappeared, a light appeared a few hundred yards straight ahead. Encouraged, everyone walked a little faster. Leaving the children at the gate of the farmhouse, Katie knocked at the door.

"We need a place for the night," she said to the bent old man at the door.

"Sorry," he wheezed. "There are two people in each bed and there are people all over the floor."

"How about your barn?"

"It's also full, and so is the chicken house."

"Any suggestions?"

"There's a big house up the road. Try them."

The "big house" was also overflowing and so were the next six places.

"Let's sleep outside," suggested Margarethe.

"And let the wolves eat us!" exclaimed Martin.

Although so weary she feared she couldn't take another step, Katie forced herself on to the next distant light. This time her knock was answered by a hearty cry: "Frau Luther!"

Katie stared, and there in front of her was the shrimp-like face of Philip Melanchthon. "Welcome! Welcome!" he cried, overjoyed at seeing her.

"How about the children?" asked Katie.

"They're also welcome." He stepped outside and motioned them in.

As Katie and the children lingered just inside the door, a slender young man of about forty walked over to them. "My name is George Gaulke," he said, "and this is my wife, Martha. We're flattered that the Queen of the Reformation would honor our home. Stay as long as you like—"

"You must be famished," interjected Martha. "What would you like?"

"Soup!" chorused the children.

While Katie and the children were enjoying the thick soup made of cabbage and sausage, George Gaulke studied her face. "We've never met, but I have a memory of you," he finally said.

"Really?" asked Katie.

"I knew Dr. Luther well. I was in one of his classes at the University of Wittenberg. When Martha and I were married he sent me a letter of congratulations. In that letter he said, 'I'm forwarding you a vase for a wedding present.' Then he added: 'P.S. Katie had hidden it.'

"Martha and I have laughed about that many times. And so *you're* the one who hid our vase! Yes, we're proud to have you at our table."

"And it's good that I hid it," replied Katie, blushing slightly. "The doctor wasn't a good money manager. He refused all royalties and liked to give everything away—even our wedding presents. It's good that I hid that vase because I would have had to pawn it to buy meat from Helmut Schmidt, our butcher."

While everyone was laughing, Martha said, "We have plenty of room, but we'll have to double up." She adjusted the knob of blond hair on the back of her head. "I've arranged for Hans and Paul to sleep together, and for Frau Luther to share a bed with Margarethe." She tapped her teeth, thinking. "Martin can sleep on the couch."

"And where will we sleep?" asked the voice of a ten-year-old boy from the top of the stairs.

"Oh, you and John can sleep in the barn."

"That's great!" he cried. "We've been wanting to sleep in the barn for a long time and you wouldn't let us. Yippee!"

At breakfast Melanchthon said, "It was only by God's providence that we all came to this house. I'm here because my wagon upset and you're here because the horse dropped dead." He took a bite of bacon and egg. "We're still several miles from Magdeburg, and I think we should continue on until we get there. They need me to help arrange for the refugees. Our next problem is to get to Magdeburg—"

"That's no problem," interjected Gaulke. "I'll take you in my wagon after breakfast."

Magdeburg, on the west side of the Elbe, was a fortress city. Here Katie met several old friends, including George Majors, a professor of theology from Wittenberg. By the end of the day she and her family had been placed in the comfortable home of a senator. "You can stay here as long as you like," said the legislator. "Dr. Luther changed my life, and I feel honored to have the privilege to assist his family."

Katie and the children were comfortable in their new home. Hans and Paul had found old friends from Wittenberg, Margarethe and Martin were having a good time with the children next door, there was plenty of food, lots of room— and the senator's wife did everything she could to make them feel welcome. Katie was just beginning to relax when a messenger confronted her.

"Frau Luther, I have bad news," said the young officer.

"Yes?" responded Katie apprehensively.

"The emperor has declared that unless we expel all our Wittenberg refugees, he will place our city under the ban of the empire."

Katie stared. "Has the Schmalkald League been defeated?"

"Not yet. The emperor has had a lot of desertions, and many of his soldiers have died of disease. But the League is not standing together."

"Has Wittenberg fallen?"

"No, but it will; and the reports are that the Duke of Alba is ruthless. He has made a vow to rid the empire of every Protestant."

"And what do you think we should do?"

"Leave."

"Where would we go?" Katie's voice was frantic.

"I don't know. But I will pray that God will guide you. I, too, am a Protestant."

After a sleepless night, Katie called on George Majors. "Professor," she said, "all of us have to leave."

"So I've been told. Where do you plan to go?"

"There is only one safe place: Denmark."

"Denmark!" exploded Majors.

"Yes, Denmark. It's the only safe place. King Christian III is a true Protestant. He loved my husband. He'll protect us."

"But Denmark is at least a hundred and fifty miles to the north!" He shook his head. "And in addition to that enormous distance, there may be Imperial troops between here and there. Remember, armies from the Netherlands are helping the emperor. Also, you don't know either the language or the way." He bit his lip and made a helpless gesture with his hands. "You'd be like a lame bird blown out of its nest by a storm." He shook his head.

"Nonetheless, God wants me to go to Denmark."

"It's still an impossibly long way, especially for a helpless woman and four children. As a friend of the doctor, I must at least try to dissuade you. If something happened, I wouldn't want it to be on my conscience."

"You're right, I *am* a helpless woman," replied Katie with a grim smile. "It's because of that fact that I should have a strong man to accompany me."

"Frau Luther, I agree. Do you have anyone in mind?"

"Yes."

"Who?"

"You!"

"Me?"

"Yes, you! After all, it's just as you said—I am a helpless woman. And, as a pillar of the Reformation, it's your duty to help me."

Majors stared. He tried to speak, but not a single syllable escaped from his mouth.

"As a professor of theology you taught that God rules," pressed Katie, looking straight into his eyes. "Do you *really* believe that?"

"I do."

"Then demonstrate your faith!"

"When should we leave?" he asked, a little sheepishly.

"Tomorrow after breakfast."

The sail-covered wagon with its six passengers had no trouble getting to Braunschweig, about fifty miles west of Magdeburg. Here Majors found a room for himself and secured a house for Katie and her family.

While Katie relaxed for a few weeks, a local senator called.

"I hear that you want to go to Denmark," said the man.

"That's the only place where we can be safe," replied Katie.

"True. But, Frau Luther, you'll never get there. All the roads going north are swarming with Imperial troops. Many of those Protestant-hating men would love to capture you and hold you and your children for ransom. Some might do worse. Men are beasts."

"Maybe so, but I'm going to Denmark!"

Using a hired wagon, Katie headed north. Imperial troops were everywhere. "I'm getting a little frightened," said Majors.

"Don't worry," replied Katie. "God will help us."

After several hours of travel, the number of soldiers began to increase, and then, just south of Gifhorn, Katie noticed the Imperial colors snapping in the breeze. Thoroughly frightened, the driver said, "Frau Luther, we'd better turn back."

"No, keep going," replied Katie firmly.

"But—"

"Keep going!"

In spite of the flow of troops and wagons crammed with ammunition and cannon, the hired wagon finally managed to groan into Gifhorn. There Majors attempted to rent a room for the night. Nothing was available—not even a place on the floor. The village overflowed with troops, many of them drunk.

Unable to buy food or secure lodging, and with an increasing fear that her identity would be discovered, Katie said, "Let's forget Denmark and head south."

The following weeks were the most difficult Katie had ever endured. Being careful to avoid the fighting, she and her children crept from village to village. In each place the news was frightening:

"Philip of Hesse's bombardment of the Imperial camp failed. Philip has been imprisoned."

"Charles V has transferred Electoral Saxony to Maurice."

"John Frederick was wounded and sentenced to death."

"Wittenberg is on the verge of falling."

"The Duke of Alba has vowed to kill every Protestant."

While all of these stories were turning over in her mind, Katie stopped at an inn to buy food. As she and the family were eating, she noticed a tiny old man in the guest room. "You look like a merchant," she ventured.

"Yes, I'm from Torgau."

"Any news about Wittenberg?"

"I have good news and bad news about both Wittenberg and the war." He cut a large section of fish and while he was chewing it continued, "The Schmalkald League might have won if their generals had attacked the emperor when he was on the Danube. They outnumbered his forces three to one. But they hesitated, and while they hesitated the Imperial forces headed north. Soon they were joined by thousands of reinforcements from the Netherlands. After that, the emperor had one victory after another.

"The final battle was at Mühlberg, just a few miles southeast of Torgau." He cut another section of fish from the tail section and loaded it with sauce. "In that battle our elector, John Frederick was slashed on the cheek. After his surrender he was taken into the presence of the emperor. The emperor ridiculed him. He called him a fat pig."

"I heard he was sentenced to death. Is that so?"

"Yes and no." The old man paused with the fish halfway to his mouth. "Ferdinand, the emperor's brother, longed for him to be executed, and the death sentence was pronounced. But that sentence was merely a bargaining point. It was finally agreed that he would not be put to death if Wittenberg surrendered without a struggle."

"And did the city surrender?"

"It did."

"D-did any of the soldiers desecrate the remains of Dr. Luther?" Katie held her breath.

"No, and the reason they did not can only be explained as a miracle."

"What do you mean?"

"The Duke of Alba, Europe's most ardent Protestant hater, had vowed that he would dig them up, burn them, smash them into tiny bits, and toss them into the Elbe. And he would have done just that except for one person. That one person was Lucas Cranach—"

"The painter?"

"Yes, the painter. Did you know him?"

"I worked in his home and knew him well."

"Well, that old man risked his life by pushing past the guards and confronting the emperor in his own tent. How he managed this without being killed can only be explained by God's providence. To the astonished emperor he said, 'I'm Lucas Cranach, the one who painted your portrait when you were a lad. Do you remember me?'

"After searching his mind, the emperor replied, 'Yes, I remember you and the portrait very well. That portrait is one of my favorites.'

" 'And do you remember the promise you made to me?' persisted Cranach.

" 'I remember that I told you that when I became emperor, I would grant you any wish you desired. Do you have such a wish?'

" 'I do.'

" 'And what is your wish?'

" 'That you will spare Dr. Luther's remains.'

"The Emperor stared. 'If I grant your wish,' he finally said, 'I will be making the Duke of Alba very unhappy, and he's my best general.'

" 'True, Your Majesty. But isn't a promise a promise?'

" 'Yes, a promise is a promise,' replied the emperor. 'And in addition to the promise, I want history to remember that I made war only on the living, never on the dead. Luther's bones, wild boar though he was, will remain unmolested. You have my promise.' "

"Oh, thank God!" Katie whispered. Then looking into the old man's face she said, "I am Frau Luther. I prayed that God would spare his remains. Does this mean that my children and I are now free to return to Wittenberg?"

"Yes, you are free to return to Wittenberg," replied the merchant as he cut another slice of fish and heaped it high with sauce.

20

The Plague

After visiting the Castle Church and making certain the remains of her husband had not been desecrated, an optimistic Katie led her family over to the Black Cloister. She was stunned speechless by what she observed.

Denied access to the Castle Church, the Spanish soldiers had satisfied their passion for vengeance by wrecking "the chief heretic's" home. Devastation was everywhere. Most of the windows had been broken, the furniture had been ripped apart, the walls spattered with filthy doggerel, half of the doors had been pried from their hinges, smashed plates littered the floor. In addition, the study had been used as a toilet, and the swollen bodies of several dogs and a cat added to the unbearable smell.

As Katie stared, her children sifted through each part of the building. Nothing had been spared. Even the cellars and the chicken house were in shambles.

Katie wept.

After a long, terrible moment, Hans put an arm around his mother. "Mama," he said, squeezing her tight, "Father wanted us to move to Zulsdorf. Maybe—maybe that's where God wants us to be."

Katie was thoughtful. She spent another half hour surveying the destruction. Then she gathered her children into what remained of the kitchen. "I've made my decision," she announced. "We will move to Zulsdorf!"

The farm at Zulsdorf and the adjoining land of Wachsdorf had not been victims of hateful soldiers. Instead, both places had been a battlefield. The buildings were gone, not a single animal was left, and all the tools had disappeared. "And so what will we do now?" asked Paul.

"We'll return to Wittenberg!" replied Katie. There was a fresh note of confidence in her voice. "Altogether, we have ten hands. That means one hundred fingers. We will use them to repair the Black Cloister. Then we'll take in boarders."

"And what will we do for money?" asked Hans.

"God will provide!"

As their wagon bumped back to Wittenberg, Katie devised a plan for restoration. "First," she announced, "we will arrange our own sleeping quarters. Then we'll repair the study."

"Are you going to start writing books?" asked Paul.

"No, I'm not going to write any books. But an orderly study will remind me of your father, and that will give me inspiration. After we've done all of that, we'll prepare some rooms to rent. God has given us a great opportunity. It's our sacred duty to make use of that opportunity!"

After a week of rising at dawn and working until sunset, three bedrooms were ready. "Now we must repair at least some of the windows," said Katie. "Do any of you boys know how to cut and install glass?"

None of them did.

"Very well, I'll get the window dealer to repair them."

"And how will we pay him?" asked Hans.

"Follow me and I'll show you." Katie led him to a secret door in the cellar. Opening it, she pointed to several shelves loaded with silverware. "Years ago I learned to hide valuables to keep your father from giving them away. Now we'll pawn these things and use the money for necessities."

As Katie continued with repairs, the children's skills improved. The boys learned to hang doors, paint, mend the broken furniture, and even install glass windows. And with Katie's help and some old remnants, Margarethe produced several sets of window curtains. Soon, Katie placed a vacancy sign in the window.

The first renters were an aged couple by the name of Kunkle.

As new rooms were ready, potential renters appeared. When a penniless man applied, Katie was frank. "I must have cash, and in advance," she said.

"But I'm Dr. Luther's fifth cousin," pleaded the man.

"That makes no difference. I must have cash." Noticing his disappointment, she added, "I do need a gardener. If you could do that, I might find a place for you. Otherwise . . ."

The man went away grumbling.

Needing a large supply of meat, Katie walked over to Helmut Schmidt's butcher shop. "Where's Helmut?" she asked as she stood behind the counter.

Esther frowned. "Haven't you heard?" she asked.

"No. We've been so busy repairing the house I haven't paid much attention to the news."

"My husband lost his leg at Mühlberg. A cannon ball took it off just above the knee. He's been in terrible pain. I've been running the shop until he returns from the hospital."

"And how are the twins?"

"John and Peter are fine. I take them to see their father every Sunday. They're the secret of his will to live."

"I think you're also a part of that secret," said Katie. She nodded and smiled.

Because Katie didn't have sufficient cash, Esther arranged for her to have credit to the extent of fifty gulden.

As the boarding house prospered, repairs on the rest of the cloister were completed. Each room soon had its occupant, with curtains fluttering at all the windows. Better yet, the dining room was filled with chattering guests, and Katie was able to pay her bills.

Although John Frederick remained in exile, Elector Maurice allowed Wittenberg to continue as a Protestant stronghold. Sometimes he even went to hear Pastor Bugenhagen preach. Wittenberg University also continued even though the enrollment sank to considerably less than one hundred.

Katie enjoyed her work. But having to get up at dawn and to continue on by the light of the third and sometimes the fourth set of candles began to wear her down. In the midst of her weariness, Hans approached.

"Mama," he said, "I think I should now go to the university at Köenigsberg."

"I agree," replied Katie. "Your father wanted you to be a lawyer, and so do I. You've made me very proud."

"But, Mama, you need me here to help with the boarders."

"Nonsense! Your life is before you. We've gotten along before and we'll get along now. Besides, God has always provided. He won't fail us."

After Hans had gone, the other children worked harder. But the strain was getting too much for Katie. Sometimes in weary moments she wondered why she, called by many the Queen of the Reformation, had to earn a living by taking in boarders. During these periods of despair, she made a habit of going into her room, closing the door, sinking to her knees and communicating with the Father. Such occasions always lifted her spirits.

Late in the winter while she was running a high fever and her prayers didn't seem to go any higher than the ceiling, Katie was so discouraged she longed to die. "Take me home, Father," she pleaded through her tears. As she was praying, she looked up into the face of Esther Schmidt.

"And what are you doing here?" asked Katie.

"I've come to help."

"But I . . . I can't pay you anything."

"Who said anything about pay? Helmut is back from the hospital and is doing well with the business. We've prayed about it, and I've decided to help until you get to feeling better."

"But what about the twins?" Katie's eyes widened.

"That is a problem. But there's a simple solution—"

"Yes?"

"If Margarethe"—she spoke thoughtfully, feeling for each word—"if Margarethe could stay at our house with John and Peter while I'm over here, I could really help you."

"Did the Lord inspire you to make this offer?" asked Katie. Esther nodded.

"Then you're an answer to my prayers." Katie wiped her eyes. "Yes, Esther," she added with enthusiasm, "you are an answer to my prayers!"

Katie was in the midst of recovering her strength when Esther burst into her room with alarming news. "Frau Luther," she exclaimed, "Wittenberg is in trouble again!"

"A new war?"

"No, it's worse than a new war."

"Has John Frederick been executed?"

"No! No! The news is much worse than that . . ."

"Then what is it?"

"The plague has returned!"

"The p-p-plague?" gasped Katie. "Are you sure?"

"Seven people on our street have already died."

Katie groaned. "I c-can't believe it," she finally managed. "I remember the last plague when this building was used as a hospital. There were victims in almost every bed. Some of my best friends perished." She shook her head. "It was terrible."

Too weak to get out of bed, Katie spent almost every waking hour in prayer. She prayed for the city, for the neighbors, her boarders—and for her children. Early one morning while she was praying, she was inspired to read the well-known lines in Psalm 121:

> The sun shall not smite thee by day, nor the moon by
> night. The Lord shall preserve thee from all evil: he shall

preserve thy soul. The Lord shall preserve thy going out and
thy coming in from this time forth, and even for evermore.

Those words became a real comfort, and she read them
again and again. Then the Kunkles were both stricken and
died. Each day the fury of the plague increased, and so many
died that their bodies were left on the street. None of Katie's
children succumbed, but each day she learned of another
friend who had perished. The situation became so grim that
within a week all her boarders had moved out. While Katie
was wondering what to do, Pastor Bugenhagen called.

"I believe it is my duty to advise you to leave Wittenberg,"
said the pastor.

"And where will I go?" asked Katie, rubbing her hands
together.

"I don't know."

"When do you think we should leave?"

"By tomorrow morning at the earliest."

Katie closed her eyes. "Pastor, I don't understand it!" she
wailed. "I've been faithful with my prayers. I've tried to be
obedient, but"—she began to sob—"but it seems that God
just doesn't hear me!"

"Oh, Frau Luther, don't say that! God loves you! God hears
you! God has plans for you!" He hesitated, and then he continued with new animation, "You, Katie, are a unique person.
Maybe God wants to use your final years as a special testi-
mony—"

"What do you mean?"

"You knew the doctor better than anyone else. You knew
him when he was discouraged and you knew him when he
glowed with triumph. Now that he's gone, people will be
watching you. If you can remain as courageous as he was
when he faced the emperor at Worms, it will be a real testi-
mony."

"I will try to be faithful," replied Katie.

The pastor shifted his chair closer to the head of the bed
and opened his Bible. "Our problem," he said, "is that God
is so much wiser than any of us that we do not and cannot

understand Him. Listen to Isaiah 55:

> For my thoughts are not your thoughts, neither are your ways my ways, saith the Lord. For as the heavens are higher than the earth, so are my ways higher than your ways, and my thoughts than your thoughts. For as the rain cometh down, and the snow from heaven, and returneth not thither, but watereth the earth, and maketh it bring forth and bud, that it may give seed to the sower, and bread to the eater: so shall my word be that goeth forth out of my mouth. . . .

"Those words, Frau Luther, are true."

"Yes, Pastor, I know they're true," agreed Katie, nodding her head. "But the doctor and I had hoped to have a few years of quiet at Zulsdorf. He worked so hard and had earned a good rest." She wiped her eyes. "Now that's impossible. He's gone. The farms are ruined. The boarders have fled. My children need an education. I'm forgotten. I have no money. The plague is all around me and is getting closer by the hour. It's killing my friends," she finished dejectedly.

"You have indeed had a lot of troubles," sympathized Bugenhagen. He patted her hand. "But you've also had a lot of blessings. This afternoon I will be conducting funeral services for all three of the Kramer children. Your children are still alive!"

"True, Pastor, true; and I shouldn't complain. The Lord will have to forgive me. I guess I'm just a tired old woman."

Bugenhagen smiled. "The Lord understands, and I'm sure He loves you just as much as He ever did. Our problem is that we don't always understand Him. As you were speaking, I was thinking of some of the blessings we've enjoyed because of His providence. His providence saved us from Suleiman the Magnificent. His providence enabled you to escape from Nimbschen. His providence saved Wittenberg and the doctor's remains from the Duke of Alba. His providence—"

"Yes, yes," interrupted Katie, holding up her hands. "Yes, God has been good. I haven't the slightest reason to complain."

Bugenhagen stopped her by lifting his hand. "Frau Luther," he said, speaking thoughtfully, "in recent weeks I've been pondering over the many ways in which Martin and Moses had similar experiences. Moses had to stand before Pharaoh; Martin had to appear before Charles V. Moses had to endure false brethren. His brother even made a golden calf! Martin had to endure Carlstadt and many others. Moses wrote books; Martin wrote books. Moses died; Martin died. But just recently I learned something new about Moses' death which put a song in my heart." He glanced at the clock. "I'll have to hurry," he said. "I have three more funerals this afternoon. But here's the story.

"After forty years of wanderings, Moses had finally led the children of Israel to the very edge of the Promised Land. Next, the Lord led Moses up to the top of Mount Pisgah. From that vantage point, he showed him the Promised Land. Standing there, Moses saw all of it—from Gilead to Dan. Then the Lord said to him: 'This is the land which I sware unto Abraham, unto Isaac, and unto Jacob, saying, I will give it unto thy seed.'[1]

"Finally, as Moses viewed the lush country with its palm trees, fertile valleys, and the Jordan River, the Lord said: 'I have caused thee to see it with thine eyes, but thou shalt not go over thither.'

"Did that ever seem unfair to you?" He smiled.

Katie nodded. "Yes, it has always seemed unfair to me."

"But, Frau Luther, that wasn't the end!" He opened his New Testament to the Gospel of Mark and from the ninth chapter read: 'And there appeared unto them Elias with Moses: and they were talking with Jesus.'

"So you see, Frau Luther, Moses not only *saw* the Promised Land, but he was enabled to *enter* the Promised Land and be *with* Jesus, the Son of God, *in* the Promised Land. And surely no one has ever enjoyed a greater blessing than that!"

"And what does this mean to me?"

"It means that someday," assured Bugenhagen, "you will

---

[1]Deuteronomy 34:4.

see Martin and Elizabeth and Magdalena again, and all of you will rejoice around the throne. We must never forget the words of Paul: 'For now we see through a glass, darkly; but then face to face: now I know in part; but then shall I know even as also I am known.' "[2]

The pastor paused with his hand on the doorknob. "Dr. Martin taught the world that 'the just shall live by faith.' That, indeed, is a great truth. Nothing would please Satan more than to get you to deny that fact either by word or action. Frau Luther, the Lord is allowing you to be in a crucible in order to be tested. But knowing you as I do, I know you will survive the test." With that, he rose, gave Katie a reassuring pat on the head and left, leaving Katie to ponder on the countless blessings God had given her. She took new courage. She *would* be faithful. By God's grace she would prove that the message God had given Martin, "the just shall *live by faith*," was still real and He would see her through this difficult time.

Katie delayed leaving Wittenberg as long as possible. Finally she had to leave. As the wagon was being loaded she paid a last visit to the Castle Church and to the graves of her children in the cemetery. Then, confident that she would soon be returning, she hurried to the wagon, mounted, and signalled the owner that she was ready to leave.

After passing through the Elster gate, the driver headed toward Torgau. From the beginning, the horses seemed nervous. Upset by their behavior, the driver cursed them again and again. Remembering how the horse had dropped dead on the other trip, Katie forced herself to remain silent. They were just passing through a village when a large dog streaked into the road and began to bark at the horses.

The horses bolted. The driver frantically pulled the reins and shouted, but he was unable to steady them. Terrified, Katie sprang over the side. She could not have chosen a worse place. Landing on a stone, she suffered severe injuries and

---

[2]1 Corinthians 13:12.

rolled into the stream running between the high banks. Struggling to keep her head above water, she cried, "Oh, God, help me!"

Fortunately a peasant nearby saw the predicament and quickly ran to her aid, pulling her onto the road before she drowned.

After the horses had calmed, the driver and the rest of the family drove back to where Katie was stretched out on the road. Paul jumped out, grabbing some heavy blankets with him. These he hurriedly wrapped around her shivering form and prepared a comfortable place for her in the wagon. They lifted her gently into the wagon and forced the horses ahead at top speed. Two hours later she was carried into the home of Kasper Grunewald in Torgau—the home they had already engaged for her stay.

"Get a doctor quick!" Paul cried. "My mother's been hurt. She almost drowned."

A doctor was summoned immediately. While they were waiting, Mrs. Grunewald removed Katie's wet clothing, wrapped her in warm blankets and made her as comfortable as possible.

When the doctor arrived and examined Katie, he found her internal injuries were so severe he could do little. The Grunewalds lovingly cared for her, and since Grunewald was a warm friend of Dr. Luther, his house was a spacious haven for her and they extended every courtesy possible.

As winter iced the rivers and whitened the land, Katie struggled back to health. Thinking of her children, she sought to live. But her battle seemed useless. Often in agony she relived the past. In her sleep, she dreamed constantly. Again and again she related to those about her the details of the night's dream. Most of them were about the great moments in her husband's career. On several occasions she sobbed, "I can hardly wait until my summons."

During the first week of December, Helmut Schmidt called. Supported by his crutch, he smiled down at her. "Greetings, Frau Luther," he said enthusiastically. His eyes

214

were bright, his voice cheerful.

"And how's Esther?" asked Katie as she laboriously focused her eyes on him.

"Haven't you heard?" There was a note of dismay in his voice.

"Is something wrong?" Katie frowned, looking at him with concern.

"Esther and the twins were victims of the plague. Pastor Bugenhagen preached their funerals two weeks ago. I'm now alone. I've closed my business and am moving in with my brother here in Torgau."

"Oh, how terrible!"

"No, Frau Luther. It isn't terrible. God has been very close to me. He is my strength." A smile dominated his face.

"What's your secret?" she asked, studying him intently.

"I've taken comfort in the words of Paul: 'For we know that if our earthly house of this tabernacle were dissolved, we have a building of God, an house not made with hands, eternal in the heavens.'[3] That passage was proved by the fall of Wittenberg."

"What do you mean?"

"Wittenberg was well fortified. The walls were high. The moat was wide. There were many cannon. There was plenty of ammunition. Nonetheless, it fell, and it fell without a shot being fired. But some years ago Dr. Luther wrote about another fortress, a fortress that will never fall."

"Tell me about it," she said, a scene from the past flashing into her mind.

"No, Frau Luther. I will not tell you about it. But I will sing about it. Listen!" Leaning on his crutch, which he held in both hands, Schmidt sang with his magnificent tenor voice:

> A mighty Fortress is our God,
> A Bulwark never failing;
> Our helper He amid the flood
> Of mortal ills prevailing:
> For still our ancient foe

---

[3] 2 Corinthians 5:1.

> Doth seek to work us woe;
> His craft and power are great,
> And, armed with cruel hate,
> On earth is not his equal.

Remembering her part in the writing of that hymn, Katie's eyes overflowed. After she had wiped the tears from her eyes, she found that Helmut Schmidt had disappeared. But the fresh glow in her heart remained. What joy and release those words had brought! God's faithfulness had never wavered, though hers had. He was her fortress, a "bulwark never failing." She had gone through many floods, but He had always been her helper. She thought back on her days at Nimbschen and the hope that had sprung up in her heart as she had read Luther's tract containing the words: "The just shall live by faith." That hope had been realized in Christ. And God had continued to bless her life beyond any of her dreams. He had given her Martin, the children, her faith, and so much more. It had been a good life.

Katie kept gradually sinking. On the evening of December 20, the children, feeling their mother's summons was near, huddled close to her bed. While they were watching her every move, she asked, "Had you not better lie down and sleep?" After that she was quiet. Then, about an hour later, she rallied enough to say quite distinctly, "I will stick to Christ as a burr sticks to a coat."

Those were her final words.

The funeral services were conducted in Torgau's nearby Lutheran church. And it was there she was laid to rest. At the time of her passing Katie lacked one month of being fifty-four years of age.

Epilogue

The plague burned itself out shortly after Katie's death. This was a signal for those who had fled Wittenberg to return. The work of the Reformation continued. Pastors were ordained, Luther's books were published, churches were crowded.

Although he had lost his enthusiasm for the law, Hans continued his legal studies. Eventually he was employed at the Weimar chancellory as an advisor. Paul became a distinguished physician. He served in various courts, including those of Duke John Frederick of Gotha, Elector Joachim II of Brandenburg, and Elector August of Albertine Saxony.

Martin studied theology, but he never became a pastor.

The Luther name continued through Paul Luther's son, John Ernest—one of six children. When Martin Gottlob Luther, a descendant of John Ernest, died in 1759, the male line of the reformer's family came to an abrupt end.

Margarethe married Georg von Kunheim on August 5, 1555. Since the groom was from a noble family, the wedding was one of Wittenberg's great events. Distinguished members of the nobility from all over Germany attended. The marriage was a happy one. But Margarethe passed away at the age of thirty-six. Some of her descendants are still alive in our time.

Lucas Cranach, the artist who persuaded Charles V not to allow Luther's remains to be desecrated, accompanied the exiled former elector, John Frederick, to Augsburg and later to Innsbruck. When John was eventually freed, he returned to his diminished territories in 1552 and established his court at Weimar. He then employed Cranach to be his official painter. Cranach died the following year at the age of eighty-one.

Elector Maurice, the one who received his cousin John Frederick's title by playing traitor to the Schmalkald League, eventually became disillusioned with Charles V because he kept his father-in-law, Philip of Hesse, imprisoned, and because he persisted in trying to force Lutheran cities to return to Catholicism.

Commissioned in 1550 to capture Magdeburg, Maurice took advantage of his opportunity, signed a compact with France and other Protestant princes and made war on Charles V. Eventually he forced the emperor to release his father-in-law and to guarantee the right of Lutheran cities to remain Lutheran. He then rejoined the forces of Charles V, but was killed in the battle of Sieverhausen.

Frustrated by not being able to destroy Luther's remains, the Duke of Alba fulfilled his passion to root out heretics while he was governor general of the Netherlands between 1567 and 1573. His "Council of Troubles" became so ruthless it was dubbed the "Council of Blood." Thousands were put to death. Indeed, he was so cruel his name is now a synonym for wanton cruelty.

Wherever it was possible, Charles V continued his relentless persecution of Protestants. He imprisoned them, burned them, exiled them. But the more he persecuted them, the more numerous and determined they became. Illness, however, caught up with him. By 1552 his limbs were so swollen from gout he was in constant pain.

His mind, also, began to erode. He was gripped by the same melancholy that had possessed his mother, Joanna the Mad. Sometimes he brooded for hours and wept until his courtiers were alarmed. But his physicians were unable to help him.

Eventually realizing that he could not destroy Lutheranism, Charles authorized the Peace of Augsburg which allowed Lutheran princes and cities to remain Lutheran. Discouraged, he divided his empire between his brother Ferdinand and his son Philip, who is remembered as Philip II, the husband of England's "Bloody" Queen Mary. Charles spent his last two years in retirement at the San Yuste monastery in Estremadura, Spain. He died in 1558.

Today, Luther's emphasis that "the just shall live by faith" is accepted by almost all followers of Christ around the world, and his hymn "A Mighty Fortress" is found in most hymnals, including those of the Roman Catholic Church.

Altogether, Luther's name appeared on nearly four hundred books and pamphlets, and it has been claimed that more books have been written about him than anyone other than Jesus Christ.

Historical Chronology

Year	Event
1415	John Huss burned at the stake
1455	Johann Gutenberg prints first Bible
1483, Nov. 10	Martin Luther born at Eisleben
1484, May	Luther family moves to Mansfeld
1492, Oct.	Columbus discovers New World
1498	Savonarola executed for heresy
1499, Jan. 29	Katherine von Bora born at Lippendorf
1501, May	Luther enters University at Erfurt
1505, July 2	Luther makes vow to St. Anne
1505, July 17	Luther enters Augustinian cloister
1505	Katherine's mother dies
1505	Katherine's father remarries
1506	Construction of St. Peter's begins
1510, Oct.	Luther journeys to Rome
1512	Luther receives Doctor of Theology degree
1513, Aug. 16	Luther begins lectures on the Psalms
1515, April	Luther begins lectures on Romans
1517, Oct. 31	Luther nails his Ninety-five Theses to door
1519, June 28	Charles V elected emperor

220

Year	Event
1520, June 5	Pope Leo's bull, *Exsurge Domine*, gives Luther sixty days to submit
1520, Oct. 10	Luther burns Leo's bull
1520, Nov. 12	Luther's books burned at Cologne
1521, April 18	Luther's *Here I Stand* speech at Worms
1521, May 4	Luther hides at Wartburg Castle
1522	Katherine escapes from Nimbschen
1522, Sept.	Luther's German New Testament published
1523, July 1	First Reformation martyrs burned
1525, May–June	Peasants crushed
1525, June 13	Luther marries Katherine von Bora
1526, June 7	Hans Luther is born
1526, Sept. 10	Buda falls to Suleiman the Magnificent
1527, Summer	Luther ill and depressed
1527	Rome sacked
1527	Luther writes *A Mighty Fortress*
1527, Dec. 10	Elizabeth Luther is born
1528, Aug. 3	Elizabeth Luther dies
1529, May 4	Magdalena Luther is born
1530, April 16	Luther remains at Coburg Castle
1530, June 25	*Augsburg Confession* presented
1531, Nov. 9	Martin Luther, Jr. is born
1533, Jan. 29	Paul Luther is born
1534, Dec. 17	Margarethe is born
1542, Sept. 20	Magdalena Luther dies
1546, Feb. 18	Martin Luther dies at Eisleben
1546, June 16	Schmalkaldic War erupts
1546, June 18	Katie Luther flees to Magdeburg
1547, May 19	Wittenberg falls to Charles V
1547	Katie Luther's farms are destroyed
1552	The plague breaks out in Wittenberg
1552, Dec. 20	Katie Luther dies as the result of an accident

Popes Contemporary to the Luthers

1. Sixtus IV (1471–1484). He beautified Rome, built the Sistine chapel, enlarged the Vatican library, and opened it to more scholars. His attempt to launch a crusade against the Turks failed. He has been severely condemned because of his gross nepotism.

2. Innocent VIII (1484–1492). Before becoming a priest, he fathered three illegitimate children. Through bribery he was elected pope. To finance his various wars, he sold offices to the highest bidder. His deathbed wish was that a better pope than himself be elected.

3. Alexander VI (1492–1503). By means of simony, this politically astute man attained the highest office in Roman Catholicism. He annulled the marriage of his daughter and arranged her second marriage. He made his son a cardinal. He launched a crusade against the Turks and encouraged the evangelization of the New World. The outspoken Savonarola was executed during his reign.

4. Julius II (1503–1513). He was a nephew of Pope Sixtus IV. He issued a bull prohibiting duelling and another which voided any papal election tainted with simony. He granted Henry VIII a dispensation to marry Catherine of Aragon. Sensitive to art, he commissioned Michelangelo to paint frescoes in the Sistine chapel.

5. Leo X (1513–1521). He received a tonsure before he was eight and at thirteen became a deacon-cardinal. In order to build St. Peter's, he arranged for the sale of indulgences. He issued a bull against Martin Luther and gave Henry VIII the title Defender of the Faith.

6. Adrian VI (1522–1523). This son of a carpenter tutored Charles V, became a cardinal, and was appointed Inquisitor of Aragon and Navarre. As pope he lost the Island of Rhodes in a war. He also did not get along with his cardinals. He died twenty months after being elected pope.

7. Clement VII (1523–1534). He was illegitimate. During the sack of Rome, he became a prisoner of Charles V for more than seven months. He refused to annul the marriage of Henry VIII to Catherine of Aragon because she was the aunt of his captor, Charles V. Henry ignored him and married Anne Boleyn. England's parliament then broke with the Roman church.

8. Paul III (1534–1549). Before his ordination, Pope Paul III fathered four illegitimate children. He created an inquisition in Rome to discipline "all those who had departed from or who attacked the Catholic faith and to unmask such persons as were suspected of heresy." He issued the bull which summoned the Council at Trent. The Society of Jesus was founded during his reign.

9. Julius III (1550–1555). He came from a family of lawyers. He sought reform in the Catholic church. He became the first president of the Council of Trent and allowed Protestant speakers to address the assembly. Having been used as a hostage after the sack of Rome in 1527, he was inclined to be merciful to those who disagreed with Catholic dogma. He even attempted to bring the English church back to Rome.

Bibliography

Those who wish to know more about Martin and Katie Luther will find the following books useful:

Acton, Lord. *Cambridge Modern History*, vol. 2. Macmillan, 1904.

Armstrong, Edward. *The Emperor, Charles V*, vols. 1, 2. Macmillan, 1910.

Atkinson, James. *Martin Luther and the Birth of Protestantism*. Marshall Morgan & Scott, 1982.

Bainton, Roland H. *Erasmus of Christendom*. Scribner's Sons, 1969.

Bainton, Roland H. *Here I Stand, A Life of Martin Luther*. Abingdon Press, 1950.

Brecht, Martin. *Martin Luther, His Road to Reformation*. Fortress Press, 1985.

Crossley, Rodney, D. *Luther and the Peasants' War*. Exposition Press, 1974.

Durer, Albrecht. *Master Printmaker*. Museum of Fine Arts, Boston, Mass.

Edwards, Jr., Mark U. *Luther and the False Brethren*. Stanford University Press, 1975.

Edwards, Jr., Mark U. *Luther's Last Battles*. Cornell University Press, 1983.

Erickson, Carolly. *Bloody Mary*. Doubleday & Co., 1978.

Friedenthal, Richard. *Luther*. R. Piper and Co., Germany. Translated by John Nowell. British Publication, Wiedenfeld and Nicholson, 1970.

Friedländer, Max & Jakob Rosenberg. *The Paintings of Lucas Cranach*. Cornell University Press, 1978.

Grisar, S.J. *Luther*, vol. 6. Herder Book Co., 1917.

Habsburg, Otto von. *Charles V*. Praeger Publishers, Inc., 1970.

Heinrich, Böhmer. *Luther in Light of Recent Research*. The Christian Herald, 1916.

James, Richard William. *Philip Melanchthon*. Putnum, 1898.

Lea, Henry Charles. *A History of the Inquisition of Spain*. vols. 1, 2, 3. Macmillan, 1922.

Luther's Works. Concordia.

Mall, E. Jane. *Kitty My Rib*. Concordia.

Manschreck, Clyde L. *Melanchthon, the Quiet Reformer*. Abingdon Press, 1958.

Mee, Jr., Charles L. *White Robe, Black Robe*. Putnam, 1972.

Schwiebert, Ernest George. *Luther and His Times*. Concordia, 1950.

Simon, Edith. *Luther Alive*. Doubleday, 1968.

Smith, Preserved. *The Life and Letters of Martin Luther*. Barnes and Noble, Inc., 1911.

Stenmetz, David C. *Reformers in the Wings*. Fortress Press, 1971.

Strauss, Gerald. *Nürnberg in the 16th Century*. Indiana University Press, 1976.

Todd, John M. *Luther, A Life*. Hamish Hamilton, 1982.